'J. G. Ballard and Brian Aldiss are, I suppose, the two most widely admired British writers of science fantasy nowadays; and deservedly so. But if one had to suggest some young pretender solid and perceptive enough to turn their joint regime into a triumvirate, the obvious name would be Keith Roberts. The best science fiction is always metaphor as well as prophecy, and *The Inner Wheel* is an imaginative variation on the theme of the supremely gifted individual in a world with no use for his talents'

Benedict Nightingale in *The Observer*

Also by Keith Roberts in Panther Books

Pavane

Keith Roberts

The Inner Wheel

Panther

Granada Publishing Limited
Published in 1972 by Panther Books Limited
3 Upper James Street, London W1R 4BP

First published in Great Britain by
Rupert Hart-Davis Limited 1970

Made and printed in Great Britain by
C. Nicholls & Company Ltd
The Philips Park Press, Manchester
Set in Intertype Plantin

Contents

The Inner Wheel

1

The voices are in a void. The void has no colour. Neither is it dark. There are formless Shapes in the void. There are soundless Noises. There are swirlings and pressures, twistings and squeezings. The voices fill the gaps between nothingness. The voices are impatient. 'Where?' they ask. 'Where . . .?'

'I told you where . . .'

'See for us and tell again . . . Where is he . . .?'

'Getting on a train . . .'

'Tell us what you see. Where is the train . . .?'

'In a station, where do you think . . .?'

There are hammers and whips and pincers.

'WHERE IS THE TRAIN?'

'T-Tanbridge. Please, THE STATION IS TANBRIDGE –'

There are flickerings. 'Gently,' say the voices. 'Gently, tell us what you see . . .'

'I . . .

'There are roses. The platforms are covered with them. The . . . train is green. The sky is very bright blue. Everything is quiet, nobody moving about. The coach stands in its bay. I see the sunlight lying across it and on the platforms. It lies in s-squares on the platforms, on the footbridge. There is a breeze now. A piece of paper blows and skips, the roses sway. I hear the little thorny sound of leaves scratching together. Please, no more . . .'

Somewhere there might be giggling. Somewhere there might be rage. 'Tell us about him . . .'

A lens moves, seeing but unseen, examining textures of glass and wood and leaves. The station is haunted in the hot, still afternoon.

'He is . . . sitting in the train. In the front seat just behind the driver's cab. He is . . . tall. He is . . . dark, his hair is dark and rather long. It hangs across one eye. His face is thin, his eyes are very blue. His hands look . . . strong. Well kept, bony. Square nails, white half-moons where the cuticle is pushed back. He uses a good aftershave –'

The giggling again. 'You like him . . .'

'Leave me alone –'

Jostlings. 'See . . . we want to see . . .' The not-colours swirl.

'No –'

'. . . dispatched in accordance with your order of the twenty-third . . .'

'I'M TRYING TO WORK –'

'Gently . . .'

'Leave me then. Leave me, I'll *tell* you . . .'

'Good,' say the voices. 'Good. Tell us what you see . . .'

'He's . . . taking out his cigarettes. Lighting one. Flicking the match in the holder. The m-motorman is coming now. He gets in, starts the engines. Puts the . . . handle on that works the brakes . . .'

'No,' say the voices. 'No, no . . . See for us, see deep . . .'

'No –'

Awfulness. The un-shapes scramble and pulse. 'Deep,' say the voices. 'See deep . . .'

'I shall . . . be sick . . .'

'DEEP . . . !'

The camera, the lens, floating close and closer. Somewhere inside the train inside the man inside the eyes are other pictures for it, closed each within each like a nest of mirages. The pictures twinkle, fade and strengthen and fade again, reduce themselves to glimmering node-points, swell. Somewhere someone bites lips till they taste salt. Only the voice is calm: it speaks from the grey place the other side of terror. It husks and limps, feeling shared pain.

'I . . . see the rain. It bounces on pavements, pours along gutters. I see houses. Rows of houses. Their bricks are bright with the rain. I see a church, or a chapel . . . All round . . . oh it's a chapel, chapel of a c-cemetery. The . . . houses all round like a high wall in the rain. The . . . men walking, the thing they are pushing doesn't make a noise because the trolley has rubber tyres. The . . . people are coming now. Their shoulders are bent in the rain. They say, "*It always rains on days like this . . .*" *I* see the f-flowers, the rain is on the flowers, on their petals. The earth is dark because of the rain. I see the . . . coffin, going down into the grave . . .'

'Gently,' say the voices. And 'gently, gently . . .'

'I see the houses again. One house. The people are inside and the great whispering cars have gone . . . The rain cries against the windows like a thing shut out wanting to get in and the people don't know what to say to each other, what to say to *him* . . . An old lady is making tea, there are sandwiches all ready, but *he* can't eat, he knows the bread is full of flesh – PLEASE DON'T MAKE ME SEE ANY MORE –'

'Enough,' say the voices. 'Gently, enough . . . We know he's coming now, he's nearly here. It's enough . . .' And the camera, the eye, withdraws itself silently, folding in, closing, shutting away . . .

'. . . to our order number cee five, oh eight six . . .'

The voices are in a void. The void has no colour. Neither is it dark.

'In a fiercely mourning house in a crooked year.'

Jimmy Stringer lay back in the seat, blew smoke, regarded the Hush Puppies that terminated his slimly trousered legs. The rhythm of the line of poetry pattered in his mind, stressed by the carriage wheels that rang now *fiercely*-mourn *fiercely*-mourn over the rail joints. A great artist had strung those syllables together sometime before he died of . . . was it eighteen Scotches, in a New York Bar? Jimmy shook his head, eyes vague. Before, the words had been just angry, lovely sounds; now, he knew what they meant.

Ahead the branch line stretched into sunhaze. A little halt swam into sight, platforms wreathed again with roses, standards and climbers that exploded like silent fireworks against the thick blue of the sky. He saw lamp standards gay to their tops with the brightness, fresh paintwork on railings and trellises, glowing flower-beds edged with whitewashed stones. The train brakes came on in a series of diminishing whooshes, the coach breathed to a stop and the driver turned off his engines.

Jimmy stroked ash from his cigarette into the tray, sat feeling the sun strike through glass to burn his cheek. Somewhere footsteps ticked, faded into silence. Above the carriage a wooden bridge spanned the single track; in front the rails curved slightly to the right and vanished between low mounded hills. Somewhere out there a town Jimmy had never seen *existed* in four o'clock drowsiness. He asked himself, *will it be any good? Will it be a place I can stay in for a while?* He told himself, *somehow it's crazy, but you're a man on the run. Can you stop running there?*

Running. There are times when the mind balks, hits a fact it can't take, throws up an equation that gives a batty answer. Then maybe the deep, thinking part of you whimpers and arches back into stasis and after a time of that any course of action seems good. So you start to run. You're not running *to* anywhere, just away from where you are. You're an electric puppet; the impossibility rides there on your shoulder while your motor nerves twitch and your body takes you away and away.

A problem is an equation. Made up of elements. Singly you can take them, it's trying to fit them all together that makes your skull sing. Jimmy remembered an element. The Studio, back in Town. Light filtering through inadequate windows, littered drawing-boards, filing-cabinets topheavy with drifts of paper and card. The yellowing fluorescents, their tubes fly-blown; flexes, Sellotaped here and there to the edges of desks, that fed tired Anglepoise lamps from a Medusa confusion. It was a place where you could work and work and see your dreams give up and curl at the edges and realize the ad game was a machine, a bloody machine that sorted the heavyweight souls from the middleweight, the middleweight from the lightweight, the lightweight from the souls that didn't rate at all. The man who sat at your elbow, painting in the shine on endless successions of bright green lawnmowers, had been a *Prix de Rome.*

An element, an aspect of existence. Further back, buried in the impossible matrix of Time, were others. His father . . . Only the image of him was fading, losing itself under a rippling and a hotness, the glaring hopeful hopeless time people call adolescence. Stringer rubbed his face. Adolescence is the time you want freedom. You take it, snatch it, eat it maybe before the folk round you grab it back. Nobody can help you. Not then. Least of all a tired old man trying to come to terms with life.

So he'd shucked his father off and gone to London to learn how to be a Great Artist with capital letters, and maybe there'd been times over the years when he'd thought the old devil wasn't too bad after all, he'd just breeze back home one day and say hello . . . But the day had never come. Instead there was a telegram. It told him, the thing he'd planned on doing, it wouldn't get done now. It told him, he'd run out of tomorrows.

Jimmy stubbed the cigarette and lit another. A coach cleared the line ahead; a signal dropped its smoky-amber arm, the driver pulled back jerkily on the Deadman's. The carriage began to gather speed. Moved out into the sunlight, nosed among the hills.

Jimmy told himself, the old man had had it good those last few years. Better than he'd ever realized. He'd made the grade, in his own way; even got his name up over the gate of the yard in faded swaggering letters. '*John Stringer, Scrap Dealer.*' And underneath, a motto, a legend. '*Everything has its price . . .*'

Elements in a random equation. Stringer nodded to himself bitterly, in the bright train. 'Yeah,' he said 'Yeah'.

He tried to remember the rain, visualize the sky outside the carriage grey, the windows streaked with spots. The exercise was impossible. Like remembering a pain, trying to work out after it had gone why you threshed and rolled and felt like dying. But that was a defence mechanism. Maybe this was as well. *Dear God protect me from the dullness and the rain . . .*

It had rained at the funeral. And afterwards. The morning after; Jimmy sitting in a little cluttered office, the man in front of him hemming and coughing and seeming as dusty and yellowed as the shelves of files that lined the walls. Jimmy listened to the voice again scratching its way from fact to monstrous fact while the rain pattered soft against the glass. Death duties of course, he understood a large amount would be lost. The affairs were confused, some little time would be needed . . . But the money that had been left for him, the money he'd known nothing about . . . yes, a fairly substantial sum by any standards . . .

Jimmy licked his lips, beginning to sense the sheer size of the problem his father had left him by dying alone like that. He said, 'How much?' He knew his voice was unsteady, knew too that whatever he said would be misunderstood. And the stranger had steepled his fingers, winced to drive his glasses back up his nose, looked at him with eyes that held every expression and no expression.

'Immediately . . . Well I would say Mr. Stringer . . . in round figures you understand, very broad figures . . . *Forty thousand pounds . . .*'

The driver touched a control and the train hooted; a long double note full somehow with the sensation of summer evenings, like the chuckle of water, the sound of a lawnmower. Jimmy shook his head again. His father had been what he never would be; a businessman. They'd told him, one of the strangers had told him after the funeral, they thought old Stringer had gone crazy when he bought that ancient halftrack. Old Kraut job it was, streaked with rust; they'd dug it out of some rotting stockpile down in the Channel Islands. Then John had bought another and another, snapping them up where he could find them, even bringing them in from the Continent. Forty quid here, fifty there, a hundred, two ... Bren carriers, beaten-up scout cars, lorries, command trucks; German, British, American ... If it was old and smashed, and had fought in the war, John Stringer would buy. Because everything has a price. Light tanks, sidearms, steel helmets, badges, *flammenwerfer* ... And it had paid off. Jimmy sneered. Forty thousand; say a big outfit wants to make a film, say they need the props and you're the only man they can come to. You can make that in a year. You've got to know the ropes of course and get to the right boys and slip tenners to odd people for not being in such and such a place at such and such a time; but these things can be arranged.

He stubbed a cigarette and caught himself lighting another almost instantly. He asked himself, angrily, *could I help being born the sort of person I am with the sort of mind I've got? Slow to hate, slower to love, the brain forging relationships like the links of a chain, slow, slow ... but when the job's done, when the links are made, they're good for the only part of eternity that interests me, my lifetime ...* He told himself, *my father was like that. He was a West Country man, he might forget but he could never forgive. Ten years of silence while he made the money he couldn't give me when I was young and silly and wanted to cut a dash. That's what the wallet in my pocket says. That's what the new cheque-book is telling me. The world owes you a living, my son ... so out thee can go, and live like a rich little king ...*

He pushed his forehead against his clenched hands. *I didn't mean it,* he thought. *We none of us mean what we do.*

The hand was shaking his sleeve gently, insistently. He looked up startled. The old lady's eyes searched his face, changing in quick shifts of focus and direction. 'Are you all right?' she said. 'Are you quite *all right*?'

'er . . . yeah. Thanks . . .' He made his mouth smile. 'Just maybe a little tired. Long journey . . . thanks for asking.'

'*Ahh* . . .' She sat back across the gangway, seeming relieved. Looked out through the window then back to him quickly, bird-like. Nodded, smiled, bobbed her silver head. 'Are you travelling to the end of the line?'

'Yes,' he said. 'Place called Warwell-on-Starr.'

Sharply: 'Then you don't know Warwell?'

'No, I've . . . never been there. I reckoned I might stay a while,' he said. 'If I like it.'

She simpered. 'Oh, you will . . . You'll *love* Warwell, everybody does. Such a *nice* little town . . .'

'Yeah,' said Jimmy carefully. 'Er . . . yeah.'

He sat back trying to think. The image that had flickered across his mind just then; the river, the trees, the flint church tower nestling . . . But he'd never seen the place he was going to, he knew nothing about it. He decided, it won't be anything like that. There'll be brutal acres of rail sidings, scrubby pink little Developments marching in all directions. Ten to one I shall loathe the dump.

Queer thing, this feeling of unreality; a detached half-awareness, a dream state in which visions and imaginings could be as real as the touchable things round him. It was as if shapes jostled at the edges of his mind, brightnesses brighter than the sky, shadows that mocked at sunlight. He shrugged. These were effects of heightened perception, of jangling nerves that now mercifully were beginning to ease. For days past life had been like a cine film shown on some huge screen. Too big, too close, too detailed. He'd wanted to pull back, get out from under, but he couldn't.

Warwell. Why the devil had he run here, anyway? His father's accountant had talked about the place, but he knew somehow the name had been in his mind before that. When? When had it started, what had triggered it? He'd wanted somewhere quiet, somewhere he could go to and be alone and think and chew at his problem, but why had one name seemed to stand out from every map he opened? Warwell, a place on a river he'd never seen . . .

For a time the rails had been winding through the low hills; round the last of the bends the way straightened and Jimmy saw how the little bridges appeared each under each like images in two opposed mirrors. Beneath the last of them the coach stopped again and there were the lampstandards once more, hidden to their tops by creepers that rioted the length of the diminutive station. The branch line was certainly damned pretty; somehow even the waywardness of it, the curving and wriggling of the tracks, soothed like a balm. As though a world was being shut away behind easy grassy shoulder of the hills; as if ahead, islanded, was all that was sweet and real. Jimmy stubbed the cigarette half-smoked. *There can be*, he told himself, *no sense of homecoming. Not to a place you've never seen.* He glanced sideways at the old lady, expecting another comment, but she stayed quiet. She was sitting staring in front of her, half-smile fossilized on her face as though she could already see the *nice* town ahead.

Jimmy told himself, it could just be . . . Could be I've met a whole series of nice, interesting, interested people one after the other. A ticket clerk, a porter at Tanbridge where I changed to the branch, an old lady on a train. All interested to hear I was going to Warwell; all keen to tell me, it's a *nice* little town. Sometimes life's like that, pointless coincidences get themselves strung together like beads . . .

The coach was moving again. The train wheels boomed on a bridge. Jimmy leaned forward, frowning, grappling at something that refused to come out into the light . . . and sat quite still, feeling icy cold. Ahead, the town made itself. More hills closed off a vista of black and white houses, steep wavy roofs. *There was the river, swinging back to cross in front of Warwell like a moat. There was a church, flint-built and nestling.*

The station was an amber box enclosing dim areas of platform. The coach glided into coolness, wheezed, stopped where the rails stopped as suddenly and startlingly as life. Stringer lifted his bags, felt the sharp rectangle of the ticket dig into his right palm. He felt out of breath and stiff, as if he was ending some huge dangerous odyssey. He passed through the barrier, turned back to see the coach hulking against the light. Beside him a girl with good legs and burning-red hair spoke suddenly. 'Heard you talking on the train,' she said cheekily. 'Hope you enjoy your stay. It's such a *nice* town . . .' She turned while Jimmy was staring, and clicked away.

'Yeah,' he said. He walked out of the station, into a sunlit square. He saw a garage, doors standing open; a taxi rank, a man lounging reading a newspaper. A few yards away the river slid cool and green and hung with willows, filling the air with some cool suggestion of presence that was more subtle than scent. Across the street a towering ugly-pretty pile of waterside Gothic proclaimed itself the George Hotel. Jimmy walked towards it, swinging his grip, feeling the sun burn on the side of his neck. From the town beyond came a buzz of sound, cars, voices; *somewhere a Wheel turned slow, unseen and unheard, its rim as big as a valley.*

2

The voices chirrup in the deep coolness of night, while the river glides black past the houses and the church. 'Wrong,' say the voices. 'Wrong, all wrong . . . He's wrong for us, who brought him here . . .?'

'I . . . I didn't know . . .'

'Wrong,' say the voice. 'Wrong, wrong . . .' There is anger, and a squirm of giggling. There are brightnesses like flames. They burn but there is no heat. There are other things.

'PLEASE . . . NO PLEASE . . .'

Laughter. A chase, an airy game of tag. The Devil takes the hindmost. 'Wrong,' shout the voices. 'He is wrong, you were wrong . . .' There is a soundless sound of screaming. There is a writhing, a gasping, a wanting to die. There is a catching, a touching, a hating . . . Then, suddenly, there is quiet. Dawn touches the river with a ghostly massiveness of light. The light has no colour. Bats hunt across the greyness like the shadows of dead leaves; island trees hang impossibly still in a world of water and air. The Starr is a mirror now a thousand miles deep, a quicksilver slash reaching to Earth's core.

And part of Warwell sleeps.

This is a *nice* town. Go ahead and ask anybody in the street, they'll tell you straight out. It's a *nice* town. Friendly, these people. And quiet. The town's quiet. Nothing ever happens, not to Warwell-on-Starr. Nothing ever has. Nothing ever will.

It's an old town. Built on a cross, so it has its North Street and its South, its West and East. East Street runs down to the river, because here that flows south and north. At the bottom of East Street is the church. It looks over the traffic lights and the big curlicued lamp standard at the crossroads, towards the Town Hall. West Street runs up by the Town Hall, climbing into the hills. East and West Streets together make the shopping centre. There's a Smith's and a Boots and a Timothy Whites on the corner and it's all very homely. Very *nice.* There's some industry here, not too much; in the main, Warwell is a Typical Market Town. There's a little cinema that runs evenings, and they use the church hall sometimes as a theatre. And once a year the Steam Fair comes, in the meadows by the Starr. It's a local convention, the shopkeepers look forward to it. There's a Chess Club and an Athletic Club, a Youth Club and W.I. There's an Archery Society (Bowmen of Starr) and a Cricket Club. They play matches summer evenings on a little ground with elm trees round it, back of the Bull Hotel on the outskirts of town, and there are stories about great bats lifting deliveries into the Starr, but nothing like that ever happens now. The traffic bypasses Warwell. There's a little police station, there's a vet and a couple of doctors and ... oh hell, all sorts of stuff. It's a *nice* town.

Jimmy lay on his back on the bed. Beside him on a chair was a saucer with ash and cigarette-butts. One hand moved slowly, trailing smoke, from mouth to saucer and back. His knees were drawn up and he held a notebook resting against his legs. In the centre of the page, growing in curly lettering from a mass of doodles, was the motto: 'This is a *nice* town.'

Jimmy sighed and shook his head very slowly, asking himself silently just what in hell was the matter. Warwell hadn't disappointed; quite to the contrary. He liked the place. It was a n— Go on, say it. It was a nice little town. After a while the niceness ate into the bone, decaying it maybe. He frowned. The dreams? They were nothing. Erotic symbolism, psychosomatic disorder ... maybe he'd got a complex because he'd never killed his brother. Never had a brother to kill ... He shrugged, still lying prone. His state of mind must be attributable to his odd situation. Plenty of money, no ties, time to burn . . . He was completely at rest; it seldom happened, and never to the young.

Maybe he'd dream again tonight. The dream was always the same. Always vague, impossible to grasp afterwards; a thing of sensation only, an affair of mounting pressures that rose and rose to wake him once nearly screaming. After that the pressures eased but he still knew of their existence the way you can know of something in a dream without seeing or hearing. The Wheel, as he thought of it, was the central part of the nightmare; and he himself was at the centre of the Wheel, on or in its hub, sensing it move, feeling the thunder of it in his long bones. The Wheel so massive that size itself seemed an indecent, foul thing. And somehow too the hub was Warwell, its houses and its church. But the Wheel was useless; it moved, it ground, but it ground nothing. Its turning was aimless, the threat of it was simply in its *being* . . .

He got off the bed. The room was small, stuck up under the decorated eaves of The George just below where a terracotta dragon glared down into Station Square. The bedsitter was all in one; at the far side in an alcove was a sink, beside it the tiny gas cooker. Facing them, the door to the toilet. A chair, a folding table; the bed took up most of the space that was left. But there had been no point in burning money, and the garret had a good view. Jimmy walked to the window, stood looking out absently. Below him was the long roof of the station, beyond it the river and the water meadows. Farther off again the hills, the distant blue cloth of trees.

He told himself, *maybe you were wrong to come here and bury yourself away. Maybe you should have gone back to Town with your problem and your worry.* Maybe he should have talked to Roley.

He nearly laughed. Ask Roley what to do with forty thousand quid . . . Roley would have told him. He could see him now, hear him almost. 'Buy a Phantom One old boy, and half a dozen whores . . .' Yes, and kill yourself with an overdose of Mammon. On your father's money. Jimmy reached quietly for his cigarettes. Roley's mouth could have mocked, but not his eyes, pale-blue, warm-cold, watching out above the tangle of beard. Roley would have understood.

He told himself, *Roley would love this town. All the niceness that's loose here, it would be like a challenge to him. He'd get through it somehow to what really drives the place . . .*

Drives?

Funny idea. Nothing drives Warwell. Warwell has no drive, no reason for being. Warwell *is*, that's all. It has its own inbuilt, sparrow-bright perkiness; the people come and go, sleep and wake up, eat and talk and laugh. They're just born friendly, all of them. Why move, there's everything here. You get bored, you can get a job; some day you'll have to anyway because the money will run low, any money runs low. But right here there'd be no problem. Here you've got friends. Lots of them. You've been here a month and it seems you know half the town already, it's like you'd lived in Warwell all your life. But that's the sort of place it is. *Nice . . .*

Jimmy stubbed the cigarette, gave in to himself angrily and lit it again. He felt like a detective trying to solve a crime that hasn't been committed. There was everything for him in Warwell. The Wheel –

He told himself irritably, stop that for God's sake. Your point of view comes from your strange circumstances, you feel floating, dissociated, because that's just exactly what you are. No worries, no living to earn for a long, long time. He wondered, was he still being too selfish? Should he form an association with somebody, anybody? Easy enough to do . . .

He went back and lay on the bed again, pillowing his head on his arm, watching up at the quiet blackness of the ceiling. He pulled his lip slowly with his teeth. *One problem I can define,* he thought. *The forty thousand. How to use it well? How make up for the years it took out of the old man's life, the loneliness, the anger?* He told himself, *the answer's here. Always here, where I am, because the problem rides with me. I tried running. It wasn't any good.*

And Warwell?

It's crazy, but the town has a problem too. Maybe if I can find it, crack it, I'll find it's all tied up with me. So somewhere, someplace, I have to find the answer to some question, I don't know what the question is but when I see it I'll recognize it, know what to do. See what? See the Wheel. The thing that drives the town . . .

You're crazy, Stringer. Take yourself off, let the tide surge you around some more.

A month in a strange town. Somewhere in all the not-happenings, the men not there on all the stairs, is the key to a question I have to decode before I can even ask it. There is no wrongness here, just not-rightness. There's a world of difference between them. There must be a question, and an answer to it. I must find question and answer before I go because somehow I know it's important to me, to what I've become, to do that . . .

He gave himself up, angrily, to analysis. Covering ground covered before, letting scenes and sights swim out of his subconscious, flare and drop back. Like the little bridges swimming into sight from the train, falling away behind. Calmly and quietly, the way life was lived in Warwell-on-Starr. But that goes for all life, any life. Life is a walking shadow, a poor player that flits and struts his – oh go to hell . . .

I can look up Warwell in a gazetteer, find it on a map. It's here, it exists, it's solid like any other town. Its buildings are stone and brick, its people are flesh and blood, they have shadows. I can read its population, six thousand. Read it's a market town, no heavy industry, used to be a centre of the wool trade. It's an urban district, returned a Conservative member at the last election.

But that doesn't help me. It doesn't stop the strangeness, doesn't check the soundless noise of the Wheel.

Weren't dreams symbols? Twisted maybe out of all recognition, but still shadows sprung from something heard, seen . . . This was how the mind talked to itself, in imagery that clothed its own secret fears.

Then take an incident, any incident. Let's start again.

The dog. Yes, she'd do.

He was walking one evening, following the slow course of the Starr. There'd been cabin cruisers tied up at the bank, voices chuckling across the water. Night was coming, bluely; and it had crossed his mind that a man rambling alone like that could use a dog for company. No sooner the thought than the act; she'd come, flickering in the dusk, a long, slim hound, dark-eyed and fast. But she was no were-thing, she'd come up close and let him touch her, she was real enough. He'd wondered about her, she was good blood and there was no name tag on her collar. She'd followed him a mile, two, circling and dancing, then she'd melted back into the dark. He hadn't seen her before or since.

Take the people at The Horseshoes. It was a strange pub to him; he'd gone into the bar, found the place deserted. He remembered standing and downing his pint and wishing more or less vaguely for talk, for friendliness, some conversation to stimulate. And they'd come. A dozen of them, ordinary enough blokes but queerly fascinating, each in a different way. They'd talked; about the river and the town, about cars and dogs and the last war. The fighting in the Western Desert, and going up through Germany with the Eighth. Inconsequential stuff, but just what he needed. One of them had produced a pocket chess set later on, giving him a startlingly good game. He'd turned down a couple of supper invites, with some difficulty. Who were those folk? Where were they? He'd never seen them again.

And then The Green Dragon affair. That was the best of all. Take that one through stage by stage, relive it. Because somewhere, somewhere, there just *might* be something you missed. Get it all, get the fine detail.

He was walking up West Street on a Saturday night. Last Saturday, just under a week ago. He'd done a round of pubs, The Horseshoes, The Bell, The Royal Sovereign. He was just a little canned, and just a little melancholy. It was nine o'clock and turning dusk; most of the shopfronts were lit and the neon signs, cars parked on the grid outside the Town Hall, people strolling, alone like myself or arm in arm. The cinema doors were open and there was a do on at the church hall, lines of cars. Down by the Starr the lamps on the bridge were reflecting long wobbling steaks into the water and there was a smell of some blossom on the air, jasmine he thought. He got to The Green Dragon on the waterfront, there was a dance. He went in, downed a couple of Scotches, saw the g—

Steady. Get an impression of the room. Might be something there.

The dance floor was low-lit, the boards shining amber. There was a shuffling of feet, just audible under the band. Mirror bowl was working, making the brown people dancing look like animals caught undersea in a jewelled net. The girl was sitting on her own. Get the picture. Colour of hair. Its brownness, the way the light catches it. Little black dress. *That* little black dress . . .

The glass of Chartreuse in front of her. Colour? Clear light green. Like her eyes.

They danced, just a little. Then drove. She had an MG Midget. Model TF, colour maroon. Slight blow in exhaust, get all details right . . . They circled the valley, as if running on the rim of a wheel. It was a fine night, cloudless and with a high, full moon. They stopped up in the hills to hear things chirring in the air, the calling of owls. He remembered the girl-smell of her. Not scent. She had no scent, but something from her still filled the car, marking the cockpit as a special place.

The woods in the valley were like moonlit hessian. He watched down at them, mouth drying. Hearing her moving, little scraping sounds of fabric. 'You can have me if you want,' she said. 'I'm very good, and I do like you.' One breast was uncovered already and she was wriggling, trying to work the dress farther down.

He stubbed the cigarette and got up, prowled back to the window. He said 'Oh, no. No, no, no . . .' Too easy, the schoolboy's dream of home. She'd been so . . . nice about it, everybody was so bloody nice about everything, the world was just too smooth. What was her name? Liz, Liz Baron . . . Like the dog, like the chess player, she'd just edged into his life when needed and he hadn't seen her since. She came, she made herself bare for him, she slipped quietly away. No yelling, no recriminations. There was a flow, like the bridges flowing past the train.

He rubbed his hand across his face, in the high hotel room. One day, one hour, he'd crack the smooth skin of Warwell, see a little of the brightness that lay beneath. Something would happen, some time, somewhere, that wasn't *nice*. And then he'd have his key, the first piece of the puzzle. He said to himself, this could be important. This could matter very much. He picked his jacket up, slung it across his shoulder and went out to find a bar.

3

Next day he bought a car.

She was blue and low and nearly new and he fell in love with the cobby lines of her, and when he'd done he had exactly thirty-nine thousand and sixty-five quid left to his name but it was worth it. The insurance shocked and upset him, but he could afford it; he signed forms and wrote cheques and by lunch-time circuited the town. Then over the river bridge and up the dual carriageway beyond, pushing the ton, feeling the world was a sweet place. And back to The George to park the glitter temporarily in the hotel yard. (Virginia creeper hung down from the roofs, setting off the icy car beautifully, but there was no key there.) He thought, maybe if I keep piling perfection on perfection all the blacks will turn to white and positive to negative, there'll be one whacking big imperfection to sink my teeth in, or one that'll sink its teeth in me . . .

Imperfection.

He took the Triumph out of town that evening, up West Street and the hill beyond. The hill she flung away behind her, away and down. He drove across Sanford Common to Gallowridge, turned off through the little village there, left a crackle of exhaust behind him climbing again to How Beacon. Five or six miles out from Warwell, on the rim of the Whee – shut up, dammit – was a little pub, The Goat and Compasses (God Encompasseth Us. We hope.) Sixteenth century, so old it was nothing to look at. Stone-flagged floors, great fireplace with ingle-nooks set each side, fireback glinting with blacking, decorated with cast sheaves of corn. No bars, just white-scrubbed tables set about and they bring the beer in from the kitchen, beer comes from the woo – *Girl, running* – Beer from the *wood* –

Foot clamped to brake pedal and the TR4 swinging and throwing gravel, lane too narrow, hedges spinning past, she was running head down to meet him and he was moving too quick he couldn't stop. *God please* –

The thud, solid and hard. Then quiet. His hands holding the wheel, vibrating with shock. Then letting go the rim, having to make himself let go. Finding the catch, opening the door, no sensation of metal under the fingers. Throat dry like a sandy tube, unswallowing. He wasn't walking, it was just his feet. He floated.

She was kneeling in front of the bonnet holding her arm. Her hair was hanging and never was there such a still silent road, and her breath was scraping in the silence like a file on wood.

The car was nosed into the bank, there were scorings, grass

and clods thrown up. He'd steered into the bank. No, his hands had steered into thc bank. He hadn't hit her. He'd stopped just ... so, an arm's breadth. The thud hadn't been her. He told himself, the bank. Not her.

He was trying to lift her, turn her wrist. Expecting gravel-rash, not what he saw. The skin furrowed, curling back at the elbow from startled sheet-white flesh that grew pinpoints of red. The brightness coalesced, ran together in thickening trickles; the arm wept blood silently, fast. She pulled it away like she was ashamed of it. Her knee was hurt too, grit sticking to the graze. He put his arm down to pull her up and she was wet. Thin jumper, wet across the back. 'Running,' she said. 'I . . . sorry . . .'

'Here,' he said. 'Here ...' (Moment of seeing and knowing he'd killed her, sitting before his lazy foot would move, they called it reaction time.) The car engine was ticking as it cooled.

She was leaning on the bonnet and gasping, propping herself by her behind. Blood ran across her leg and somehow he knew brilliantly just how she was feeling, sort of dumb pain in the knee and stiffness spreading up to the shoulder from where she'd torn her elbow. He was asking her where he could take her; she was shaking her head, trying to push hair back from her eyes. No, no . . .

He said absurdly 'You're wet. Look here . . .' Opening the car door. (*Imperfection ... Who runs themselves wet, on a still summer night . . .*)

She tried to push away, brightness splashed his shoes. Jeeze, he thought, Jeeze. there just can't be an Awkward Pause, not now ... The thought galvanized him, he made her sit in, slide across from the wheel. Awkwardly, everything awkward ... There was a towel, he'd shopped in the afternoon, hadn't taken the things out of the car. Couple of shirts, hand towel. He put the towel in her hand, helped her wrap loosely. 'For your skirt,' he said. Skirt was a pretty little denim hipster, marked already. He got in the car, started up, pulled the bonnet out of the muck. Moment of panic, something would clank down there and he wouldn't be able to drive . . . But the Triumph was OK.

He headed back the way he'd come, moving fast, the girl lying beside him looking white. The hospital sign, he remembered seeing it. Place was off the road, stood back a hundred yards behind trees. Little old house, new low wing built on, he'd have called it a cottage hospital; probably wasn't called that now, probably was some Unit or other. He swung up to the front of it, ran round to lean on the porch bell. They were very good. Accident . . . yes, yes of course, take her arm . . . No it's all right now, have a seat Mr. . . . er. .

'Stringer,' he said Croaked. *And I hope to God there isn't dirt on my nearside front* . . . No, she's with me . . . No it didn't happen on the road, she fell . . . *Why the need to cover for myself and her? Because, he told himself with terrible clarity, because of the Wheel. Because then for a moment it showed itself; just the rim, filthy and shrieking, shoving up out of the soil. Until it ground back, into the quiet.*

Twenty yards away from him through a pair of open doors six perky men were being given supper, cheeking at the nurse with the trolley. The scene was brightly lit, a vignette set against the softly blueing dusk of the corridor. When the lights came on he saw other vignettes. A tall vase of red flowers on an occasional table. A copper jug in an alcove. A stack of magazines, *Field* and *Lady*. The whole of experience was for him now a series of glowing unconnected pictures against a dark backdrop. Like the images he had always imagined filtering through the compound eye of an insect.

When they brought her back to him she was chalk-pale. Sister was lined and bucktoothed and very lovable right now. 'Take her straight home,' she said. 'Straight home . . .' And Jimmy agreed. Yes, of course, tetanus, one couldn't be too careful, she'd had a shot, now she must be taken straight home . . . The arm was bandaged, neatly and whitely, the leg they hadn't bothered with, it was just wiped. He put his arm round her waist. She was still wet, he could smell the sweat now mixed with the other-world tang of the dressing. Leave it a couple of days he was told, and straight to her doctor if anything goes wrong . . . 'Yes,' he said. 'I'll see to her, she'll be all right. And thank you, Sister, very much indeed . . . Yes, yes of course . . .' And finally he could drive away into the night.

She said, 'I'm terribly sorry.' They were on the road, her hair was moving in the breeze, he was driving back to Warwell gently, mind busy. 'I must have put you about,' she said. 'It was very kind . . .'

He was just beginning to realize again that he hadn't killed her. 'I wasn't going anywhere,' he said. 'What's your name?'

'... Anne Nielson.' First the pause, then she didn't ask him his.

'What were you doing, Anne? You came so quick, I couldn't do a thing ...'

'I was running.' She shuddered. 'You hit the bank, if you hadn't hit the bank ...'

Leave it, leave it ... 'Where do you live?'

'In Warwell.'

'I'll take you home.'

'It doesn't matter.'

'It's no problem,' he said. 'Really, I insist.'

She's nearly blonde. Older than she looks. Running. Warwell. Six miles, seven ... Not from Warwell, couldn't have run from Warwell ...

'Please,' she said. 'Something silly. I'd like a drink.'

'*What?*'

She said, 'Nice long double Scotch. That's all ...' Her hand was on his sleeve.

He shipped the TR4 on to the hard standing outside The Dog and Badger. Nice little pub, he'd been there once before. 'Anne,' he said. 'This is all wrong.'

'Please. That is if you d-don't mind. I'm all right now. It was just the shock.'

So women are tougher than men. He opened the door, helped her out. She flicked her hair. 'God, I'm a mess ...'

Conventional remarks the order of the day. The fear had gone, she was female again. Had been a frightened child. So had he. He ordered the Scotch with misgivings. Waited for her. She'd excused herself to tidy up. He thought, she's tall. Taller than I realized. The saloon was empty, he stood looking at sporting prints on the walls. The pub was quiet; once a car passed, moving fast, then there was silence again while she didn't come and didn't come and didn't come.

He went to the side door, looked out. A lamp in the road showed him a wicket gate swinging. He walked back into the bar. Waited another quarter hour before admitting he'd been taken for a sucker. He realized then the true direction of the misgivings and felt nearly happy. Obscurely, he seemed to be back to familiar ground. 'Ah,' Roley used to say. 'The thrust and parry of Sex; the feint, the quick *riposte* ... The posturings, the *lunge* ...' Jimmy knew all about sex. (He was seventeen and feeling the cold. She was all of thirty and the more she took off the fatter she got, get stripped she said and he said I am stripped and she giggled and did something that made him screech, sex, *pshaw* ...) He poured the Scotch into a potted palm. He simply wasn't inventive enough; Dali once cut his finger on a glass and filled the glass with the blood and put in one real and one imitation cherry, set the apparatus on a table and asked everybody to watch it then stole quietly away, but all he could do was pour his Scotch into a potted palm. Jimmy recognized the fact that he was becoming cynical, finished the beer, got into the TR4 and drove home.

He paced the little hotel room, from sink to bed and back. An hour, two, telling himself of all things she's just twelve months too old to wear a hipster, but isn't she sweet; then he became aware, oddly, of the quietness in the town, the one oblong of light showing from under the tall eaves. He put the light off, pulled collar and tie und –

Down in the square a car engine started, wound up high in first. He ran back to the window, saw the bulk of the motor and the white fan of headlights swinging out the top of Station Road. Listened to the noise fade in the night.

No connection, he told himself. None. He pulled collar and tie undone, lay on the bed, lit a cigarette. Watched the pink reflection of it on the ceiling. All problems were soluble, including the present one. And he had a name to work on. Presuming the name was correct.

Don't presume though. Not a thing. Work from the facts. Anne, running. Wet through. She hadn't seen the car. Damn it to hell, she hadn't seen the road ... She was running or staggering along the road, head down. Where had she come from? No way of telling. What was she running from? From nothing. Empty fields, sunlight.

He imagined himself lacing up and projecting a mental film. The last few seconds when he already knew he'd killed her, the action recorded dispassionately by the camera of eyes and brain. He saw himself straining to hold the car, the girl stumbling at the bonnet.

Two images joined. He'd been to a coursing meet, just once. Seen the hare hit the wire and bounce back squalling, right under the dogs. He remembered its movements. Spastic, disorganized. Anne, running. Yeah, something had been there. Something that could hurt her worse than her poor scraped arm.

Queer to be thinking like this, in terms of Anne. Her pain, her fright. Everything in terms of Anne. It was as if she fitted into a gap already there in his consciousness. But that was crazy, he'd only seen her a few minutes, she'd been sweating, scared half to death. Scared of him, he told himself. Why?

Find her again then.

How? Population of Warwell was six thousand, nearer seven with the new estates. And she didn't live in Warwell, something told him she'd lied there, the answer had come too pat. Work in Warwell, then maybe? What as, clerk, typist, secretary? Get a Classified, start ringing the firms 'Excuse me, but do you have a Miss Nielson working for you?' Oh go to hell, and pick a few needles from haystacks on the way. His mind turned slowly, tiring itself with thinking. The car that had passed The Dog and Badger. He knew it had picked her up, a hundred yards or so down the road. Just how in hell had she fixed that runout? No answer. Never would be, till he found her again. The Wheel, the thing that ran this town. It wasn't going to give itself away. It was too big, it was too subtle; above all, look how it covered itself, it was too scared . . .

He found he was sweating in the dark. He wondered if he was going crazy. He'd always been a little mad, it was the artist in him. All artists were mad, everybody knew that. So most of them went mad quietly to fit the image, at heart they were conformists.

The car that had taken Anne away. The same car had circled back, mysterious and quiet, sat humped in Station Square watching up at his light.

Stringer, you're rambling. There's no proof of that, not even a basis for assumption. Your nerves are shot, you're getting the jumps. All this talk of a Wheel. Hallucination, vision . . . more like simple nuttiness. He told himself nobody has robbed a bank, nobody has done a murder, gunned their pal down in the street. All they've done is run a clean, quiet, friendly little town. And maybe made a girl bolt across a field.

They? Who were *They?* The people who'd hunted Anne. Maybe. The people in the car.

It was no use. *They* were there and the Wheel, grinding in his subconscious. He could feel it, it was almost as if the building shook. What would it do, now he'd seen it move? The Wheel was for grinding, grinding . . .

Anne . . .

He slept; and the dream came.

Not like any dream he'd ever had. Not like the dreams of the Wheel. Their horror lay in their vagueness; this one was clear and bright and pitilessly precise. He was standing on a station platform. He looked round slowly, recognized Tanbridge. The little wooden footway over the tracks, the banks of roses. But the tracks were rusty now, they gleamed in the stark light orange-pink and shocking as dissected veins; and the roses were dying, they thrust out from their trellises like black spiky skeletons. The sun was shining but it held no warmth, it was like the pale orb of a half-eclipse. And the light was fading slowly from the sky.

He became aware by degrees of a huge sense of desolation. It swamped him, bore down till it felt like a weight across his back. He could barely force his feet to move. He dragged himself across the platform, over the bridge. Wood broke and crumbled under his heels. He touched the flowers and they crumbled too, dropped into flakes that a wind picked up, tossed into the sky like black snow. There was a railbus waiting and a . . . sort of motorman. He made himself get aboard, fighting revulsion at every step; and the car was so old, the seats of it were blackened and brittle, its wood was dull, splotched over with mildew. Even the mirrors had grown continents of green and ginger spots. He heard the buzzer and the answer from the cab; he thought the coach would never move but it did, creaking and moaning. Out past a dead signalbox, into the hopeless light.

On the road the little bridges had fallen, they shoved up stumps like decayed teeth. The train cried, but there was nothing pleasant in the sound; the hoarseness of it whirled up and away like the last noise on a dying planet. There were people by the track, first ones and twos then more then a great dim crowd of them pushing forward, jostling, holding out their arms. He saw folk he knew. His parents, people from Town, old

Roley; but the faces were transformed, skulls seemed to glow and smirk through the flesh. They shouted and mouthed, but the carriage couldn't stop; and it seemed that as it moved darkness followed it, pulled like a skirt to swallow the throng. The coach reached Warwell with a final bang and groan; Jimmy touched the door, it crumbled sickeningly in his hands. He walked through what was left of the barrier. Dust blew in swirls, and ancient leaves of paper. He looked back; but it seemed already centuries had passed, the train had rotted on the rails, spread rust round it and out along the tracks like the stain of a haemorrhage. A glower of light showed behind it, horizon burning silver, zenith of the sky dark, dark . . .

He tried to hurry into the square. Roofs and houses had fallen, trees stood stark, the river had gone, left the bare cracked mud of its bed. He thought he was the only living creature on earth but he was wrong, there was Anne. She stood on the steps of The George Hotel, in her jumper and denim skirt. The wind gusted round her, lifted her hair; when it blew from the building the old dying stench of the place came with it, like Victorian sweat. He was walking, pushing with feet made of lead, but now the square was a mile across and there was no sense of progress. She called to him, high and piping, a gull-noise shredded by the wind. Tried to move, stumbled and fell on the path. And his car was there, the bright TR4, standing by the kerb. As he stared the rust ran along her like a wave, a dark shadow visible to the eye. Burst through the bright skin of her in patches that joined and spread like fingers. She sagged, tyres wheezing, came down on her sump and sagged again. Gear clusters rolled, the box walls no longer able to hold them; the little wheels ran flashing, browning as they went, fizzing away to dust, to nothingness to blow along the wind. He gasped, fighting for breath. Three steps more, another yard . . . He could nearly reach Anne, he was on his knees stretching his arms. Their fingers met, gripped . . . and the Change, the huge Age that was romping through the world, caught her. He saw her shrinking, fullness sagging, clothes loosening round old limbs that were twisting, withering. He screamed, but there was no sound. Cried, feeling the tears on his face burned by the desiccating wind. She was a rag, a hank of hair; then cloth and flesh fell away, bone showed, browned, blackened, crumbled. He scrambled forward madly, clutching; tatters flew in the sky, the wind yowled and mooed; skeletons of hounds coursed the brown wound of the river, their bone-voices boomed into dark and there was nothing, the buildings empty shells, no Anne, just dust, dust, dust . . .

He sat up on the bed wet and quivering with shock. His throat was full; he staggered to the basin, retched. Then again and again till there was nothing left to come, but still his stomach churned and the stink was in his nose, sweet like old flesh, ancient bone. His vision sparked in darkness; he slipped, landed on his knees, weaved his head from side to side. The sickness passed enough to let him get up, sprawl across the bed. Then the bed moved. There was a roaring in his ears; it was the Wheel, churning . . . he tried to scream again and there was no sound, just Power, Power, more Power than he could have dreamed.

The noise faded and he was still. A last thought stirred in his mind. *This was why she ran* .

4

The lorries woke him, clattering in Station Square in the early dawn. He mumbled and rolled over, lay for a time trying not to remember. Then he got up and padded to the window, stared down rubbing his face. The drags stood rattling, cab doors ajar; there was shouting, blue diesel fumes jetted from the exhaust stacks. Each vehicle was pulling a road train of trailers, their loads bulky under lashed-down tarpaulins. It took Jimmy a minute or longer to realize what was happening. The steam fair was arriving.

He leaned on the sill. He'd been looking forward to the fair. he'd intended buying some sketching gear, turning back into an artist for a few days before he moved out of Warwell. But the night before had changed all that. The flavour of the dream persisted; images came in front of his eyes, he saw skeletons riding Gallopers and Switchbacks, swaying on the Cakewalk, jigging to the noise of a calliope. He rubbed his face again violently and the pictures faded. The lorries moved off, but he couldn't sleep any more.

He sat on the edge of the bed and smoked till he'd finished

the packet. Then he shaved, changed out of his rumpled clothes. spent a couple of hours walking by the river where he could see the town in the distance, the clustering of the houses. His head throbbed, his eyelids felt heavy. The air was clear and keen, but didn't it carry some faint tang? Just a hint, a suggestion, but it was enough. To Jimmy it seemed the very wind blew from some place of corruption and oldness.

He ate no breakfast. The black mood persisted; he found himself hating Warwell and its inhabitants, everything about the place. He went to the car meaning to drive out somewhere, clear his head with speed. He couldn't touch her; some part of his mind knew if he lifted the bonnet the rust would be there, a red well of it, waiting to strike through and burn. On the front seat was a smudge of dried blood. He set his face and turned away, walking aimlessly.

Watching the skeletons. Talking and laughing, shopping, eating. Drinking coffee in the Tudor Room and the Buttery, cleaning windows, driving cars, sitting in buses, pushing prams. Other skeletons lay in the perambulators, little gristly things that mewed and writhed. He sat on a seat outside the Town Hall, wiped his forehead, saw sweat on his hand. He clenched his fists; he was trembling, he asked himself what's the matter with me, have I gone crazy? It was all he could do to stop himself yelling, telling the people didn't they realize, didn't they know they were all bone and slime, they were getting older, they were *dying* ... He put his face in his hands, tried to stop the shaking. Feeling the traffic grind and grind like one great Wheel, seeing the fish-eyes roll, hearing the bird-gabble of skulls, tongues clacking inside the bone ... He felt he was going to pass out again, or vomit on the path.

God, he'd never felt like this since ... *when?* His mind groped for a parallel. Warwell, the river and the valley, church spire and Town Hall cupola thrust up from a writhing of goblins and demons, a medieval maggot-heap ... Away from the Starr he knew the world was *good*, there were grass and trees and high quiet roads. He had to get away. He was half-way to his hotel, scurrying to pack his bags and pay his bill, when he realized. Knew suddenly and with complete sureness that he wasn't going crazy.

He leaned on a wall, gasping. Shoppers stared, edged past. He wasn't conscious of them. *Nature imitates art,* he thought. Subject for a college thesis.

See the film of Moulin Rouge. *The ride back to your digs on a London Transport bus. See the women and men, the turn of a wrist, tilt of a nose just so . . . Lautrec folk all of them. You're soaked in a way of seeing, you look through somebody else's eyes.*

Quick now, think. For God's sake *think* . . . The skulls, the bones, the flaring light . . . Something Germanic, *Die Brücker,* the Blue Riders? No, older than that, farther back. Holbein? No, not Holbein at all. *Bosch* . . .

And by God that was it. Old Hieronymus, the Adamite. The *Millennium;* incarnation of all evil, writhing, pallid . . . He'd studied it once for a holiday task, reached the stage where he could look through the painter's eyes, see the world and its people as the master had seen it all those years ago. Now he was seeing it again.

A chain of logic had completed itself without his direction. The fantasies that had swamped him, rose bowers that had glowed, sweet organic nestling of river against town; these things he had been *shown,* as now he was seeing their obverse. Somebody, *something,* had tried to lull him with women and talk and drink and beauty, bright canvases all of them dangled in front of his face; and it hadn't worked, he'd gone on searching and prodding, as Roley would have done, and he'd touched the makers of the dreams and they were frightened. He'd touched them through Anne.

Crazy, his brain yelled at him, *crazy, crazy* . . . But it was too late. He could feel now the strange Will pushing, insisting, making a living canvas out of Warwell. And the rage came, dulling his mind to impressed thought. He told himself, *they* were doing this. The people who'd taken Anne away, the people who ran this town, made horror and impossible beauty and used them like weapons. Whoever they were, they'd half killed him last night. And worse; they'd destroyed Anne, stripped her to the bone, rotted every cell and tendon of her. Shown him, mercilessly, the things nobody should see. Now, they'd given themselves away.

The noise that had swamped him receded. He straightened up with an effort, stared round at the bright town. Saw the shops, sunlight, the four crossing roads; the valley cupping streets and houses like a grassy hand. The town was finite; so was the enemy within. And it was a child, he told himself, that feared a painted devil.

He started to walk. It was like wading against a hot river that pressed relentlessly. Suddenly he was very tired; there were weights on his back, on his legs and arms. He couldn't drag himself another yard, not another step. He countered the fresh attack with the image of Anne. Anne alive, full of blood and electricity, with a woman's body that could make sweat and tears and milk. He told himself, *Anne isn't dead.* Convinced himself somehow that if ... *they* could drive him out then she would die, in his mind, and that death would be final. He moved against the pressure, holding the thought and the picture of Anne, wanting Anne and holding the rage. Peering into shops, offices, into garages, through walls that seemed half transparent. Not feeling the sun, not hearing the gabbling. Somewhere was the enemy, impossible but real. *Keep sending,* he thought. *Keep sending till I come. They* responded, stepping up their force.

If you're real, if you're human, pray for yourselves. Because when I find you I'll break your bones, I'll pull you joint from joint ...

Laughter echoing, the little town ringing with it. The noise vaunting up like cracked bells in the sky.

Show yourselves ...

Searching and circling, endlessly. Every house, every street. Walking, staring, feeling. No sense of time; in dreams, time ceases to matter. *Find them,* he told himself. *Because they're here.* Odd times he thought what he was hunting had stopped bothering to hide itself; it made a shape ahead of him in the air, it was a pressure, a noise, a coldness and hotness joined. He saw the Town Hall through a golden haze, and the river and church. He said to the sky, *show yourselves* ... But it was hopeless. *They* were in the town, owning it and exulting, but they had no focus. Never would have, until they chose. He asked himself, *how many of the people here, the vacant faces playing chess and making love, felt what I felt and were drawn then lulled and fed like cows?* Lunch-time came and passed, offices emptied and refilled. *Vacant and harmless,* he told himself. *Like cows.* And the sun moved. The wind played in the trees. The river flowed.

How long can you keep a rage in concert tune? Not for ever, the effort would kill. And they *know that. I'm burning, bleeding off strength, but I have to keep on now. If I give in the skeletons will come back and all the rest and I'll forget I'm watching somebody else's picture and then God help me, God help me indeed . . .*

They were laughing now, tickling and prodding, squeezing out the last of the anger. He stood blinking and seeing the Town Hall clock. The hands marked a quarter after five. He knew suddenly he was through. His legs ached, his feet felt like they were blistered raw and he'd found nothing, no Anne. And the ghosts still babbled, the skeletons walked mantled with flesh as it was in the beginning, is now and ever shall be . . . But no praying please, there is nothing to listen. *Move, ghost, ghost yourself, in our little shadow world of the river and the town here in old Warwell. Soon, you'll leave . . .*

He turned away, helplessly; and *they* were with him again, skipping and taunting. *Why give up so soon? Here, along this street here . . . or, that one over there, perhaps what you're looking for is there . . .*

He moved dumbly, mind blocked with fatigue, not able now to raise even the image of Anne. He'd forgotten what she looked like. The Pied Piper drew him gently, away from town centre where the officers were emptying at the end of the day, the buses pulling in and drawing off.

He turned back into hell and noise. Dragons burned on rooftops, streets shone bright with blood. He was swearing at himself for a fool. He'd been led round and about all day long, *they* had let him use himself up. Now for just a little while he had to swim against the tide, go where *they* didn't want him to be. he'd forgotten why.

He saw her through fire and din, glimpsed the white scut of the bandage. She was boarding a bus outside the Town Hall. he started to run back to The George to get his car. The car was rust, would fall to bits under his hands . . . Yes, he said impatiently, he knew that. He got in the Triumph still knowing it, started up, gunned her across the yard and under the arch. She didn't come apart.

He caught the bus as it slowed for the brow of West Hill. Steady now he told himself, *steady.* Hang back, stay in sight, sooner or later she has to get off . . . The air round the car seemed nearly thick with rage, but *they* couldn't touch him now.

The lane opened on the left, there were houses set back a couple of hundred yards. He saw her leave the bus and slammed the Triumph forward, terrified now of losing her. Must take her by speed, he knew she'd run . . . He raised dust skidding into the lane. She was fifty yards away, looking back already. He accelerated, hit the anchors, came over the top of the door. She was scampering now and he was running head down, the houses were close and he'd never moved so fast but the gap wasn't narrowing. He was back in nightmare; the enemy were throwing everything they had, he felt his flesh pierce in holes and boil away, the wind bite among his bones. And every step was a century long and he'd touch her and she'd shrivel like in the dream and he couldn't take that again, not again . . .

She was down on the verge, he nearly fell across her. Shoe in her hand swinging, spike heel coming at his face; he ducked and got her wrist and she was strong, she rolled over and back and arched her body, hissed like a cat. He banged her arm at the bank and again harder, her fingers uncurled, the shoe rolled in the ditch. Then he was kneeling, still holding her wrist, breath coming harsh and her hair across her face, she was panting and the wind and terror had gone. He wanted to tell her she hadn't shrivelled, hadn't died, that she had blood and sweat, but there were no words. 'In the dream,' he said thickly. 'Dream . . .'

She stared, and he saw the tears coming; then, 'I know . . . it's all right . . .' And impossibly she was in his arms, he was holding her and she was holding him back and moving against him, texture of wool and hair and smell of being close, he was rubbing her hair and damn it to hell she wasn't even pretty, lines across her cheeks from not getting enough sleep and the hair over her ears nearly starting to be grey. 'Anne,' he said. 'Anne.' Damn it to hell and gone, he'd thought he was chasing a bit of tinsel but that wasn't Anne.

He pushed away. He said, 'Your shoe went in the ditch . . .' and 'Here . . .' Finding a handkerchief. 'You've got a snotty nose . . .'

Trying to laugh. 'I . . . sorry,' she said. 'Thank . . .'

'Keep still.'

He'd reached the shoe out of the ditch, she was standing, he was holding her ankle. Just the start of her, at the foot, was wonderful. 'They gave up,' he said. 'They went away.'

'No . . .' She was shaking her head, she nearly wasn't wearing any make-up, her eyes were grey and sea-wet. 'They're waiting,' she said. 'It's you that has to go.'

His hand was holding her waist, steering her. *Not to lose her again* . . . He listened to his voice make words. 'They sent me a girl. Elizabeth. But I didn't want her.'

'You mustn't s –'

'When you're an artist,' he said. 'Cross-grained by nature, just can't take what's . . . given. Mind . . . have to make your own shapes from what you see . . .'

'You're not making sense. I don't know what you mean . . .'

But you're walking. Towards the car. I'm making you do that, I'm stronger than they are . . . He'd done a hundred hours' thinking in the last few minutes. He said, 'I know about *them*, you see. Isn't secret, not any more.'

'You're a . . . liar . . .'

'Anne,' he said. 'Anne, I *know* . . .' Firmly, nearly believing it himself. Knowing if he frightened her now she'd run again and this time he wouldn't catch her. 'I know about *them*,' he said. 'And you. Anne, don't you want to break out of this stinking town, don't you want a life of your own any more?'

'The shoe,' she said. 'It wasn't . . . I didn't mean . . .'

Keep pushing. The fragments come, and they make a sort of sense. He hugged her gently, trying to stop her wanting to run away. He said, 'I'll show you how much I know. *They* . . . heard me. A long way away. They wanted me here. But afterwards . . . I wasn't right. They sent the girl and the dog and the man who played chess. Maybe they made everything, they made the . . . car be where I should see it. But it wasn't any good. So they sent . . . last night . . .'

'No . .'

He went out on a crazy limb. 'I lost a father,' he said. 'I thought my mind was going to explode. What happened to you Anne, how did they hear you –'

She started to panic again. She was trying to fight him. *'Go away,'* she said. *'Go away go away go away –'*

He shook her, having to shout. 'I can't. I'm in too deep –'

'You don't know what it's like,' she said. 'Oh, God,' she said. She was crying badly, trying to hide her face. '*Oh God* –'

He was sitting with her in the car, his arm was round her shoulders. He gave her a cigarette. 'Listen,' he said, dry-mouthed. 'I found you again, didn't I? When *they* didn't want me to?'

She nodded dumbly. He took her hand, rubbed the knuckles. 'Then trust me. I know what I want, I'm crazy, I have a wonderful life . . .'

'They'll kill you . . .'

'Then I'll rise on the third day. Anne, I *believe*. People, us, I believe in . . . oh hell, everything, *they* can't stop us. Don't you want to get free again, not even try?'

'Can't.' She banged the car dash miserably. '*Can't, can't* . . .'

'Not by running,' he said. *Still the crazy pattern, fitting* . . . He said, 'You can't run from *them*. That's what they like, isn't it? For you to try to run. You were running last night –'

'*No* . . .'

'Anne,' he said. 'I've got to meet them.'

'No!' She choked on the word that time, made a noise like a bad gearchange. Puffed at the cigarette, hand shaking. 'It'll be Paul,' she said. 'Next time, it'll be *Paul* . . . Last night was only Albert, he has the sort of . . . Gothic sense . . .'

'What does Paul do?'

Shuddering. 'He makes . . . things . . .'

'Were they why you were running?'

She nodded mutely. Cat had got her tongue.

'They can't hurt you.'

The nodding again, furiously.

'What can they do to you?'

'*Things*,' she said. '*Things* . . .'

Don't let the rage start, not again. A man in a rage can't think. And you need to think, by God how you need to think . . . Two names, he told himself. *Paul, Albert.* He nearly knew what he was fighting. 'Anne,' he said. 'Can you shut them out?'

'S-sometimes . . .'

'Tonight's a special time,' he said. 'Be ordinary, Anne. I want to take you out. Got a lot of talking to do . . .' This was the only way, soon he could draw *them* into the open. He said, 'It's about this pub . . .'

'Pub . . .'

'Down in the West Country,' he said. 'Long way off from here.'

Crazy how a problem can drag on for years then unsnarl itself in an instant of time. He'd said to himself, once I find an answer to Warwell, I find an answer to everything else. He'd been right. He asked himself, what if my father didn't hate at all? Then all the long years would be an act of faith, a blessing not a curse. 'To thine own self be true . . .' Aloud he said, 'Anne, if you're the person I think you are you'll understand this. There was an old man once who wanted his son in business with him. Wanted to put "*and Son*" over the gate, was all. I said something that took him apart. Afterwards, the money, I didn't understand. I was a smart little Townie, I didn't understand . . .'

'B –'

'I never stood up to anything,' he said. 'Not till today. Just ducked out and thought I was being smart. Dad knew that. just wanted me to wake up, that was all.' A pause; then, 'He'd have liked you,' he said. 'Very much.'

'Jimmy, the pub –'

'Oh,' he said, 'That . . . it all worked itself out, it sort of came clear.' But you have to be married or they won't give you a li –

'*What?*'

'Married,' he said. 'Oh, I am being patient. For a start I kept thinking it was crazy, love at first sight and all that mush, but it isn't love of course you live through that pretty early on. Need's a different thing, rotten thing, can't do much about it. I'm sorry for your friends, they don't stand a chance –'

'*What?*' she said. '*What?*' And he thought Christ it'll be the shoe again but it won't be as bad this time because it'll only be her rage driving it. 'I can see you now,' he said. 'Standing back of the bar cheeking the locals . . .'

'*Jimmy . . .*'

It sank in, the second time. 'Oh,' he said, 'she knows the fellow's name all along. Nice little espionage service they have down here, not bad for the sticks. Congratulations, m'dear, now it's a hard life but rewarding –'

'What –'

'The pub, God I shall have to spell it out for you. Up with

the lark and all that and scrubbing the loos before you can have your supper but it's very rewarding, human contact you know, invaluable to the artist, write a book about it. Seven days a week but you get the afternoons free and we'll have a glass roof in the snug for the pigeons to land on –'

'Jimmy please –'

'Geraniums,' he said. 'Now my maternal G-Granny was a great one for geraniums, you keep the soil loosened round the roots or you have to be careful not to loosen the soil round the roots or something but they're great for the outside, window-boxes, very fetching. Snap up the tourist trade. And there's Roley of course, did I tell you about Roley?'

'*A*...'

'Guy I worked with,' he said. '*Prix de Rome.* We had a pact. First one to get a pub gives the other a month's free beer. Now Roley can smell free beer from a hundred and fifty miles so that'll be OK but I can send him a letter just in case. You'll like him, he's great, he'll turn up in something twenty feet long with rivets down the bonnet and the first thing he'll do is ask you to bed with him but not to worry, he says that to all the g –'

'You're ... mad,' she said, struggling. He kissed her mouth; he nearly couldn't help it, she was whipping her head about, turned straight into it. Then he couldn't stop, he had to kiss her eyes and hair.

She lay still, like a toy with a busted spring. Eyes shut in pain, tears still squeezing out under the lids. The tears were salt, he could taste them. 'Anne,' he said, 'I know I'm mad. But not as mad ... as this town.' He lifted the hem of her skirt gently. Her legs were straight and smooth and there was no mark, no sign of a graze. '*They* saved you from the car,' he said. 'But they threw you too hard, they had to do it hard.' He touched the bandage on her arm. He asked, 'Did you have to keep wearing it? Was there somebody might have noticed?'

No answer.

'Why did they mend you?' he said. 'Were you bothering them?' He shook her suddenly, trying to make her react. 'Don't you see I can't stop now ...?' He swallowed. 'Anne, will you trust me?'

Again the silence.

'I can't leave you here,' he said. 'For *them* to perform ... indignities ... on your body.' Then very quietly, 'Do I make myself clear?'

She spoke bitterly, not opening her eyes. 'Dignity, indignity ... Do you understand about dignity, Jimmy? Do you think you do?'

He tidied her skirt. 'Darling,' he said. 'Last night they ... opened your grave, I don't know another way to say it. I didn't know about them. Like you said. I was lying. But I know this. for what they did ... *I'll choke them ...*'

Her voice sounded remote. 'I had a twin sister,' she said. 'The thing that killed her, they could cure it now.' She licked her mouth. 'I guess,' she said, 'I guess I shouted pretty loud. Afterwards ... I couldn't get away. My parents don't know where I am. I changed my name.'

'We'll go see them,' he said. 'Soon, now.'

She looked at him, finally. Deep tiredness in her eyes. She said, 'I'll take that drink I missed out on. Were you very mad?'

He drove her home. A whole hundred yards.

5

They weren't by the river. *They* weren't out on the road. *They* weren't anywhere, any place he drove. Anne sat beside him tensed and waiting; he hadn't fooled her, she knew what he was doing. there was something in this town, something he loathed, and she was his key to it. He felt crazy, now. He'd driven up the hill that afternoon, come back down with a wife; it was a prodigy, against the natural ordering of things. He waited for other miracles. They didn't come.

There was a temptation to run, turn the nose of the car at the open road and shove the throttle. But it was no good. Whatever this thing was, he couldn't hide from it; he knew that instinctively. He looked across at Anne. How much did he know about her, truly? Everything, he told himself. Everything and nothing. She'd come to Warwell, settled in a shared room over a country pub, got herself a job as secretary with a firm that marketed radio spares. That was all she'd told him and he knew she'd say no more. She couldn't, because she was involved more deeply than he. She was part of the thing that had hounded him.

She was sitting stiffly, hair blowing out. She was wearing a sweet summer dress. She held the bandaged arm blatantly somehow, like a badge. *They* had done that to her, and worse. Run her wet, ridden her like a horse. Jimmy gripped the wheel, trying to squeeze the impression of his hate into the metal.

They were waiting at The Dog and Badger.

He saw the lights of the pub showing ahead against the evening blue of the sky, felt Anne tense as soon as the place came in sight. A car was parked in the little pull-in; he drove alongside, sat and looked it over. Jaguar, XK150. Saloon, black. He remembered the howl of an engine the night before. And the car that had wound up passing The George. The big car. XK? Could be . . .

He set the brake, turned his engine off, walked to the passenger door. Anne got out, stood pressing herself against him and vibrating. He didn't need to ask. *They* were inside.

He walked towards the saloon door, stopped. He said quietly, 'All of them?'

'No . . .' Shivering. 'Two . . .'

'It's OK, Anne,' he said. His fingers found her damp ones, curled round them. 'It's OK . . .'

'The Little One,' she said. 'Mind the Little One, she throws things . . .'

'Interesting. Got a temper on her, has she?'

'No!' Violently. '*She throws things* . . .'

The bar was quiet. Just like the night before. The sporting prints hung on the walls, the counter glassware shone. He stopped just inside the door, and stared. *They* stared back. The two of them. *She* was small and cute. Little skirt pulled far too high, curly short hair, eyes of baby blue. Red horseshoe of mouth, smiling. *He* was dark, hair black and wavy, oiled till it glinted. Wide-set strange eyes, flat, hot-brown. No expression there at all.

Anne walked in behind Stringer, hesitated. A pause; then the little One lifted her arm. Snapped her fingers.

The girl moved past Jimmy like a sleepwalker. Stopped beside *them*, and turned. The three faces watched and somehow they were the same, God they were the same –

He got her wrist roughly, pulled. Anything to break that trilogy. She came to him; he could hear her panting in the quiet room. He rang the bar bell for service, someone came. He didn't see who. He opened his mouth, but it was the Little One who spoke. 'A large beer,' she said sweetly. 'And a Scotch. Double. The one the lady didn't have last night.'

He paid for the drinks. He couldn't take his eyes off *them*. 'Anne,' he said. 'Who are your friends?'

'Hazel . . .' She was swaying, he was scared she was going to fall. 'Hazel, Johnny . . .'

'Uh-huh,' he said. Nodding. 'Hazel. Johnny.' He made himself look back to her. 'Drink your drink, poppet. Then go sit in the car. *My car*.'

She didn't move.

There was danger here, he could feel it shift and coil and raise his back hair. He could fight what he could see but he wanted her out first. 'Anne,' he said sharply. '*Do as you're told* . . .' She picked the glass up, lips pale. Swallowed jerkily, coughed, touched her mouth, looked at him in pain, walked out. He heard the door close behind her then the click of the catch on the Triumph. His ears seemed preternaturally sharp. He took a breath. 'Hazel,' he said. 'It's rude to snap fingers. Anybody ever told you?'

No answer. Just the staring, innocent and intense. And the smile curving, curving, it would touch her ears. The cat was looking at the cream.

He drank his beer, eyes watching over the rim of the tankard. *What would they do, pull a knife, a gun? Nothing you fool, nothing like that. Nothing you could understand* . . . He finished the pint, walked forward stepping carefully on his toes. His body felt light, balanced. He leaned on the table in front of *them*, resting on his knuckles. And still there was the smile, same smile now on two heads. The rage was back, furring his throat; he made himself be calm. 'We came in,' he said. 'We had our drinks. Nobody stopped us. Now we're leaving. Anybody going to object?'

Silence. The smiling silence.

'Don't click fingers,' he said. 'Not at Anne. *I* don't like it.' he picked the Little One's hand up from where it lay on bright formica. Was an ordinary little hand, nails bitten down. He twined his fingers and twisted, slowly closed his grip. He'd always had powerful wrists. Hazel rose slightly in the chair, arching her body, smiling still. 'Do you want to be broken?' he said. 'Or you Johnny, do you want to be pulled apart? No? Then get off my back. Get right, right off. As of now.' He stepped away, sidled to the door. 'That was a promise,' he said. 'Not a threat. I don't threaten.' He closed the door on the smiles. got into the TR4 and found he was shaking. He reached across, took Anne's wrist, pressed. 'It was all right,' he said. 'Don't worry, it was *all right* . . .'

It was late that night before he dropped the girl at her lodgings. He drove back down to Warwell feeling better than he had in weeks, stopped in the car-park in the middle of town. It was past midnight, the yard gates at The George would be shut; he'd been with his Anne a long time, talking and dreaming and watching the moon. He got out of the car. He'd leave her where she was, she'd come to no harm. He pulled the tonneau cover across the cockpit, clicked the studs in place, fastened the zip. He straightened up, looked round. The town was utterly quiet; the moon was still high, riding a clear sky. The central area of the car-park was brightly lit, round it the pointed shadows of buildings were inky black. He started to walk across the open space, heading for the gates.

He stopped. The noise . . . It had sounded loud in the silence. a shuffling, scraping. Not a footstep. He looked behind him and to each side. Nothing. He felt the hair prickle again on his neck. Wished he'd brought his car torch with him, but it was back at The George. The sound came again.

Very deliberately, he took his handkerchief from his pocket. he wound it into a ball, gripped it in his fist. In the mob the boys had used pullthrough weights, but the hankie would have to serve. He pushed pennies between his knuckles, wadding them against the cloth. He looked round him again slowly; and there was the noise, in front and to his right.

He turned and stared. Twenty yards away, lying in the moonlight, was a plank. Three or four feet long, six inches broad by a couple thick. A moment before, it hadn't been there.

He extended one foot carefully. Felt the toes touch the ground, took a step. As he moved so did the plank. It rose on end, hung swaying slightly. It was between him and the gate.

'Uh-huh,' said Stringer. 'Yeah . . .' And started to walk.

A long time back when he was a tiny kid there was a dog he had to pass on the way from school. He remembered now how he'd edge by the place where the thing lived, walking on the opposite side of the road. Sometimes the dog would come, with a pattering rush. Sometimes not. But always as he walked he could sense without looking the open garden gate. Feel the presence of it like a hot breeze against the skin. The sensation was there now. He kept his eyes ahead, stepped past where the plank hung and rocked in moonlight.

He felt it move. Saw the quick flash of it from the tail of his eye, ducked. The wind from it lifted his hair. It spun back; he jinked, started to run. Wasn't quick enough. The end of the wood thudded into his chest, it felt like the blow had stopped his heart.

The Little One . . . The Little One throws things.

He doubled again knowing he couldn't win. Couldn't fight . . . this. A blow across the back fetched him to his knees. It came again, over the base of the spine. And again, *bang*, into his ribs.

Bang . . .

Bang, bang . . .

His breath was sobbing. There was a huge sickness, there were stars, flashings, *Anne, please* . . . The car was close now, he was fumbling at the cockpit cover. Something sailed past. A clang on metal; he grabbed, there was a wrenching, his palm tore agonizingly. He was in the car fighting with the ignition, key wouldn't fit, wouldn't turn, wrong key . . . He saw the missile swooping end-on, jerked his head back behind the screen, flung his hands up. The last blow blotted out the car park and the moon.

A paleness, filtering between his eyelids. He opened them fractionally, felt how his brain, photo-sensitive, reacted to light with pain. He lay still while the throbbing eased. Then he sat up. The pain came back, exploding downward into his body. Ribs, hips . . . He groaned, put a hand to his face. A scraping, and more pain. He saw dimly the flesh on the palm was ragged, splinters were showing. He shut his eyes again, squeezed, opened them, waited while gliding images fused. The roofs of buildings showed in dawn light, the tall hogs-back of the cinema. The white ice-glitter in front of him was the broken edge of the windshield; glass was strewn across the bonnet of the car, in her cockpit. He swore uselessly and looked round. No sign of the plank.

His jaw felt nearly broken. He fumbled with the rear view mirror, turned it till he could see. Cheek and chin were grazed; the plank would have smashed his face, it had missed when he jerked his head. Blood had run down his neck in an untidy stripe, spread a brown fingershaped stain into the collar of his shirt. He put his head in his hands, sat still awhile. Felt a little steadier, groped for his cigarettes.

The man was standing beside him before he realized. He felt the aura, half-turned, saw the dark blue of the uniform, froze still holding the match. He tried to speak. His mouth felt like it was full of felt. 'I . . .' he said. 'I . . . a stone. Afterwards . . . didn't feel so good . . .'

'I see sir . . .' The policeman had his thumbs hooked in his pocket flaps, he was rocking gently on his heels. 'This your car?'

'I . . . yes . . .'

'Made a bit of a mess of it haven't you? Got your licence with you by any chance?'

He stared up, trapped, and saw the eyes. Long somehow, like the eyes of a cat. Almond-shaped and hazel. His throat worked as he swallowed. The eyes, and the face . . . He'd seen the face before. Three times. He licked his mouth. 'I'll . . . go,' he said. 'Go. I . . . had enough, officer. Don't want any more . . .'

He'd done the right thing. The man stepped back, strange eyes dancing. 'Yes, sir, I should if I were you. I'm just walking round the block now. When I get back . . . don't be here, will you?' He turned on his heel and moved away.

The cigarette smoke tasted bitter. Jimmy threw the thing away, switched on the ignition. His hand shook when he touched the key. He revved the engine, brushed fragments of glass from the windscreen edge, drove out of the park. His mind was blank.

The town was still sleeping and quiet. He turned left at the traffic lights, crossed the Starr. Saw the fairground way off, rides jacketed with green tarpaulins. He reached the dual carriageway and opened up a little, heading for Midhampton ten miles away.

The airblast from the broken screen cleared his head; when he reached the town he could think again. He found a car-park with toilets open, washed his face, picked the worst of the splinters from his hand. There was a sweater in the car. He put it on. it had a polo neck that hid the marks on his shirt. He went back to the washroom mirror. His face was pale and the grazes showed brightly, but it was the best he could do. He went looking for a garage.

He'd been anticipating some sort of trouble, he was carrying fifty quid in his wallet for emergencies. He found a Standard-triumph agency, hung round till they opened, told them a tale and left them working on the TR4. He got himself breakfast; he didn't feel like food, but he thought he ought to eat. They had trouble locating a spare screen, it was mid-afternoon before they were through. He filled his tank, paid them and took the car out on the road. Turned the bonnet north for Warwell.

It was like the dream repeating again. The same lane, winding between tall hedges; the same girl moving along it. She was walking listelessly, head down, jacket over her shoulder and handbag swinging. He'd pulled the car out of sight in a gateway, she was abreast of it before she saw him. She stopped and put a hand to her throat. Her mouth opened and shut but right then she was bad at making noises.

'Yeah,' he said. 'And on the third day, he rose again. Only I couldn't wait. Sorry, Anne ...'

She tried to run then but he was too quick. He'd been expecting that. He caught her wrist, spun; she thumped on the grass bank, her hair flew across her face. 'You know,' he said, 'I must like this sort of life. Great when the pain goes off ...'

She was wriggling. 'Please, Jimmy ... *hurting* ...'

'Yeah,' he said. 'I know ...'

'They let you ... let you g-get away ...'

'But now they want me. They know don't they, they know I'm back, you just told them ...'

'*Jimmy* ...'

'*Didn't you?*' He was bending her wrist. '*Did you tell them, Anne?*'

'Hurting,' she said. 'Please ... Hurting, *please* ...' She was trying to squirm round her arm.

'I'll break it . . .'

'I can't stop them . . .' She was nearly screaming. 'They're . . . inside, all th' time . . . they . . . make me walk, talk, do . . . things . . . can't hold them out, I *can't* . . .'

'Who are they . . .'

She started to whimper.

'It's OK,' he said. 'Anne don't, it's OK, please don't, it's OK . . .' He let go of her and she rolled away from him, lay curled up with her shoulders working. 'They . . . want you,' she said. 'I've got to tell you.'

He lifted her, gently. 'Anne,' he said. 'Who are they?'

She hung her head and panted. 'They're . . . everybody. Paul, and J-John Taverner from The Bull . . . And David, Johnny, the Round Table . . . Hazel, Maureen, they're in the Inner Wheel . . .' She looked up, eyes tear-bright. 'You were best with the women,' she said. 'You knew about them all the time . . .'

He stayed quiet, letting the words sink in. The imagery of the dreams, the thing his brain had tried to tell him. Phrases heard or seen, cast back as monstrous parables. He swore, very softly. 'God,' he said. 'Isn't there a thing in this town that's clean?' Then he picked her up the rest of the way and started leading her toward the car. 'Anne,' he said. 'I think you'd better tell me now. Everything you know.'

6

The house looked upstream from the tip of a little wooded eyot. He'd seen it many times on evening walks, a bone face peering along the Starr. The sun was setting now in a blaze of orange, sheets of colour flooding across the river. The building was silhouetted; lights burned in some of its windows, shining pale against the glow. On the far bank the steam fair rumbled, organ sounds drifted across the river and the scents of electricity and crushed grass. A metalled drive wound to the bank. There was an open space, cars parked. Among them a black XK.

There was a spidery bridge. He walked across it holding Anne by the wrist. Their footsteps sounded loud in the quiet. The door of the house was unlatched; the girl opened it and stepped inside. He followed her into a cool hall. White and blue tiles covered the floor, there was a carved Swiss umbrella stand, a bowl of flowers. A faint lavender scent pervaded the place.

He felt hollow now; somewhere inside him anger and fear were mixed. He climbed a stairway. A stag's head watched down mournfully from the landing. Anne stopped outside a door. From inside Stringer heard a hum of voices; and there was something else. A tenseness, a strangeness that touched like a warm breeze prickling his scalp. The questing power of *their* minds.

The girl was swallowing, twisted her hands. He squeezed her elbow and opened the door. She walked through and he followed her, stood while the door closed itself behind him. He saw a white room, tall windows burning with the sunset light. Grouped chairs, a polished table. Faces watched him; and there was quiet.

These were no Rotarians. He saw Johnny at the back there and the Little One, next to them a man who had served him petrol at the Central. The landlord of The Bull, the policeman who had checked him that morning. A railway porter, a little old lady; a girl with good legs and burning-red hair.

He knew them all from what she'd told him. In the timeless time while he stared and they stared back he heard her voice again, hurt and stumbling, as she sat in the car.

'Paul's the . . . leader, if there is a leader. Paul owns the house, the big house on the island. It's Paul that makes the . . . the things, the things that run . . .'

'It's all right,' he said. 'Go on.'

'He's an . . . accountant, he's quite well off. They're all . . . different, they all do different things. Don's a policeman and there's Albert, he's Albrecht really, he's half German, he works in a b-bank, he's the one who can make things . . . rot, die, he makes the dreams . . . And Gerry sends them, Gerry and Maureen. Gerry's an electrician, Maureen works in the telephone exchange . . .'

'Then you're all telepaths,' he said.

'We're all . . . different.' She was still crying, not wiping at the tears. They fell steadily, splashing her wrists, running down her throat. Somehow it was like watching somebody bleed. 'Different?' he said.

'Yes . . . The Little One, Hazel, she's the . . . hands . . .'

'She hates me.'

'No . . '

'She tried to kill me She wants me dead.'

'No,' she said. 'She . . . doesn't care what happens to you, Jimmy.' *As long as it's funny . . .*

'Johnny runs a television shop, he helps her . . .' She started to pant again. 'Jimmy, I was . . . seeing for them. In the car park. I couldn't help it, they'd got hold of me, all of them . . .'

'In the car park,' he said. 'It's all right now, stop . . .'

'I'm their . . . eyes,' she said. 'Oh can't you see how useless it is Jimmy, they won't let me go. They can't . . .'

'Softly,' he said. 'Anne, how did they all come here? How could it have happened?'

'I . . . don't know. I know about you and me but the others . . . It's a sort of drift, one comes and another and . . . we can just tell . . '

'You thought I was one, didn't you?'

'Yes,' she said, 'No . . . oh, I don't know . . . Paul said to . . . give you things, anything. Make you happy. Afterwards, when we couldn't . . speak to you. He said it was best. But it didn't work . . .'

'Paul's a smart cookie,' he said. 'Give a man everything, that's the way to stop him. It rots him . . . I'm just too cross-grained, Roley would have been the same. There's still a few of us about.'

'It knew you knew about it,' she said. 'It was watching you, all the time . . .'

'*It?*'

'There aren't any words,' she said desperately. 'Not to say what it's like. It, us, the whole thing . . .'

'The *Gestalt,*' he said. 'The Wheel. I was dreaming about a Wheel.'

'Yes . . .' Biting her lip, hands fluttering. 'Like a . . . person, eyes and brain and . . . legs and arms, the whole lot sort of adding up like an Indian statue . . . You could feel it Jimmy, I knew it wouldn't work when they tried to . . . make you like everybody else, I t-tried to say . . . Jimmy that's what's so important, it's like . . . well an animal somehow, I mean it isn't people, not just us . . .'

'I know,' he said softly. 'It's all right Anne, don't cry any more. I know. It's the Wheel . . .'

He walked forward across the carpet. It seemed it was time for an extravagant gesture, something crazy. This was a thing you read about, laughed over, a thing that could never happen. It was the impossible, walking and talking. It had happened. Here.

He smiled and clicked his heels, bowed stiffly from the waist. He said, *Homo Superior,* I presume . . .'

The river glided, the sky turned from orange to summer night blue. Bats moved over the island, a heron came in to land, stood for a while by the bank like an old stone imitation of a bird. Jimmy talked. He described his life, the chain of events that had brought him to Warwell. *They* listened, and watched. *They* fetched him whisky, a bottle of smooth Glen Grant, and everything was very civilized. 'Go on,' said the man called Paul time and again. 'Go on . . .'

Paul. Lined pink tortoise-face below wavy silver hair, well-cut suit in a brown pinstripe. Paul had dignity. When Jimmy finally ended he leaned back and pulled at his chin, nodded. 'I see,' he said. 'Yes, I see . . .'

A long wait. Then the accountant started to speak again, musingly. 'There have been others like you,' he said. 'Sometimes I think our . . . skills are latent in every thinking brain.' He smiled thinly, not in humour. 'A few have been able to integrate themselves with us. As you can see. The rest . . . We have managed to make them content.'

'Great,' said Stringer brutally. 'Keep a man on the nest till his knees start to bend feed him beer till it comes out his ears . . . I just love,' he said, 'your public spirit . . .'

From somewhere, a giggle.

Jimmy felt the quick choking rise of rage, kept his eyes from the corner where the Little One sat watching him blue and rapturous. Fought the impulse he had to take her by the throat and squeeze and watch the eyes change at last with the knowledge of death.

Paul shook his head. 'No,' he said carefully. 'That has not been our way. It mustn't be yours.' On the table in front of him was a bone paperknife; he picked it up and toyed with it, turning it in his fingers. 'Mr. Stringer,' he said, 'you will not be appeased. Yet you are not one of us. What are we to do with you?'

Jimmy looked across to where Anne was sitting mute, hands

gripped between her knees and eyes on the carpet. He said coldly, 'You'll do nothing with me. You have nothing to do with me.' he reached his proposition. 'Miss Nielson,' he said, 'has had enough. I want to buy her out.'

A silence that deepened. Then, 'I see,' said Paul again blandly. He steepled his fingers and peered at Jimmy. There was no reading his eyes. 'Mr. Stringer, your . . . manner has at least the virtue of honesty. I must try to match your forthrightness.' For an instant his tongue touched and moistened his lips. '*How much is she worth to you?*'

Useless to barter. Jimmy knew in this room his brain was clear glass; the answer that had formed there had already been read. He listened to his own voice speaking steadily. It said, 'All I've got.'

Still the charade. 'How much is that?'

A sharp intake of breath from Anne. Jimmy swallowed. 'Thirty-nine thousand,' he said. 'And the car. Call it thirty-nine-five.' He asked himself, *Pop, have I done it right? Is this a good way to spend your life?* The quietness inside him was its own answer. The words were out now, and he still didn't care.

The snigger came again. Paul glanced behind him and the noise stopped. He turned back to Jimmy. He said vaguely, 'How payable?'

'Any charity you care to name. Come gentlemen, these things can be arranged. You own the bloody town.'

'Thirty-nine thousand pounds,' said Paul. His eyes focused, he shook his head slowly. 'I'm sorry,' he said. 'She belongs with us.'

'*But she hates your guts . . .*'

'An over-dramatization, I think,' said the accountant mildly. 'Anne?'

No answer.

'*Anne!*'

She jumped like she'd been stung. 'Paul I . . . yes . . .'

Jimmy was on his feet. 'Whatever you did then,' he said gently, 'don't do it again.'

Silence.

Anne said miserably, 'I can't be b-bargained for Jimmy. I'm not a horse.'

'What were you doing to her?' asked Stringer. 'The night I nearly killed her?'

The Little One spoke up chirpily. 'We wanted to do a little job,' she said. 'Johnny and me. But she was naughty.'

The rage in Jimmy was misting his sight. 'So you sicked Big Brother on her,' he said. 'Because she wouldn't help you stir dirt.' He rounded on Paul. '*Call that belonging?*'

'Mr. Stringer . . .'

'Paul,' he said. 'You're an intelligent man. So ask yourself, to keep an . . . organism alive, does a grown man have to crawl? *To that?*' He pointed. His voice rose, riding the other down. 'Something I'll tell you right now. You're sick, you know that?' He stared round the circle of faces. 'The brain is sick. Sick with this . . . rubbish jolting into it. You're divided against yourselves. And you know what that means to a mind? They call it schizophrenia. That's what you've got. The first *Gestalt* brain in the history of the world is going round the bloody twist –'

Surging. The rage, the roar of the Wheel, threats of oldness and death and things worse. He closed his eyes, rocked. Anne had her face in her hands. 'That's enough,' said Paul sharply. 'All of you, *that's enough* . . .'

Silence, through all dimensions.

The older man got up and walked round to Jimmy. Put a hand on his shoulder, steered him away from the table and across the room. 'Listen,' he said, 'and try to understand. In what we do, we have no choice. Mr. Stringer, if I laid a pocket knife on the table there, and put forty thousand pounds into your hand, would you allow me to pick out your eyes?'

Jimmy was silent.

'We have done nothing wrong,' said the accountant. 'Understand that. We do nothing but exist. Now think what that means. Try to imagine yourself the only one of your species. Perhaps there has never been a unit like ours, or ever will be again. Mr. Stringer, we did not ask to be born. Yet we . . . came into being, in an environment that was never meant for us. A hostile world.'

'Don't chop logic,' said Jimmy viciously. 'You own this town. you drive it, you shape it –'

Paul shook his head, and he was sweating. 'We own nothing. we . . . direct certain aspects of life in Warwell. We have to. and believe me, for us it is very simple. We could do much more. Warwell is our . . . home, our shell if you can think of it in that way. And I swear to you, nothing but good has come from that domination.'

Jimmy was staring out the window, seeing and not seeing the distant lights of the fair. The noise of the rides reached the house thinly. He said tonelessly, 'There's blood on your hands.'

'No, Mr. Stringer. Not yet.'

He brushed the man's arm away, turned to peer into the faded blue eyes. 'Paul,' he said. 'This I believe. You're a sincere man. Or maybe you were once before this . . . thing got hold of you. I'm sorry for you, because you're in deadly trouble.' He raised his voice to include the others in the room. 'Give in,' he said. 'Get to a . . . hospital, somewhere they could understand you. help you. You're needed; there's no power like yours in the world.'

He read their answer in the silence.

'OK,' he said. 'Now I'll tell you this. I don't hate easily; but I hate for a long, long time. And I'm defying you. Get off my back. Go to hell where you belong, get out of my way.' He shoved past Paul, went to Anne. He said simply, 'You coming?'

She lifted a stained face. Shook her head wordlessly.

'Uh-huh,' said Stringer. 'OK.' He walked across the room, opened the door, looked back at Paul. 'You know what you're doing,' he said. 'I don't have to spell it out for you. I'll tell you what I'm going to do. I'm taking that girl out of this. I don't know how. Not yet. I don't care. But I'm taking her if I have to break all these bastards down one by one. You're not a corrupt man,' he said. 'Not yet. But you will be. Because evil is a sickness that spreads.' He turned away. 'I'll talk to you again,' he said. 'When you've cleaned your house.'

The doorhandle was snatched out of his hand. The door smashed shut; he pulled at it briefly and knew no force he could raise would open it.

Across the room Paul's face was grey. Behind him the Little One smiled a blue china smile. Anne had turned away, she was covering her face again. Suddenly he needed to touch her, but he couldn't move. A barrier had built itself in front of him; he could feel the heat and nearness of it though there was nothing to see.

Paul walked back to the table, stood leaning on his knuckles. he said, 'I don't think you fully understand your position.' His voice shook slightly; he moistened his lips again with the tip of his tongue. 'As I said, we exist; and Warwell is the ... fortress we have built for ourselves. What our true function may be we don't know. Perhaps we are a random particle in a random universe, and have no purpose. But we wait, and we hope. Sometimes, we pray.

'Mr. Stringer, we are a living organism. Like any other breathing creature we defend ourselves if attacked. We fear mutilation, we fear death. *You must not threaten us ...*

'There is no blood on our hands. Your somewhat theatrical phrase can have no meaning for us. We are neither good nor evil. We exist, we endure. If you force us, we shall kill.'

Silence in the room, total and absolute. The light, the bright threat spreading from face to face now the thing was finally said. In the quiet, a ride at the fairground hooted. *Whup* it said. *Whup-whup-whup ...*

'You cannot fight us,' said the accountant. 'We could break your bones where you stand, we could burst your heart. You cannot warn others of our existence; to try would be to fail, and we should know.' He looked back towards the window. His lips were set; he was the judge pronouncing sentence. 'You must not stay,' he said finally. 'You have till the fair leaves at the end of the week. You will not be molested. Should you remain beyond that time you will be destroyed.'

Jimmy tried to make his brain work. 'Anne,' he said. 'Anne.'

She quivered but she wouldn't look at him.

'No,' said Paul. 'No more. Please leave us now. I'm sorry.'

The door opened for him. He stepped through and down the darkened stairs. He carried with him one last impression. A pair of bright blue eyes, the smiling red horseshoe of a mouth.

7

Stringer wiped his face, felt the sweat on his forehead mingle with the rain. Looked up at the blind grey sky. He was unshaven, eyes dark-rimmed from lack of sleep. The drizzle soaked the shoulders of the mac, ran down inside the collar. He didn't notice it.

Round him were the massive rides of the fair. Water beaded painted wood, spread dark fingers across tight-stretched sheets of tarpaulin. He reached the Switchback, leaned his hands on the curved wall of the machine. Above him, over the chin-high tarps, gargoyle faces peered. Golden cats and cockerels, motionless in the dead light, eyes bright and painted, blue like the eyes of china dolls. The rain made a faint hissing, nearly inaudible; and it was Saturday morning.

He hung his head. *Paul*, he thought for the thousandth time. *Paul* ... Can you ask a man to gouge his eyes out, cut off his hands? Can you expect him to do it? He thought, now they'll punish Anne. They'll hunt her again, send unspeakable things to hop across the fields, snuggle in her bed. He thought, Paul doesn't understand. And then, Paul does understand. But how can you ask a man to cut off his hands ...

Saturday morning. He groaned, wanting Anne, the warmth of her, her young-old face. His time was nearly out. At midnight, with the chiming of the church clock, the fair lights would snap off, the rides run down in darkness. Then *they* would come for him. Not Paul; but Johnny and the Little One, they'd come. and afterwards, they'd make his Anne dance to a tune. Afterwards? No, before. They'd start tonight, they'd show him what they could do.

He saw Paul's face again in his mind, old tortoise eyes wary, mouth pursed saying no, no ... The *Gestalt* was not evil, but it was sick. Sick of a pair of china eyes, a horseshoe smile ...

'*Gestalt*,' he said, and banged his fists on wood. '*Gestalt, Gestalt* ...' His life was tied now to Anne, the brain was his enemy. Unbreakable, undefeatable. How to fight it ... He told himself, for every perfection a fault. For every strength, a weakness. Find the flaw. Use *Gestalt* against itself, somehow there's a way. Kill the brain, poison it. *Poison it? How, what with* ...

He lifted his head, wet hair dangling. Round the sides of the great ride, baroque cowboys galloped; under his hands, an Indian was plunging from his horse. The head was thrown back impossibly, a round hole in the forehead spewed a thin stream of blood. The face was contorted, mouth stretched with pain.

Jimmy's eyes widened, slowly. He stood and stared a long time, hands slack now at his sides. Then he turned and walked rapidly away, purposive now that he knew what he had to do.

East Street, on a fine June night. The rain cleared away, the air warm. Turquoise streaks still showing in the western sky, silhouetting the church. A solitary balloon floating a quarter mile up, somebody stabbing at it with the silver finger of a searchlight. Shopfronts blazing in town, crowds jostling down and back from the river. Noise of the fair coming across the water, hootings and the music of the rides.

Stringer pushed along crowded paths seeing the traffic, saloons balked and bad-tempered, open cars moving with their toploads of youngsters or cruising slow, hunting for pickups. Seeing the endless people, kids with faces candyfloss-sticky cradling coconuts and dolls, girls in blouses and skirts and tight jeans and summer frocks, faces laughing, kiss-me-quick hats on their heads and papiermâche sombreros, the boyos with the plaid shirts and jeans, leather jackets, Norton and Matchless studded across the shoulders and crossed bones and skulls, the ton-up Joes.

Searching all the time, hunting till he saw her. Boyo on either side of her and she arm in arm, the pickups laughing and burly, sporting black cock-combs of hair, she in step, body wriggling and being a whore's body, only the eyes desperate, bolting like the eyes of a hare. She saw him and there was pain, but she couldn't stop. She passed on down the street, throwing her head back, laughter pealing from her, heigh-ho come to the fair . . .

He huddled in the doorway of a shop, brain spinning. Watching the crowd that seemed now to surge forward and back dizzyingly, faces like foam-flecks on a sea. *They* were close, he knew they were close. *They* were in her body, controlling it, pulling the wires that made the marionette step and prance. The punishment, *the fun* had started.

He saw them. Johnny cutting a dash in fawn tapered slacks, white shirt framing Gigolo-darkness. Turning and laughing now, showing his teeth and braying. The Little One in a froth of summer dress, hanging on his arm and smiling, always she must smile . . . He stepped into the crush behind her praying she wouldn't turn then *knowing* she wouldn't turn. Knowing she had forgotten him already. *She doesn't care what happens to you, Jimmy; as long as it's funny . . .*

His hands made themselves into balls of bone. He said through his teeth, 'It'll be funny.'

The serious drinking hadn't started yet, The Green Dragon was nearly deserted. The river terrace nestling by the bridge piers was empty. Water chuckled under the stone arches, the noise of the fair came loud across the Starr. Jimmy edged forward, keeping to shadows. *They* were standing together by the steps down to the landing stage. She holding his arm and looking out across the river, smiling he knew, smiling . . .

He said quietly, 'Johnny . . .'

He whirled, and Stringer hit him. All the rage, all the hate exploding from a point and that point in his fist, at the end of an arm that swung, cracked . . .

Perfect timing. He felt no impact but the body flung itself back and down, thudded against the bridge. Then the rock spun at Jimmy's head, missed, half-numbed his shoulder. An iron chair rose from the terrace, whirled at him; he knocked it aside and ducked knowing others would come and stones and bricks, converging on him as a centre. Watch the Little One, she throws things . . .

He reached her in two strides. She tried to bolt but she wasn't quick enough. He hit her twice, for the beating and for Anne. Her body wrapped itself round the blows, '*Ip*,' she said, '*Ip* . . .' And he'd got Johnny's arm, he was twisting it high behind his back, hauling him up by the wrist. '*Where is she* . . .?' said Stringer. '*Where is she* . . .?'

"Eeehh . . . Yeehh . . .'

'C'mon boy, *where* . . .'

Raspberry dribble on the chin and spilling down the shirt, teeth bared, thin high noise coming between them. Stringer twisted again and the Little One started to scream.

'*Fair* . . .' said Johnny. Gritted. '*Fair* . . .'

'*Where, in the fair* . . .'

'*Bastard* . . .'

Twist, and feel the bones flex . . . '*Where* . . .'

'Gallopers . . . The big ride . . .'

'Good boy. What's she doing?'

'With the . . . boys . . .'

'What happens, Johnny? What happens now?'

'Fun . . .' He was wheezing. 'Then afterwards . . . real fun . . .'

It was possible to see red, everything in bright flat sheets of colour. 'Johnny,' said Stringer. 'You're going to have a very bad night.' He heaved his victim at the flight of steps. And as he shoved, *pulled*.

Sharp high cracking of bones and the body crashing, arm flying out loose. Then there were two of them down there both holding an arm, both rolling and shrieking. *Gestalt* . . .

Jimmy ran across the bridge, flung himself into the traffic. A skidding, close noise of a hooter . . . He fended off a bonnet with his hands and there was a crash, a grinding. *Good,* he thought, *good.* Confuse the issue . . . Then the fair was ahead, the brightness and noise. Floating haze of faces orange-lit, jostling and shoving, hands grabbing. Thunder from the Switchback and the Scenics, rich din of organs, smack and clang of shooting galleries, shrieks of Laughing Sailors. Somebody yelled at Jimmy, punched his back. He ducked, swerved, saw Anne. She was reeling, holding her arm. He reached her and clung. People were staring, he shoved his way through them. She was gritting her teeth and moaning. 'Jimmy, what . . . what'd you d-do . . .'

'Broke all your good right arms,' he said. His breath was sobbing, the lights were spinning in front of his eyes. 'I . . . sorry,' she said. 'Pass out . . .' He yelled at her, 'You *can't* . . .' Then, 'Just a little way . . . Just a little way, Anne, *come on* . . .'

They were clear of the fair. He had the car parked close; he bundled her into it, started up, bucked his way across rough grass. Out back of the fair was a lane, he burst the paling by it and the hedge, wallowed, got away. Anne was clinging to the dash one-handed, the other arm lying useless in her lap. Halfway to Midhampton she was still whimpering. *God* he thought, *what range does this thing have* . . . He was in the outskirts of the town and swinging round the first rotary when she sat up and yelped with relief. He shouted to her.

'*What happened* . . .'

'They put him out . . .' Her eyes were wide now, terrified. 'Jimmy, they'll take us. You can't get away . . .'

'Great,' he said. 'Hold them out Anne, *you must* –'

'Trying . . .' She was rocking in the seat again, there was sweat on her face. 'The car,' she said. 'Don . . . The police will stop the car, he'll make them . . .'

'Damn the car . . .' There was a main line station ahead, he swung across the forecourt, braked with a squeal, jumped the door.

'Jimmy . . .'

He slapped her bottom. 'Move, Anne. Run . . .'

'*You can't* . . .'

He yelled at her. 'I know. I can't win. I can never bloody win, I'm used to it . . .' He grabbed her wrist. She was panting again. 'I knew it would happen,' he said. 'They'd send you to the fair . . .'

'How . . .'

'Heard them make their minds up,' he said. 'It was starting. It was in me, it grows . . .'

'But you c-could . . . be a part. Jimmy, you could –'

'Of that?' He shouted again. '*That* . . .?'

She was shuddering. 'You hurt the Little One. She'll kill you . . .'

'Paul won't let her. Anne, we've got to try . . .' Hammering on the ticket office window. 'Express,' he said. 'West Coast sleeper. Ten minutes. All worked out . . .'

Anne was stamping like a hound. 'Hurry,' she said. 'Please . . .'

'Been rung in,' he said. 'Six minutes . . . Anne it's OK, we'll make our own *Gestalt*.' They'd told him Platform Ten; there was a tunnel, he took the steps at a run still holding her arm. The suitcases in his hand were bumping his knee. 'Jimmy,' she said. 'What . . .'

'What?'

'Cases . . .'

He gasped. 'Luggage. For the hotel. Keep your hand in your pocket, haven't got a ring . . .'

'*Jimmy* . . .'

'No more. *Hurry* . . .'

Cool here, under the tracks. The tunnel stretching ahead, their footsteps clattering. Long lines of lamps glowing yellow, looms of dirty cable on painted brick walls. She was running trusting him, eyes screwed shut. They'd make it, they'd make it, they'd ma–

She wrenched away. He clutched at her. She swerved, moving fast, throwing her legs out, running the way women don't run. She passed the last flight of platform steps. He followed her but she was too quick. There was a barrier, waist high. He took it on the run and the top bar cocked up as he jumped, caught his foot, sent him smashing down, rolling over and over *Contact*, he thought. *Contact*. Anne . . .

The Little One raging, using Anne's eyes at last, holding her body, making it run. He staggered to his feet. He was in a loading area, dim-lit. Goods lifts to one side, piles of parcels. A flight of steps. He leaped up them into the open air.

A siding. Acres of rail, shining. Ahead he saw a white moth still running. He forced his legs to move again, heart hammering. Across the tracks skidding and slipping, barking his shins on steel.

The station buildings were behind him now, and the lit face of the clock tower. He staggered on seeing signal-eyes glaring miles off, reflecting green and red streaks down the rails. He glimpsed Anne again and the train, the lit numberplate on the loco sailing out of the night. He heard the noise of it, the long double scream of the horns, then it was passing, blowing him back from its hugeness. Thunder rhythm of the wagons, *wrench-bang wrench-bang wrench-bang wrench-bang* loud then softer, the red lamp on the guard's van receding, swaying away down the line.

'Anne!'

She was lying huddled, the wind moving her dress.

'ANNE!'

He reached her. Her arms ... Wrists clamped to the sleepers, a foot from the steel. The wrists had hands on them.

He took his jacket off, put it round her, lifted her inside it. she was shaking. She held her hands out in front of her. 'That far,' she said. 'That far. *Not on the rails* ...'

'Anne ...'

She looked at him. Tearmarks showed on her face. 'Jimmy,' she said. '*They've gone* ...'

He started to walk back down the tracks, holding her, not letting her stumble, feeling the wonder grow. The Wheel, the thing that ran a town; somehow at last it had stemmed its own sickness. It was brooding now, thinking, searching for purpose and sanity. Some day, some place, he knew it would send for him again. He felt a huge thanksgiving and a hope in the presence of the Thing that, for a need, had blinded itself. No, it wasn't human, not the *Gestalt* brain; for in the end, when it had found itself, it had chosen mercy.

When it called, he hoped he would be ready.

The Death of Libby Maynard

1

'*Libby-Libby Maynard, Libby-Libby Maynard . . .*'

That voice is the first thing ever. It floats at me from mist; a four o'clock mist, blue and cold. In the mist are houses and streets, patterns of damp unlit concrete roads, shaggy grass verges dotted with rowan trees and Spanish oaks. The houses brood, little blue and mauve-roofed semis, blackout patches over their eyes. Between them, past the front garden fences and green and black painted gates, scurry children. The boys run, legs thin and pale like grubby pipestems, kicking stones, scuffing the toes of their cheap wartime shoes into a mash; the girls move in twittering groups topped by the bright shapes of pixie hoods.

'*Silly Libby Maynard, silly Libby Maynard . . .*'

Two children separate from the rest. One is skipping and taunting; the other, smaller, stalks along triangular-faced with rage. She sports scruffy black plaits, she wears a bulky little tweed coat and long grey socks. From the sleeves of the coat hang mittens, each attached to an end of the same worn tape. They are decorated on their backs with dirty white rabbits; their wool is damp, beaded with minute drops of condensed moisture. The child chews a mitten, barely noticing in her fury the bitter blue taste of the dye.

That thin little thing, walking a blue-lit street so long ago, is me. The time is 1942, and I'm seven years old.

It seems strange that I can still recall that scene so clearly. I can taste the gathering fog; I can see the nearly leafless trees, the wet paths, blades of grass in the paving-stone cracks, the occasional thick worm thrust out from between the slats of a garden fence. The eyes of children, small and sharp and close to the ground, notice such things. I hear my feet batter on the path. I am running now, the rage inside me red and bubbling. my name is *Elizabeth*, *Elizabeth* Maynard; and I'm going to kill Alice Kelly.

Alice is my best friend, the focus of a complex pattern of

hate and love. She is pale-faced and thin and wears clothes without utility marks. My clothes all have the little symbols stitched inside collar or cuff, two segmented brown water-lily leaves stamped on an inch of white tape. Alice's father is in the Royal Air Force; when he is home on leave he fetches her from school by car. The car is very black and long and he is tall and wears a uniform the colour of evening stormclouds. Alice's voice is high-pitched, her knees are nobbly; her hair is mouse-brown and she always manages, somehow, to smell of urine.

I'm halfway home, scuttling alongside the tall fences. My breath is beginning to hurt as I draw it into my lungs but Alice is very close. Ahead of us a fog bank lies like a thick blue tongue, floating inches from the road, pushing slowly forward as if from the mouth of a dragon. Little boys zoom in and out as it advances, half-afraid, wings stretched out stiff from their shoulders, soprano machine-guns chattering. Beyond the fog is a corner green. Once it was guarded by thin looped iron railings, but they were taken away to make aeroplanes with; a path has been worn across the grass, broad and puddled, and there are other paths in the bushes and rockeries where the boys play. Some of the bushes have little bright orange buds among their thorns, like the flowers we call 'eggs and bacon'.

Alice scurries across the grass knowing I will catch her before she reaches the road. She darts aside, terrified, vanishes in the mist. I take my satchel from my shoulder and hold it loosely, swinging it by the strap. Between the rings that hold the strap to the canvas part is an iron bar. I call to Alice to say what I'm going to do to her.

She is out of sight but I know where she is. I watch the shapes her panic makes, glowing in the fog. She is crouched by the wall behind the bushes, among dog-turds and leaves and broken glass. I stalk forward, wanting her to run again, but she will not move. She raises her hands as I lift the satchel, wincing and grinning, saying, 'Please, Elizabeth . . .' I growl a little and threaten. I can see now what she is afraid of. An image is clear and sharp in her mind; a little boy, head split by a brick, running bright-handed and bawling. She is afraid I will hit her too, and make the blood come.

The fear responds to my movements, the colours shifting and running as I raise and lower my arms. Alice is a theremin, from which I can raise whimpering notes. Intrigued, I forget I hate her. When the fear stops she loves me for letting her go. We walk home the rest of the way together. The colour of love too is bright and distinct in my mind. I think of it as blue, but it is not blue. It is a colour beyond the spectrum, beyond any explaining.

I am a full telepath. I was born with my talent; at least I cannot remember a time when I was without it. I learned at a remarkably early age to conceal my abilities. No doubt as a toddler I babbled the thoughts of those round about me; but I escaped detection, and by the time of my earliest real memories I had already closed myself into an almost impenetrable shell. Why I did this I have never been too certain. I was guided by instinct; I experienced a strong urge to hide my talent, a compulsion not unmixed with feelings of guilt. These feelings I found reflected in the people around about me; for that reason and others, I was seldom lonely.

Everybody was afraid, children and grownups alike; this was one of the earliest lessons I learned. Children feared blood and worms and bats and ghosts, bullies and teachers, their parents sometimes, examinations, beginning-of-term, black soldiers; and a whole range of chimeras, some based in reality, others imaginary. Grown-ups were afraid of bombs and income tax, cancer and frigidity, invasion, death, the police; their fears seemed to me less real and consequently less interesting. Although at will I could be party to their inmost thoughts much of what my brain received was unintelligible; I in fact developed the knack of recognizing an 'adult' concept at present beyond my range of experience, and filing it for future reference. For some time I was disinclined to use my gift 'upwards', as I thought of it, disliking the nuances and uncertainty of half-understanding; I employed it solely to make my daily life easier, picking answers from the brains of my teachers when it seemed they thought me too dull, analysing the orders of my parents into those which must be obeyed and those not meant to be taken seriously. Essentially I was a child with the ability to appear at the right place at the right time, to do and say exactly the correct things to my elders. I would rapidly have gained something of a reputation as a prodigy had I not been at pains to conceal too complete a perfection by occasional calculated falls from grace. I dunked the family cat in the garden tub a moment before I knew my mother would appear round the corner of the house, I allowed my class mistress to catch me making drawings on the forbidden and sacred blackboard. As I said, such lapses were carefully contrived and I invariably escaped serious punishment; my mother disliked the cat, and the drawings were of flowers and trees, subjects dear to the heart of the teacher. As a result I gained a reputation for a certain charming waywardness.

Some studies in fact caused more trouble to me than to my less talented classmates. During religious instruction in particular I was able to sense the boredom in the mind of the mistress as we read and dramatized our bible stories; oncc indeed I detected an eager string of images associated with a young man she had met at a local amateur dramatic society. Her thoughts of a few mornings later were even more illuminating; so much so that I shut my mind with a shocked snap, and was ever subsequently able to acquire the easy faith of the average infant. In our wrestlings with mathematics and geography I was also frequently conscious of the disinterest behind the smooth manner of the teacher; the secondary thought-streams were confusing, blurring the sense of the spoken word much in the manner of static overcoming a radio signal. At the best of times this changing pulse and flutter of background brain rhythms tended to disturb me; the entire learning process might have been rendered intolerably difficult had I not developed at an early age the trick of focusing my mind, again somewhat like tuning a radio to a specific wavelength. By this means the pipe and chatter of thoughts round me could be reduced at will, or even silenced altogether. Only sleepiness rendered my talent less easy to control; if I allowed myself to become overtired local thought-streams would begin to wash in through my guard like the frightening waves of a sea, inducing a spinning sensation of helplessness. In so far as it was possible I developed the habit of sleeping long and regularly to avoid this, thus further enhancing my reputation for what my elders referred to, for want I suppose of a better term, as godliness.

Properly harnessed, my gift proved of inestimable value, saving me on many occasions from trouble of one sort or another. I remember one evening soon after my fight with Alice I detected a man lurking in or near that same corner shrubbery. I was alone at the time, a little late for some reason; most of my schoolfellows had already passed, and the street was deserted. I was unable to see my ambusher but in the quietness his thought-stream, which was singularly bright and vivid, shone ahead of me like a torch. I could tell that he had heard my footsteps, and that he was eagerly anticipating rushing from hiding as I went by. I recollect I was somewhat puzzled. It seemed he had in mind a sort of game; but certain of the ideas he had, in particular one of fumbling very hard beneath my skirt, struck me as both pointless and painful. The thing was altogether too violent for my taste; I accordingly turned back, reaching my home by a more devious route. I was made even later as a result, and was severely scolded by my parents. I was tempted in self defence to mention the encounter but held my peace, fearing if nothing else a revelation of the gift I had always instinctively concealed.

After that I sensed the watcher many times and was hardly surprised when a girl from my class was successfully captured. She never returned to the school; I asked my parents what had happened to her, curious to find in what respects their account would differ from the truth. I was given the excuses usual under such circumstances; I listened to them abstractedly, following the thoughts that ran beneath the words. The concept of rape had little meaning for me but what I understood suggested that my initial feelings had been correct; it seemed what had happened to my schoolmate had been both uncomfortable and distressing. I took considerable care after that, determined not to suffer the same process, but the thoughtstream had left the area entirely. I derived great amusement from the anxious journeyings of parents who for some time afterward escorted their children to and from the school; I could have told them their efforts were pointless, but I was mature enough to realize I would be ignored.

I had almost forgotten the incident when some months later I was sitting with my mother in a teashop she often frequented. I disliked the place; it was invariably overfull, the sea of alien thoughts bumping and jostling my mind. Mother however was always anxious to be seen eating in public; the process was associated in her mind with certain half-formed notions of class distinction. On this occasion I was indulging in a private game; I sat picking at the dry scones that were virtually all the place could offer, swinging my heels under the table and looking no doubt the picture of innocence, while I alternately opened my mind and rammed it shut in face of some mounting, bright-textured jumble of ideas. Slowly, within that confused welter, the taste and colours of a single stream of consciousness separated themselves. As the entity formed, flickering and glowing, I had no doubt where I had encountered it before. I looked round quickly and found I was being watched by a grey-haired, well-dressed man at the next table. I was rather surprised by his appearance; I suppose I had expected him to be in some way distinguishable from the people round him. He smiled, it seemed a little tentatively; I stared back with all the concentration I could muster, trying to bring him to awareness of my own consciousness and the accusation it was levelling. I was interested to see his mental patterns change convulsively. One of those beastly, fumbling thoughts had just started to form; it was cut off abruptly. In its place was the vividness of fright, as clear and distinct as the ringing of an alarm bell. I withdrew from the discordance. My acquaintance was rising hastily to leave; his sleeve caught a cup, spilling tea across the table and on to the floor. I tweaked my mother's arm and pointed. 'Look,' I said. 'There's the man who did that thing to Jane Streatley –'

I was hushed of course instantly and bustled out of the place. My mother was highly distressed. It seemed the police had established to their own satisfaction that there could have been no witnesses to the assault; I had certainly been away from school at the time, in bed with a cold. I was angry for a while, insisting on the truth of what I had claimed, till I realized that apart from risking punishment I was in danger of jeopardizing the secret I had been at such pains to preserve. From that time onward I gave no hint of my gift, either to my parents or to anyone else.

My talent grew steadily. The war ended; there were parties in the streets and bunting and fireworks, we trudged miles carrying plates and cups and were given wedges of cake and yellow half-melted icecream. Trucks even arrived at school one morning, great long-nosed things with wheels higher than our heads, their bonnets splashed with broad white stars. Another party was held on the sports field, run by American soldiers. To us they all seemed very tall and strange, speaking in twanging voices we could barely understand. They gave us sweets to take away, and tins of chocolate powder; most of us had never even seen the stuff before.

We had in those days an ordeal known as the eleven-plus, an examination designed to sift junior school leavers into their appropriate secondary streams. I say 'designed' advisedly as its chief effect seemed to be to throw its prospective victims into a mental turmoil that stretched for weeks and months ahead. exam nerves were naturally foreign to me but I was nonetheless distracted and annoyed by the antlike activity round about. I worked well on the great day, picking what answers I needed from the brain of the invigilating mistress. I finished with a very high mark indeed. That was intentional; I wished to make sure of a place at the local High School, whose uniform I much admired. In my eagerness I almost over-reached myself; I understand the completed papers caused some slight stir, happily soon forgotten.

I was glad to leave my school. Despite my caution I had long since been noticed as an unusual child, and the strain of holding myself to the proper pace of my age group was beginning to tell. I am inclined to believe I would have been a forward pupil without the aid of my gift, though of course telepathy had always coloured my perceptions to such an extent that that is difficult to decide. I know for example my mathematical ability was unusual; I had progressed to the use of simple algebra by the age of eight or nine, though how much of my understanding came from self-reasoning and how much from the continuously presented thoughtstreams of adults I find impossible to say.

When I joined Carshalton High I was a skinny little rabbit of a creature, all plaits and eyes, though the female characteristics of my few pounds of body were already showing signs of development. I was interested in this, and waited puberty with something like impatience. I had begun to realize that on a deep level I was bored. Possibly characteristically, I set myself to analyse the causes of my dissatisfaction. They were not far to seek. My sixth sense, in the use of which I had become so proficient, enabled me to avoid unpleasant encounters, to gauge exactly the reactions of those round about me, to shine effortlessly at any intellectual exercise; but equally it removed from my day to day existence the possibility of surprise. I began to consider for the first time how many of the emotions that colour the lives of five-sensed people are based on and compounded from that magic ingredient. Fear and pleasure, the two most powerful stimuli, alike demand it; how often, in their simple way, my parents had tried to surprise me with Christmas or birthday gifts! I had learned to simulate the emotion with some skill; when the long-hidden doll or bicycle was finally produced my eyes would dilate, my voice would squeak, I would pant, become inarticulate; I even learned to blush, with pleasure or confusion, but invariably I lived a lie. When other children leaped from dark alleyways, holding as like as not a grotesque mask before their face, I had schooled myself to squeal and run, but my heart could not skip a beat. I felt that I would give much to experience even fear, that I was not in fact superhuman but a sadly lacking shell. Emotion would have completed my life, given it roundness and a function. Others might strive for some academic goal, sweat and study to attain it; inevitably, I realized, no goal would be more distant from me than the nearest trained mind.

I had little difficulty integrating myself into my new environment. Carshalton was a vastly bigger establishment than my last school, catering for well over five hundred pupils. Space was cramped, classes large and unwieldly, discipline not always what it might have been. For my private purposes this was all to the good. Nobody had time or inclination, in all that hurry and confusion, to bother themselves with a four-foot rat of a first former; with suitable care my odd abilities might remain undetected for years. I chose my examination rating, about a third of the way down the form list, and held to it assiduously. As ever, there was no problem in picking out what I needed to know or learn.

I think it was this very surfeit of facts and the means to acquire them that first set me thinking about art. Here surely I would find something imponderable, something that had to do deeply with existence yet could not be plucked wholesale from the first available brain. Although an English High School is not the best of training grounds for this type of ability I nonetheless pursued the notion vigorously, drawing and painting extensively in my free time. I derived, and still derive, considerable pleasure from the acquisition of manual skills; in fact I felt toward art rather as I felt toward sport, in which I was also beginning to take a keen interest. Both were fields in which I could compete on equal terms with the people round me; there was a delicious uncertainty in the outcome of a long or high jump or track event that provided just that element of surprise I had been sorely missing. I also considered for a while the possibilities of chess; but one contact with the complicated mind of a senior, the bout of giddiness as I struggled to correlate alternate and conflicting possibilities, taught me that that at least was an area of human experience best avoided by the younger telepath.

When I was thirteen my father, who since my birth had worked as bank clerk in the same little midland town, finally screwed his courage to the sticking-place and accepted a managerial appointment in a larger branch some fifty miles to the north. My mother, instantly seizing on the advantages of our new financial status, determined that I transfer not to the local High School but to Saint Catherine's, a private school some twenty miles from what would be my new home. I followed the mental processes of both my parents with interest for some days. Finally the decision was made and the subject broached to me, for all the world as if my opinion mattered or would carry any weight. I agreed without argument; partly from the certain knowledge that it would be fruitless, partly because I had in turn become tired of Carshalton and the whole atmosphere of State education. I was sanguine enough to realize that I would enjoy the same advantages and disadvantages wherever I might be, and sure enough of my increased control to tackle a smaller establishment again; I looked forward with some enthusiasm to what I sensed would be an interesting experiment. I felt a need to explore a new social sphere where my talent would perhaps bring me fresh concepts to work on. The gift that should have brought me into closer contact with my fellows had so far tended to isolate me; in my enforced loneliness I had begun to feel I must be singled out for some special purpose in life, and was vitally concerned to discover what it might be.

I entered what was for me a new world, a world I had scarcely dreamed existed. Saint Catherine's School was a rambling, stone-built place standing well back from a main road that was its link with the nearest town. Its grounds were enclosed for the most part by a high wall; that wall came to symbolize for me the detachment not only of myself but of all the people who lived and worked behind it. To me the place was like some strange hospital, from which pain and need were seldom absent; for every pupil at some time or other went through what seemed to me the punishments of the damned. Loneliness and homesickness were emotions with which I'd seldom come into contact and to speak truly I was ill-equipped to deal with such violent assaults on my consciousness. I in fact suffered similar feelings myself for the first few weeks although I had imagined myself immune. Contact between pupils and their parents during term-time was strongly discouraged; but there was in the reception hall a round oak table on which gifts and letters might from time to time appear. Some snivelling member of the lower school was frequently to be found hanging about in the vicinity of the hall, hoping in vain for some word from home. I haunted the place myself; I remember very clearly the faint scent of lavender polish that always pervaded it, the sheen of the copper plates that lined one wall, the bowl of flowers invariably placed in the geometric centre of that fateful table. If I had wanted the sensation of emotion, then I had it; I was paid out, firmly enough, in coin of my own minting. I had of course discovered a major drawback to my gift; the telepath is painfully or morbidly sensitive to atmosphere, and more than usually open to infection by group hysterias.

After the initial period of strain I managed to readjust my shielding to cope with the disturbances but the early part of my first term was a considerable trial. When I was finally able to take stock of my surroundings I found them even more extraordinary than I had at first supposed.

The pupils at Saint Catherine's were fairly sharply divided into two classes. The majority of the girls came from backgrounds similar to my own and were bitterly conscious of their status. They were always prepared to believe themselves mocked by those of superior means; these suspicions were in the main well founded for there was a leavening of wealthier children, all of whom were constantly ready to demonstrate their superiority, usually with some sublety. The process was not altogether new to me; what did surprise me was the depth of passion aroused by comparatively trivial incidents. It seemed at times the very walls of the place might glow with heat; it was only after weeks of bafflement that the answer dawned on me. I, and those about me, were adolescent. I hadn't thought that growing up would be like this.

This revelation alone was enough to preoccupy me for some months. I was on the threshold of something very strange indeed; I gave the discovery my whole attention, becoming for some time a kind of pint-sized combination of computer-complex and radar listening post. Ours was, with the exception of an elderly and shuffling caretaker, exclusively a female society; yet within the tiny matriarchy of Saint Cath's, sex not only managed to rear its proverbially ugly head but became a rampaging force. This was the true meaning of the night whimperings and unease, the misery and black desolation I had sensed. Love, unasked-for and unrequited, filled days and nights with grief. The phenomenon of the crush; how strange, I thought, that a process that can pulverise what we term the soul, burn a man or woman or child to a husk, should be so casually described by a piece of jocular and outmoded slang. I felt passionately about this at the time; I feel passionately still. I looked into minds torn by love, and I shall never forget what I found; those Dalinesque landscapes of madness, molten and rotting, feral-shadowed, distorted as if glimpsed through globes of blood. Comfort yourselves with platitudes, if that's your way, tell each other these torments do no harm; but don't tell me.

Hard on the heels of my discovery came a notion of some genius and magnitude. The idea was I think first triggered by fear; for I had established to my own satisfaction that I was far from immune to emotion, and now I felt myself attacked. Would it not be possible, I wondered, to use my gift in an active rather than a passive sense, to create mental states advantageous to myself rather than simply moulding my reactions to the thought-streams of the people round about? Certainly there were great possibilities, but the practical side of things baffled me; until, oddly enough, I visited a circus.

I was home for the Easter vacation, and the circus was a holiday treat. The climax of the show was of course the big cat act; I remember sitting tensed in my seat, staggered by the brilliance and simplicity of the idea that had come to me as I watched. I could sense the unease and bafflement of the great animals, represented as nearly as I can describe by a sort of formless redness; over it, quelling and subduing, the will of the trainer rose calm and bright as a sword. If he felt fear or uncertainty, no hint of it came through his mental guard; and in that alone lay the secret of his skill. Why, I thought, he's just like these rich girls who so bother me; for all human beings are to some extent telepathic, whether they realize it or not. That's how confidence tricksters and lion tamers and salesmen all work; the brain stamps out a pattern, a rigid scheme of impulses, and it's that we detect and not the person behind it. If I were to design for myself such a mental mask, and project and project to the world round me . . . it had worked before, I'd proved it. Why not again? What would they not believe? After that I couldn't wait to get back to school.

We had at that time a singularly beautiful pupil at Saint Cath's. Her name was Moira Summersby; she was a year or so older than myself, the daughter of a family of wealthy West Country farmers. She was a slender, classically lovely creature with soft brown legs and a cloud of floating dark hair; and she was the most adroit and accomplished sadist I had yet encountered. Some one or other of the juniors was perpetually in love with her; and Moira was adept in the handling of her victims, at keeping them in the appropriate state of blushing chaos. They would be encouraged with little kindnesses, sent to run errands that made the silly creatures glow with pleasure, cuffed flat with rebuffs calculated not quite to break their spirit; then the whole process would begin again, with all its pain and grief and confusion. It was a game of which Miss Summersby never tired; I had watched her at it long enough, hating her for the agony she caused so carelessly. To be truthful I was more than a little afraid of her. I had felt the stirrings within myself, she seemed to me as to others the epitome both of womanhood and motherhood; had I been frank I would have admitted I wanted to sleep with her, feel her arms round me, my head against her breasts. I had shed tears of my own; it was only my gift that had kept me from her clutches. Now, Moira was to suffer what she had inflicted; I think in my childish way I saw myself as some form of avenging angel.

On the slow train journey back to school I sat alone, intensely withdrawn, completing in fine detail the picture of the Elizabeth Maynard to be. Gone were the memories of a working class background, by the time I had finished; gone the little private estate where my parents lived, the roads and concrete streets of childhood. My new family, like Moira's, came from the West; our ancestors lay in splendid painted tombs, they had crossed with the Conqueror, fought at Hastings and Waterloo. I invited brothers and cousins galore, a sister at finishing-school in Switzerland, a port-swigging martinet of a father. He was Something in the City, I decided, when he chose to work; but he had no need to, being wealthy in his own right. For good measure I gave my mother an independent income too; though later I made her a ballerina, and had my father fall desperately in love after seeing her dance *Sylphides*. We owned cars and dogs and horses, and a great house with a mile-long gravelled drive. As an afterthought I sited it on the edge of the sea so there could be boats and a private beach. I 'remembered' seafishing and yachting; once started the process was self-perpetuating and I enjoyed myself thoroughly. It was a shock when the train reached its destination and I had to climb out to the dowdy platform and make my way, well encumbered by bags and satchels, to the school coach. God, I thought, frozen into my dream. That old place again; what a *bore* . . .

The fraud was wholly successful. Had Moira owned my gift she would of course have seen through it readily enough; most of the silly ideas weren't even my own, I'd picked them years before from my mother's fuzzy brain. But my quarry was five-sensed, dumb and blind; all she detected was the aura, the total effect of assurance and superiority. I was not the child who had left the school a few short weeks ago; she was intrigued, and frightened in her turn. Sensing her uncertainty I moved to the attack, projecting my incipient love, letting it grow and bloom within certain rigidly-controlled limits. My victim rose to the bait. She had to; it was designed to be irresistible.

Then began a devil's dance, all the more atrocious for its wordless silence. I had to be broken; but I wouldn't break. I stepped round the little traps laid for me, the carefully prepared humiliations, one after the next, subverting Moira's friends, shattering her own faith in her unholy skill. Had I been more mature I would have realized I was kicking a cripple; the beautiful and talented Miss Summersby was a potential lesbian, incapable of taking pleasure in anything but domination. I realized nothing save that the game was afoot; and I was playing it well.

Something, as they say, had to give; and it wasn't me.

The end came abruptly, one oppressive summer evening. There was in the school grounds a curious half-maze, half-grotto of considerable extent, constructed largely of vast blocks of limestone flung and tumbled apparently at random across the slopes of a wooded dell. Deep, beaten paths ran and twisted between the megaliths; there were caves, dripping with water and thick with moss. At the centre was an open space of grass, overlooked by an ancient partially-ruined summerhouse. In the spring the dell was a haze of bluebells; in any bright weather the little closed vistas enchanted the eye with subtleties of colour and line; but in the rain, when the paths streamed with yellow mud and the puddles at their sides grew to bogs, under overcast skies or on evenings of wind, a positive miasma seemed to rise from it, a shadow of some ancient, shapeless sin that made it a place of dread. I was far from being the only person to sense this, and the whole grotto had some years before been put arbitrarily out of bounds. Such a prohibition of course acted as a stimulus on the more daring spirits at Saint Cath's; Moira herself had made the dell peculiarly her own, exploring and plotting its strangeness till she knew every rambling path by heart.

This particular evening was as I said oppressive and dull, sheet lightning flickered above the clouds to the accompaniment of sudden muffled cannonades of thunder; weather in which the grotto would normally have been studiously avoided. But Moira was in a highly abnormal state of mind. I had stayed close to her most of the day on some pretext or other, puzzled and not a little alarmed by the thoughts that churned to the surface of her mind like bright fish, slipped away nearly too quickly for me to grasp. Her suggestion of visiting the dell was thrown down nearly in the nature of a challenge; I agreed, not altogether willingly, and we slipped away from the school, arriving, after a circuitous and careful route, at our favourite point of entry, a spot shielded by a massive beech where a strand of the wire that ringed the little wood could be unhooked from its post. Moira ran ahead of me in the deepening gloom, down those paths she knew so well; I followed, puffing a little and snagged-at by creepers, till we reached the central area of grass. We raced each other to the summerhouse, as was our custom; it was there that a chance word of mine – I truly forgot the initial cause of the quarrel – finally released the flood of Moira's bitterness. She accused me of plotting to ruin her life, of taking away her friends – that much at least was true – and of a score of outlandish crimes that took me completely by surprise. The words, and the brilliant, horrid bursting of hate that came with them, completely unnerved me. However I faced her boldly and made some sarcastic answer, having in my mind the beginnings of a notion that happened to be true; that of all the punishments that can be inflicted on a man or woman indifference and mockery make the deepest wound. I turned away, smiling, to leave her; and in that moment was convinced, briefly at any rate, of the physical reality of Divine intervention. The storm broke with a bolt of lightning, intense, jagged and violet-blue, that seemed to rise nearly from the ground on which we stood. For an instant the farther shapes of trees and rocks showed in a dreadful chiaroscuro before the accompanying concussion either flung us or sent us cowering to the ground. When I could hear and feel again Moira's arms were locked tightly round me; her face was pressed against my shoulder; she was sobbing and muttering in swift, senseless incantation '*I love you, I love you, God make you see. God make you see I love you . . .*'

My state of mind, of nearly ecstatic terror, can I'm sure be better imagined than described. She was hysterical of course, though that realization was little help to me at the time. One thing only was of paramount importance; to get myself, and her, out of that horrible place. That I did, finally, though the nightmarish run through torrential rain, always with the physical sensation of hands, or claws, at my back and neck, is still a thing I don't care to dwell on. Moira spent the best part of a week in the diminutive sanatorium of Saint Cath's, being fussed over and generally spoiled; I joined her on the second day with a streaming (and I'm surely largely psychosomatic) cold. When we were passed fit again we found many of the trees of the dell were already in process of being felled; and later a chain-link fence was thrown round it inside the older, insecure barrier. That made little difference to us at least; I'm quite sure neither of us could ever have brought ourselves to set foot inside the place again.

But the effect of those few seconds of terror was permanent. I had glimpsed myself through Moira's eyes, a glowing, shimmering creature; that itself, in retrospect, was a considerable shock. I remember standing before a washroom mirror and staring, staring, as though I had never seen myself before. In a sense of course I had not. The stranger watched back steadily; I saw the fine, glossy-black hair, the level forehead, the eyes of old deep lavender blue, the firmly chiselled mouth and chin. This was self-awareness; it would have come to me late or soon, six-sensed or five. But not maybe in such a strange and frightening way.

Something of my gift, I decided, revealed itself in my face. I began to cultivate little tricks of expression, veiling my eyes, letting them show suddenly their full and startling brilliance. Moira by this time was completely subjugated; the gorgon had seen her reflection. I filled her waking thoughts; she would have died for me, slowly and with pain, had I so desired. Now was the time to exact payment for what I believed had been her crimes; but oddly enough the rage was gone, dissipated by success and my new discoveries. I now felt for her nothing but compassion; I used her gently, careful not to hurt. Deeply suspicious at first, she was gradually soothed; and we became what the world is pleased to term friends.

I had by this time almost completely lost touch with my parents. Their letters and gifts arrived regularly; but they told me nothing more than such trinkets would tell a normal member of the human race. I found it disturbing to be reduced to a beggarly system of guessing and reading between the lines to arrive at an estimate of the mental state of my own father and mother. In its way it was a salutary lesson; and I was due for another. It was weeks before I saw my father again; when I did, I was shocked by his appearance. He was much thinner, and his hair, that had been speckled with grey, was almost totally white. There was something at the backs of his eyes that sent me burrowing hastily into his brain; what I found there nearly shocked me into vomiting. He had an incurable cancer.

The months that followed showed me a new aspect of his character. My father was not a man on whom providence had seen fit to bestow any striking physical or mental gifts; he was a mild soul, kindly and unambitious, whom I had hitherto regarded with a kind of half-amused tolerance. Yet he contrived, by means I can still only guess at, to keep the nature of his illness from my mother (and, he thought, from me) while he quietly put his affairs in order, made what provisions he could for our future. His letters still arrived for me week after week, full of transparent and hideous gaiety; I remember one contained a postal order for some little thing I had said I wanted to buy. At that I broke down completely; Moira caught me in my dormitory, weeping bitter tears. To my horror, I was unable to stop. My violence frightened her; I made her swear never to mention the incident, and realized with amazement that she would keep her word. For once, she was out of her depth; she thought, for some extraordinary reason I have never been able to fathom, that I was pregnant.

My father was finally admitted as a terminal patient to a research unit attached to the local General Hospital, and I was given permission from school to visit him at weekends. Right at the end, he understood something of the creature I had become; I remember his eyes searching mine, over and again, his lips shaking and fighting for words as he lay wasted on his pillows; but his thoughts were so masked and disfigured by the drugs they had given him that they were hidden even from me. They fought for him, distracting him with strange machines that boiled and burned, but it was useless. Even to touch his brain seared mine; it was nearly a relief when he slid into coma. But then there was the jumping and flickering, like a lampflame guttering on its last drop of fuel, slower, slower . . . I ran from that dim ward, unable any longer to tolerate the evidence of my senses, too shocked to block my mind. I remember I stood on a high place, a driveway, the building behind me like a great cliff burning with light, lights of cars below me winking like red and yellow jewels, all spangled with the tears that squeezed from my eyes. I felt the night wind touch my skin with ice, heard the distant crying of a train. They came to fetch me, but they could have saved their effort. I knew when he died.

My mother took it well. Silly woman that she was, there was in her something of that same unexpected steel that had been in my father. We convened a family council of two, after the funeral when the brooding people had gone. I was to go on with my schooling, that much was sure; her mind screamed against it, wanting to keep me with her, but her will overrode it. There was a little money, an insurance scheme that would allow me to complete my education; later there would be grants to be had, my father had investigated such things and left letters of advice. Reading them, my mother shook her head. 'It seems,' she said, 'that somehow he is still here.' For that platitude I wanted to shake her; grab her shoulders and shake and shake and scream at her to realize, *my father was gone.*

Who better than myself to know?

I returned to Saint Catherine's. Moira's love should have been a great comfort; but now I loathed myself for it. Deep and real as it was, it had been purchased by a shabby trick; who was I, I asked myself savagely, to hold a whip, make these animals called humans jump at my command? Moira could not understand my altered attitude; she put my coldness down to grief, which was at least partially true. I was treated with great kindness by everyone. I remember my form mistress taking me aside one day; she had some little project, silly in itself, that she felt might divert me for a time. She talked enthusiastically enough, while I nodded and voiced my agreement; but beneath the words I felt her brain wonder to God how a child could have aged, in as many weeks, ten years. I could have told her, had I a mind; I was still fighting my way, agonizingly, from the shadow of Death.

During my time at Saint Catherine's I had learned to ride; the school owned no horses but had the use of a small local stables. I rodc a great deal in the weeks that followed, usually with Moira. We were without doubt the two best horsewomen in the school, though our methods were laughably different. Moira loved horses for their own sake; her control and understanding of the animals were beyond my comprehension. I handled them in a way I handled most things, mechanically; to me the process was little different from driving a car. My mind, touching the mind of my mount, found little coherent thought but a reservoir of strength; by tapping that reservoir, listening and feeling as a motorist listens to his engine, I learned to ride extremely well. I was never thrown, though in all faith I was hard-handled enough; that neural link was far too fast for the animal brain of my mount. It had always been pleasant to feel how the great mass of energy that is a horse or a pony could be made to respond to me, coming more and more surely to rely on my touch and voice; now I concentrated desperately on improving and refining my control. Anything to stop my brain remembering and reliving the process of extinction. Moira and I scooped the board at a local gymkhana; our headmistress was delighted but slightly aggrieved. She felt morally bound to put up another cup; it set Saint Cath's back some few pounds and became known, unofficially and irreverently, as the Libby Trophy. As far as I know it is still competed for; I hope those who win it get more pleasure from it than it ever gave me.

During my last year at Saint Cath's I was invited by Moira to spend Christmas at her home. The offer was made in plenty of time to accept or refuse and I broached the matter tentatively in a letter to my mother a few weeks before end of term. I could tell by her reply that the idea distressed her but she insisted I go down with my friend. This after all was part of what she'd planned and schemed for. The vacation approached rapidly; so quickly indeed that the last week arrived almost before I realized it and I was immersed in a whirl of packing, of suitcases and railway vouchers. The school coach took us to the station and Moira and I boarded a train for London. We passed through the terminus at three o'clock, when the city was already lost in a roaring pastel fog, crossed by taxi to Paddington and were soon gliding from the noisy, half-seen cave of the station on board a West Coast express. As London fell behind my spirits revived, for the first time in many months; we sat in a crowded, steamy-windowed compartment, cracking nuts and giggling in a thoroughly unladylike fashion as the wheels clacked away the long iron miles. We left the train at Taunton; outside the station we were met by a chauffered Bentley and by ten o'clock I was relaxing in my own room at Compton Deverell.

On my first morning I was taken on a tour of the house and farm. Or farms, since much of the huge acreage was worked by tenants of the Summersbys. The house itself surpassed my expectations. My dream had taken on reality; it stood foursquare and proud on a rising swell of ground, mullions and twisted chimneystacks clear and detailed in the sharp air. From somewhere in the outbuildings came the clank of a pail; the clatter of a tractor engine drifted in across the fields, mixed with the mewing cries of birds. We viewed the farm from horseback, crossing the rolling ridge of high ground at a gallop; I remember the noise of the wind that brittle morning, the smell of the cold air, the blankness and brightness miles off that told of the presence of the sea. Sensitive as ever to atmosphere, I rapidly decided this and this only was the life for me. There was about it all an exactness, a fitness, a proud and swelling oldness; I had the feeling of having at last come home.

The house, I was interested to hear, was very fashionably haunted. There was a mass of evidence to support the manifestations, and the usual legend of eighteenth century murder and mayhem. I was seized instantly with a strange fancy; surely I of all people must be able to attest the presence or absence of those detached spirits we term ghosts? I spent many hours with Moira exploring the ancient wavy corridors of the place, the unused pantries and butteries, the crotchety attics, braced most of the time for the trailing rush of a disembodied thoughtstream; but my expectations were disappointed. I do not say, there are no ghosts; in fact I conceive some such unhappy accident to be wholly possible. But there were none at Compton Deverell.

Other incidents I can recall with equal clarity. The Summersbys bred Salukis, great feathered hounds with all mysteries in their eyes; I spent an hour making friends with the favoured stud dog, coaxing him grumbling from his nest by the kitchen fire. Moira was highly impressed but of course the performance posed no difficulties; his mind was even shallower than the mind of a horse, with less rudimentary reasoning power. Once we went to late mass in the local village church; there was the powered warmth of the Bentley afterwards, and rugs for our knees. I went hunting, a Christmas meet; I can see the line of horses stretched out across the brown ground, the distant scarlet splashes of jackets; I hear the muffled rumble of hooves, the thin bright yelping of the horn. There is the surge of the living engine beneath me, the red shrieking of the cornered fox; and I am blooded before they daub my face.

Two days before we were due to leave, I met David Craigie.

His people owned a biggish farm some few miles west of Compton Deverell. He had been invited for Christmas, but some arrangement or other had prevented him from coming. I remember him being shown into the morning room. I was on my knees in front of the fire, jean-clad, surrounded by records; in the alcove the player was clattering out some silly-season sensation. He was tall and burly, blond-haired and smelling of frost and tobacco; I was open to his mind, all guards down. I used my eyes and veiled them before I thought, felt his brain jolt. (Does that convey anything? *Jolt?*) I rose; a record slipped off my knee, rolled across the floor. Moira was coming forward, laughing; I half heard what she said. It was hello David, and Elizabeth, and her friends call her Libby, and laughing. I was dazed; something extremely strange had occurred.

He was talking again, covering up with a sort of desperation while his brain spun.

'Is that your bay up in Haycraft? Walleyed great brute . . .'

'Did you hear Gee came off the bike . . .'

'What?'

'Yes, darned clot; been asking for it long enough . . .'

'What?'

'Oh, nothing fatal. Well plastered up though. Be out of things a week or two, darned clot . . .'

And Jessie Cartwright had broken her engagement, that made the third; and old Blackwell's eldest had taken a foot off with a damn twelve bore and damn near died, and Young Farmers were co-opting that ghastly Mallory clot from Broomfield, you know, the TR chappie, because Jo Crompton's folk were movig up to Yorkshire . . . The voices faded, lost beneath a roaring that came from my own ears.

I had often wondered whether it was possible for a telepath to feel love. I had answered myself, no. Because love is the rationalization of a complex of patterns and pressures, a blind answer to a hormone-laced compulsion; we rut, as goats and stags rut, and have to dignify it with a phrase. Now I knew I was wrong. There had flashed in on me in that moment of awareness some unphysical pattern I could adore, some distillation from the mind of man; there is no comparison that will truly serve. I have said that Libby Maynard saw the colour of hate as red; but 'red' is an empty metaphor for what she experienced, the hues of rage exist in no spectrum conceivable to man. How describe the colour of love? It is the colour of a cave of ice, a tinkling gorgeousness full of bright shards of thought. Something of the sort I knew I had seen. I would not look again; I told myself there was no need.

The wheels of the train drummed, Taunton to Paddington, Saint Pancras to Derby; the iron beating ran in and out of tune with my brain, becoming for me the beat of hooves, of horses running free across the hills, while Moira stared dark-eyed and jealous. Images jostled in my mind; Compton Deverell, the ghost-hunt, the Bentley, the church, the empty fields; firelit parties, fruit and silverware, the colour of the sinking winter sun. Saint Catherine's when we reached it seemed truly dowdy and old, my father and all the past lost behind a tinted mist. I was young, and stupid; and I had fallen gloriously from my perch. My days were filled with love, my nights with thoughts of it. I waited for the letter Dave had promised to write, haunting that hall with its oaken round table where the parcels appeared so mysteriously like the bottles in *Alice in Wonderland*; while the days passed and faded, winter turned to the blustering wetness of March.

There was letter after letter from my mother, full of news, titbits of information, little complaints. How I ran to grab them from the table, how I hated them and their stupid, brutal postmarks! I never answered them; the great loneliness of all souls was on me again, blacker and more bitter than before. The whimperings that went on and on through the old walls of the place, I joined my moanings to them. I leaned my forehead to wet windowpanes, and mingled my tears with the rain.

And the letter came. So much, so very much more than I deserved. I read the postmark over and again before I could bring myself even to slit the flap. Cleared through Taunton at four fifteen pm: lovely, glowing Taunton! The wind blew from the West, piercing the walls of my room.

I saw Dave again and again, through spring and early summer. I travelled down and back with Moira; lonely, withdrawn Moira, who now had no love in her life at all. I could have loved her enough to make up for what she had lost; but she was sunk into an apathy from which not even my skills could rouse her. So much, I thought fleetingly, for the puppet-mistress; but my brain was too full to hold even thoughts of Moira for long. I had no need now to project the image of serenity. I was serenity, walking the earth; I was a mile tall.

The Lord giveth, so they say; and the Lord taketh away.

I had decided, during a discussion with David, that from Saint Catherine's I would go on to Oxford. He had laughed good-humouredly enough at my confidence; I smiled, and let things be. The way I operated, matters like that were not left to chance. My way stretched before me now clear and golden; college, a short engagement, a 'county' wedding; and the life of a farmer's wife down in the West Country, in the free wind and rain, a life of love and richness. I won my Oxford place, gained it on the highest academic rating ever to leave Saint Catherine's. My mistresses were staggered; for years I had lived the life of Reilly there, trundling along at my studies, keeping just ahead of possible trouble; but in a few short weeks I had grown up. I used my gift explosively, indifferent to consequences; so I came to sit in a city of spires, the city they say of eternal youth. I walked grey cloisters walled from scurry and din, stretched hands up to the sun and said 'All this is mine.' I'd come a very long way.

'Silly Libby Maynard, silly Libby Maynard . . .'

Somewhere a little girl still skipped in my brain, taunting and calling; calling, calling, through lonely winter-blue streets.

I was lying on a beach of smooth brown sand when the world came to an end.

Above me, high and sunlit, are cliffs. If I crane my neck I can just see the nose of David's red TB MG parked up there close to the edge, cloths draped over its sunward tyres. If I raise myself on my elbow I can see the sea, moving slow and heaving like the breath of the world; sun reflections play across it, silver skeins dazzling and lancing. Above me the sky is a flawless vault, haunted by the mighty ghost of the sun; it seems to my sleepy brain that I could fly up into the nothingness, fall away swift and effortless as a bullet from the Earth and all things known.

We have been swimming; I lie and let the water and salt dry on my body and listen to Dave's voice as he talks. He looms in the brightness like a brown monolith; his voice seems alternately to fade and grow near, pulsing like the waves of the sea. He is building a little pyramid of pebbles, on my flat bare stomach; each tiny stone and piece of sea-glass is a year of life, a promised time of happiness. I slide easily, almost unconsciously, into his brain, find there reassurance and the coiling, quiet shapes of love. I am, I think, the luckiest person alive; for what girl or woman, what *human*, ever owned an assurance like that? Of course I shall marry him, of course I'll wait; were he not five-sensed and blind, he would read the answers in my brain. The rapport is nearly complete; now I must make it perfect. I never met a human before whom I *knew* would understand.

I pushed his hand away from where it likes to stray and tease. I sit up, laughing and scattering the pebbles. 'David,' I say, 'I want to talk to you. Very seriously.' Loving him, and mocking; for they were the words he used to me. We lie shoulder to shoulder, pressed together, and I make patterns in the sand as I talk. Stars and triangles, circles and squares; smoothing each away, doodling with my finger in the tiny glittering grains. He listens, and I can feel him laughing. I tell him everything, right from when I was a child. The laughter becomes audible; I protest he isn't listening but he shakes his head. 'Libby,' he says, 'what are you trying to do? Don't you see what it would mean if all this nonsense were true? You'd be a monster . . .'

In the sea-washed afternoon is a little white-hot point of fury, bright and surprising. It's strange that my rage could have risen so quickly, strange that it should burn so steady and clear; like something long submerged, coming at last into the light. I fight to stay calm, because suddenly the quiet air is charged with disaster; but it is impossible. I own a unique gift, a great and terrible talent; there is power in me, more power than these five-sensed folk could ever dream. I will not be mocked; not by any of them. Mocked or patronized . . .

He is still talking, and laughing. To him this is just a game; soon. I'll show him how I mark the cards. 'Whew,' he is saying. 'Just fancy having your brain picked. Libby, you should have slapped my face . . .'

He's very close to something sacred and still it's a joke; I want to hurt him back for the way he's hurting me. I can feel the power in me building, fed by this first true anger of my life. I wonder if I should tell him to me he's just a toy; young and not-serious, like a sort of bumbling well-shod teddy bear. That's how I see him now, all at once; a new David, egotistical and stupid, painted in clear sharp aniline colours. 'David,' I say, 'I do know. All the . . . things you want, just what you want to do with me. I want it too. Very much . . .' I move against him, wanting him to stroke me, soothe away the rage, but he pulls back uneasily, I'm in his brain again, I see the sudden fear; the fast slither and flash of it, like a worm of red mercury. Gone half-glimpsed, buried away like something foul. 'David,' I say again; and I know my voice is snapping icicles and frost, I know the gift is showing in my eyes, shifting and glinting. '*Think* . . .'

'What . . .?'

'Think,' I say. 'Think of anything. Just hold the things in your mind then take something else. Quick as you can. Try and beat me, Dave . . .'

It's like taking pennies from a blind child. In a sense that's just what it is. That's the first image; a penny. No, a florin. Newly minted. It turns, catches the light, flashes silver. Then a . . . boat, power boat. No, he's changed it. A yacht. And cars and bosoms and flowers, rainclouds, lightning, the sun . . .

And the fast red clamour of fright. Like alarm bells, obscuring and overriding. He's on his feet, as if something jumped from the sand and bit; but I can't stop. I have to go all the way now, hurting him, terrifying. His thoughts are jumbled and confused but I clatter them out like a loudspeaker clamped on his brain. I'm his *doppelganger*, squalling and spitting in the sunlight; I'm locked to him, so tight I can't unhook when he goes scrambling for the cliff. His fear is hurting now, burning like acid, driving me wild; two sets of eyes glare, two pairs of legs and arms scrabble on stone. Through him I see my body alter, and that's the worst of all. A pink-pawed monster pants and scratches on the rock; I scream to him, using my voice, tell him David please, please to God I'm not a monster. I'm not, I'm not . . . and I miss a handhold he was reaching for and my body goes sliding and bouncing and tearing itself. The shock snaps the link; I see sand wheel and the sky and a bird like a paper scrap before pains jars up from my knee and down from my knee and through me. Faintness flickers black across my eyes and I'm lying panting staring at the sunlit edge of stone above, something trickling and running on my leg and blazing with pain.

I look at the blood and up to him. I touch and my hand comes away marked but it seems I can't believe. He ties a handkerchief round my leg but his fingers are shaking so he can barely make the knot. We sit awhile and watch the blood come glowing through the cloth and a man tells me I want to go to hospital with that then David fetches my coat and dress and somehow I get clothed, put away my silly pale animal's body. I don't touch his brain and he cannot look at my eyes. Whatever happened there between us finished us for ever; we both screamed and crawled, now we're like twin poles of magnets, needing to swing away. I remember getting into his car, then my leg starting to shake then all of me. And him bandaging properly and me holding the first aid box dumbly on my knees. Did I talk to him? I can't say. My brain said, *you are a shell. Thinking and breathing and talking, but no man for me. Like a pretty, sweetbreathed icon, dead and cold. Soft and flat inside, and dirty like a sewer.* And he said in return, *For they are like unto whited sepulchres, which outwardly are fair, but within are full of dead man's bones.*

No, we didn't speak without voices. He wouldn't have said that, not even to me.

I think we said goodbye to each other. I know there was a train; miles and miles of track and rail, and the tracks wobbling and shimmering with heat and the dust and dirt blowing up from the big iron wheels. I was on the train, but I didn't know where it was going. Then I was not on the train. For the first time I seemed able to step outside my body, watch it trudge and shuffle along. In my ears was a great singing and susurration, echo of an unholy hymn; the thoughts and hatings and lovings of a million million beings, all up and down across the world. I made the trudging Libby lift her head and laugh so the black sky, raining now, rained into her face and eyes. Soon she couldn't walk any more, because of the pain in her knee. She whimpered a little because she was lost. She leant head down clutching a wet green lamp post, seeing the beads of water scurry and run and join; then it seemed that after all the road was familiar, that she was nearly home. She saw the little houses round her, the yellow reflections of lamps spindling on wet paths. Yes, just at the end of the street was a school. And a little girl, Alice was her name, came skipping and laughing from the dark. Alice would take her home; and they would mend her knee and help her, put her to bed in a room with an electric fire that glowed in the night like a burning ship at sea. She tried to take Alice's hand but it melted into blackness. There were other faces round her now, a ghostly ring of them; they stretched and distended and gleamed like faces made of lampflame. *It's a big world, Libby,* I told her. While she hung her head and sulked and her hair swung wet and dark and the shoulders of her coat and her pretty gloves blackened with the rain. *It's a big world,* I said. *It laughs and cackles with a million voices, and the voices are like the sea.* She nodded, seeming to understand. She knelt down; moved her leg to be more comfortable, where the hurt part touched the grass. Her gloves were muddied; she wiped them feeling confused. She was thinking of a place called Compton Deverell, then of a funny round table in a little hall. There were letters on the table; she tried to reach them but her fingers scuffed them off the edge and they fell into the darkness between the planets. She began to cry then, lying huddled, wanting Moira and the bunny-rabbit gloves somebody had taken away.

The faces came closer, bending and swooping in the rain; there were hands, some trying to touch and turn her, some trying to pull the other hands away. She tried to scream, but nothing came except panting. She wanted to tell the faces not to touch and pat her with their thoughts, to leave her in the dark. Till there was the white, flying noise of ambulance bells, tyres on the rainslicked road; and stand back there and move along, and the people chatting and mumbling at the strangest thing that ever happened, in their funny little street, in their funny little town.

I woke slowly, to a green-painted ward and the cool thought-stream of a nurse. She stood tapping her foot and considering; before I was fully conscious I knew my mother had been informed. She came in haste, tearstreaked and anxious, found me lying in a sunny bed in a sunny little room. From the windows I could see the roofs of lorries and cars moving along a road; I watched them quietly, as a child might watch the bright beads of an abacus strung before its eyes. My brain, bruised, reconstructed by slow degrees the horror of that day and night, but I felt curiously untouched; the drugs they had pumped into me kept me floating, away from contact with the world and pain. In time I was allowed to go away. I suffered my mother to take me north, sat in the train compartment while she pecked and probed and the fields slid by and the telephone wires swooped mile on mile, hynotic and unending. I watched them listlessly, as later I watched the clouds move ragged and pointless across the window of my room. Some mental fuse had blown; trapped once more in the cast-iron ring of middle class existence, I was barely aware of the walls that closed me in.

When I felt stronger I took to walking the little, pretty, dead roads of the estate. I was still confused; to think, consciously, demanded more effort than I was prepared to make. I realized, incoherently, that I could never return to Oxford; no shred of my past life, of the old Elizabeth, could be allowed to remain. I had finished with Saint Catherine's, with Compton Deverell, with David and with Moira. She, I realized, was the only true friend I had ever made; and I had destroyed her. She had hated me for taking David from her, but that would have passed; now, when I had given him back, she would hate me till the sun burned cold.

I would wander too through the quiet house, while my mother was out working to earn our keep. One day, turning out an old drawer, I found my brushes and a sketchbook. Something about the touch and feel of them stirred me, it seemed for the first time in years. I walked out of the town that afternoon, to the flat high moorland and the empty rolling of the clouds. I drew for hours, alone in the sun and rain, trying to catch the desolation before me that coincided so exactly with my own emptiness and despair. Curiously flat, those drawings were; mechanical, empty, dead. I have some of them still; I see I discovered, in the high clouds and hills, the circles and triangles and aimless formal squares I had once scratched with my finger in the sand of a beach. Something I included myself in the drawings; a tiny lay figure, antlike and black, head bowed as my head was bowed in hopeless concentration.

As I worked my mind, recovering slowly, began to understand how misguided and absurd my life had been. I had tried, through all my years, to live as a human being; oddly talented maybe, but human for all that. Now I saw more clearly. Whatever I was, however I had been spawned, one cold fact stood out. Human I would never be; that sobbing crawl up the cliff had taught me that. As I recalled it, in every hateful detail, I was conscious that for the first time the visions of Somerset that had filled my brain for so long were shimmering and fading. Lonely I had been born, and lonely I would die. From henceforth I would seek pleasures, if any pleasures remained, on my own high plane; for me love and gentleness were delusions, chimeras that could only mock and hurt. I had made a terrible mistake, and it had nearly destroyed me; I would never, never, never make it again.

2

Libby, circa *1957.*

A tall girl, graceful and striking. She has put on both height and weight; four years' worth of glossy black hair manes down her back, hangs perpetually across her sombre eyes. For school she dresses simply in sweater and jeans. The jeans are neat, tight but not extravagantly so, faded from scrubbing; she wears them with deep cuffs that accentuate the slimness of her ankles. In summer she sports topless sandals or rope-soled canvas sneakers, in winter flat-heeled shoes of dark red or dark green leather. Her hands are well-kept, nails trimmed short, the cuticles pushed back to accentuate their squareness. She uses them continuously while talking, conscious of the slenderness of the fingers, the broad, boyish palms; they flutter before her face as she speaks, hypnotically, like sinewy butterflies. She usually carries with her a dishevelled, paint-splashed shopping basket, one of those deep, woven affairs in vogue at the time. It is well filled with bric-a-brac; from its top protrudes a worn quarter-imperial sketchbook, there is a purse with small change and a pound note pushed in the lining, a house key, a wad of used weekly bus tickets; bottles of wash and ink, Waterman's Midnight Black, Winsor and Newton's Fixed Indian; putty rubbers, pencils, cobblers' heel; tatty squirrel brushes, precious sables with their points protected by rolled tubes of paper. An old spectacle lens that serves as a reducing glass, a book of lettering; dog-eared postcards of a Bosch triptych, the Dali Crucifixion, a page from the Book of Kells; a copy of *Under Milk Wood*, a pamphlet on Anglicanism, another, well-thumbed, on the Doctrine of the Bodily Assumption. There are cigarettes and matches, rattly pencilboxes full of odds and ends; drawing pins and razor blades and stumps of wax candle, broken bits of pastel and Conté crayon, a six-inch typescale. More personal belongings jostle with the rest; a compact, a mirror, a comb, a lipstick, seldom-used mascara; a broken charm bracelet, a bundle of old letters, a bunny in its plain white carton. In matters of that nature I was notoriously indifferent to display; though I never affected the monthly pallidness and dishevelment, that curiously patient expression of tight-lipped martyrdom, that set the boys to twittering and made a social accomplishment of dysmennorrhoea.

As usual, I had found conformity my easiest course; an art student I have become, an art student I would be. I was I suppose fortunate; after my unprecedented rejection of my County Major the authorities mulled over my case for some months before agreeing to underwrite a new career. There were of course conditions, one of which was that I attend school in Northerton, the county town. Rather grudgingly I was granted my fees, travelling expenses and a tiny allowance, some few shillings a week, that would keep me in materials. I would be hard pressed at times, but I was in no position to bargain. I could live; that, for the moment, was enough.

We were a small establishment, seldom numbering more than a dozen and a half students; our Principal, a mild-mannered man and no great disciplinarian, lived in constant fear of rationalization. The school suffered as a result in output and reputation; escapades that under more normal circumstances would have secured certain expulsion passed unremarked and I saw a great deal that widened my eyes, though I had formerly considered myself wise in the ways of the world. I rapidly came to understand the resentment of those I jostled in bus queues and on the streets; in the minds of Northertonians, to be an Art School girl meant only one thing. You were a whore.

Such a society of course suited my talents ideally. I had long known I functioned best in an atmosphere well charged with emotion; and emotion from this time on was to be my stock in trade. Ambition, that for a while had been submerged by grief, had returned in quieter and more deadly shape. I knew very well the potential power of my gift; I would use it now to regain what I had come to consider my birthright. Deep in my consciousness the image of Compton Deverell swam once more; one day, somehow, I would win back what I had lost, I would own that place or its equal, I would have my green acres, my horses and cars and trees. Sometimes in vicious reverie I saw myself drive Moira physically from her home, as she had driven me from her long-shared life; at others there was a grand reconciliation, tearful on her part, lordly and condescending on mine. Then I would touch the smooth scar below my knee and think of David Craigie and the anger would rise, slow and consuming, misting my sight till the lines of little houses beyond the jerking windows of the bus swam in red haze. I might I suppose have sold myself in any market I chose; but I was no chattel, to be knocked down to the first rich bidder. I would rise by my own efforts, by the money I made and multiplied; I was indeed lost in a thorny wood, and like another bitter soul before me my one recourse would be the bloody axe.

But first there was a great deal to learn. I needed a sound practical and theoretical knowledge of art; once that had been acquired I could branch out in any of a half dozen directions already shaping in my mind. For my first year I studied hard. To my natural dexterity I added of course the immense advantage of telepathic understanding. My work improved rapidly, so much so that I was soon back at my old game of hanging fire. And savouring the cosmic truth that those cab-horses proverbially pissing across Turner's canvases had more to do with the Fact of Art than all the old ladies of our evening classes, delineating so carefully their bowls of violets and daffodils.

My enforced inactivity gave me time to concentrate on several pressing social matters. The chief of them of course was sex; in the bitter environment in which I found myself I had ample opportunity to study its manifestations. We were I suppose an amusing collection of young people. The boys (or males, in the new cold terminology I acquired) came mostly from working-class and unpretentious homes; the girls on the other hand seemed to represent the very worst sweepings of the *petit-bourgeoise.* That phrase I had previously regarded as a sort of music-hall joke; now I rapidly came to loathe it and the mentality it represented. I knew the value of money, far better than any of my fellows; I had mixed with folk of quality and discretion, and one day, on my own terms, would do so again. Northerton was no finishing-school; these preening daughters of big-time pork butchers left me cold. I managed to disguise my contempt effectively enough; that trick of mirroring that I had first practised on Moira served me well. The boys were more interesting. Their experience of women varied widely; but all seemed to desire me, violently and more or less continuously. I was undressed and raped a hundred times, to my intense amusement, always in silence or to the faint accompaniment of those ever-scratching pens. I had of course long since realized sex would be my most potent weapon, though I still lacked, aggravatingly, the essential practical experience. I gave the matter of virginity some thought before deciding to sacrifice mine. I eventually concluded that having no intention of marrying into Royalty self-denial served no practical purpose, and was most certainly depriving me of a valuable part of my armoury. I set out to remedy the defect, casting round for a suitable mate.

The choice was not difficult. Griff Edwardes was the most experienced of my intake; a valid technique was obviously a requisite, if I was to be violated I intended to profit from the exchange. He was a stocky, thick-necked boy, bass-voiced and beautiful-eyed, a great womanizer, rugger player and drinker of beer. I was intrigued by him, and grew quite attached to his curious mind; it fascinated me to see how well his noisy good humour concealed the boiling inadequacy beneath. I could see no reason for such unhappiness; his father was a moderately successful unchartered accountant, Griff was never short of a pound for drinks or cigarettes; he had certainly had his pick of Northerton girls in his time yet still he drove himself unremittingly, striving to dominate by fair means or foul any company in which he might find himself. The thing was like some congenital disease; I became obsessed for a time with the oddest variations on the notion of Original Sin, and had to take myself firmly under control. These were deep waters; I'd been in over my head once, it wasn't going to happen again.

I had been keeping Griff in a state of uncertainty, projecting my sweetest and most desirable image whenever he concluded I was an experienced *femme fatale*, reversing my role when he seemed about to suspect my gross innocence. Experienced though he was, he could make nothing of me; those tiny hints, movements of an eyelash, a foot, ways of standing, walking, that to him and his kind spoke plainer than the plainest print, were invariably absent, or bafflingly misapplied. His lack of success with me had of course intrigued him. He had tried insults, he had tried blandishments, he had tried sheer charm; and was in fact beginning to despair.

I decided I would fall from grace during or after my first Arts Ball, and took up the option he had been offering some weeks before that annual event. I held to my programme, though I am painfully aware that had I been a five-sensed virgin I would have found it virtually impossible; his vivid thoughtstream, the keen and animal Wanting, his crafty and skilful petting, all rapidly conspired to abrade my nerves. He seemed to set me jangling and humming, fill me from toes to head with hot, sensitive wires; the idea of translating theory into reality, of experiencing at last the process that caused so much fuss and dislocation, came to occupy more and more of my waking thoughts. I designed myself a costume for the ball, a skimpy thing all rags and flinders of bright blue satin, spent hours modifying and refining that appurtenance of sin. I experienced a certain giddying excitement, preening before the mirror in my room, taking in a dart here, a tuck there, as I prepared to take Northerton, and young Master Edwardes, by sudden storm.

It was overall an exciting time. Students laboured in the ill-lit basement of the school, building massive flats of lath and paper for the floorshow that was traditionally staged; size buckets stank and bubbled, brushes slapped; we hammered and bolted and nailed while devils' heads and hands, painted in vast swirling strokes of red and blue, collected in eerie stacks against the walls. We devised curious machines, more spectacular than effective, that we trusted would recreate with fidelity the flames of hell; floodlights, spots, drums of cable were begged and borrowed, posters and tickets printed, rehearsals staged. The ball was held in a big dance hall some three or four miles from the school; half a dozen of us scoured the countryside round Northerton in a pair of borrowed vans scrounging for mistletoe and holly to decorate it, jounced back into town with our bristling, outdoor-smelling, frost-crackling loads. The day before the show school was all but deserted; working parties converged on the Palais, hoisting grotesque wall panels under the eagle eye of the manager, pumping up innumerable balloons to fill the great square net they lowered from the roof. The floorshow was a wild affair of men and girls tossed through the demon's mouth into a cauldron of boiling silk flames; I danced in my costume afterwards, three-quarters stoned, twirling and spinning and showing my behind, driving myself quite frantic.

I was dazed finally by an excess of impressions; I seemed to be at the centre of a roaring technicolored sea, the excitement of five hundred revellers cutting unstoppably through my guard as a dozen or so gins took their cumulative toll. I clung to Griff in direst need; he wrestled me to the edge of the floor, where I broke away from him and ran. The walls of the place seemed to tilt, to right and left; I gulped and skidded, doubting my ability to survive the gauntlet. I reached my haven with seconds to spare, and was most inelegantly and inaccurately sick. The process left me with a thunderous headache and a pale determination to die. Black coffee and an indefinite number of aspirins sobered me somewhat, but the darting and spitting of so many thoughts around me had me delirious and confused; I needed little urging to seek the open air. Griff steered me, hand under my elbow, fingers gripping my arm; past pillars complicated with spotlights and holly, by half-seen tables littered with glasses and wet trays, with stoles and parti-coloured drifts of streamers and sequinned evening purses. Beside us the fancy dress dancers paraded remote and untouchable as figures in a dream; folk known once well enough, turned now to gnomes and dwarfs and strange new wild princesses, jerking and capering, nodding their great wise heads under the electric confetti of the mirror bowl while the band played some weird troll-song and their feet lisped on the shining polished floor. Then we were in the car park, steering between the waiting Morrises and Fords, their windscreens blind with frost; my breath steamed in the icy air, the cold knifed at my throat, moved brightly on my legs and arms.

The gin had not finished with me; I seemed poised now between sobriety and drunkenness, solemnity and mirth. My head spun; I craned back to see the hall behind me, the long high yellow line of the clerestory; and I was certainly giggling again then, at some nuance of wit that seemed at the time fit to stop the world. But something moved up there, black and momentary, crossing like a ghost the lit eyes of the windows, and I began to fight and weep. They were preparing to drop the balloons, an event of cosmic importance that must on no account be missed. I balked stubbornly, trying to dig in my heels, beating at the hand that held my arm; but the fingers had turned to bands of steel. The sounds of the revel reached me faintly, flaring among the other flarings from the hall; round me now were black pools of shadow, lines of house-backs staring and dark. I pointed waveringly, some shaggy new resolve formed in my mind; I felt a vast and sudden sorrow for all fleeting things, all the little folk round about who were not drunk or alive or in love. It seemed the whole world by some great mercy of God should be made to dance and sing; I was blathering that out as I was bundled inside the van of a friend of Griff's whose name was Mike and who was blond and in Advertising and who had come up from Town. Waving my arms and struggling, all bare hips and thighs and little flashy pants, shouting quavering and high but firm in my resolve '*Bring out your dead* . . .' While within the hall those tinsel figures of memory plodded round and round, passed now not through the throats of cardboard, of painted devils, but to some deep Limbo, a stark place of forgotten promises and sorrows, hopes and dreams.

Griff was very good with me, oddly considerate and gentle. I remember his mouth closing over mine; but soft and slow so I had time to adjust and open wide and wide. And sliding into his mind, and brighter seas mounting and dazzling, and the burning hurting things his hands did, and kissing and rubbing till nothing was enough and nothing would serve and nothing was left but shock and sublimity and bursting sweet pain. And when it was done Griff sitting on the sodding jack and swearing and me wanting to go again and laughing and crying and licking him to try and make him start. While the polyps of figures swayed and surged to Auld Lang Syne and God saved the Queen and the cars chuffed and revved, left the place at last to icy loneliness and dark. What whisperings, what manoevring got me my coat and bag and neglected dress I never knew; but Griff bundled me and wrapped me, shaking and dazed, and him telling me, half-alarmed, to get a Chrissake move on; very careful he was and loving, with a stupid girl who'd shown herself so gauche. The van swayed and juddered, accelerating with rocket force through dark town streets while I mumbled and called for beer, and someone wrestled and hugged and someone else played bugle, high and clear and sweet, all the long way home.

I carried away for Christmas a *ménage* of impressions in which Griff's scent, the vivid pleasure I took from his rustling-clean linen and breath, seemed combined with those dwarfs who had nodded so wise and strange in the moving lights. Spotlights turned towards me, staring with their great hot colour-changing eyes; my feet whispered on polished wood, the crowd jostled and roared and gleamed. And there was another image, odd and unconnected; an old and humpbacked car standing on a driveway bright with frost, engine running, expelling a steady white cloud of vapour like jetted breath. The car stood before Griff's house; I saw it with my physical eyes, noted and passed on, but the vision would recur. The Christmas Car, I called it to myself; epitome of winter and of school, all frosty mornings and lovings, sorrows and passions and frightened passing pains.

Reality, after that strange night, struck me with an odd and obsessive force. Why was it, I wondered, that my mother's house was so small? I saw, and continued for days to see, odd details in a new and alien light. White ceilings with their upside-down cracks and stains, amazements of wallpaper, chipped paint landscapes of skirting and picture rail; tiny marks of forgotten dustings, scuffed places on floors, the interplanetary and sober depth of the switched-off tellyscreen. The exact spatial relationship of a flower vase and a pair of spectacles would hold me hypnotized; a ball of bright wool, laid by accident on a white cloth, could send me scuttling in panic. I had had maybe a lesson in art; I understood now emotionally what before I had learned by rote, how Vincent could have come to paint his Yellow Chair. Nights I lay sleepless, revolving these basic strange images; the gnomes, the tablecloth, the Christmas Car. And faint far horns would blow, voices from fairyland, some place that struggled, on the edge of consciousness, to be. I felt strangely blocked and polar; I recalled without difficulty my plans and schemes; but also I remembered deep quick pain, and touching where there was unrepentant blood. The memory rang time and again with the deep force of a drum across my mind; it seemed I might never tire of its savagery and strangeness. A tooth had been drawn from me; I relived the creaking snapping instant, so horror-filled, so quaintly desirable; while a part of me cried that my white temple, my body was defiled and another answered remembering a vast and timeless giving that seemed in that lost moment of wisdom a purpose of life itself. Against these factors, each so disparate, each so strong, I balked; not knowing gladness or sorrow, trying to understand, never understanding. I jumbled the images and reselected with care, very thoughtful, very slow and cool. I walked invisible tightropes, stepped dainty feet in line to breakfast and to bed; as if by careful attention to details, tiniest nuances of dress and speech, an almost religious preoccupation with the formality of existence, I might avert some catastrophe that I realized absurdly was already in the past. That was Elizabeth Maynard, *Christmas Elizabeth* I tried (tasting the syllables). Very formal and correct, pained, most white and cool. Behaving, I realized wryly and at length, like any other freshly-deflowered virgin. For all my mess of senses.

I had a card from Griff, end product of a litho project he'd been playing with for half a term; a rugger player straightarming his opponent, blood splashing from the victim's nose, a caption *Merry Christmas*. Inside was a hastily scrawled invitation to a New Year dance. I ignored it; lost in my musings, I had for the moment no further need of stimulus. Griff could wait; I stayed home with my mother through most of the vacation, watching the endlessly flickering television, hearing the wind moo and bluster in the chimneys of the house, sipping the bad sherry and worse port that seem an inescapable part of working-class festivities. In the mornings I would cycle out, maybe six or eight miles from my home, to sketch. I drew a great deal, discovering to my surprise a new and totally unwomanly vigour of line. I had it seemed become preoccupied with the chastisement of my already-ruined body; in icy or too-hot bathing, in sitting huddled in the freezing moorland wind till knuckles and knee and ankle joints stiffened with cold. Later, in my own good time, Griff would soothe away the pain; but properly, undressed in a deep, warm bed. The image infused and richened my dreams; I felt the fresh stirring of a tenderness I had thought banished for ever; so that I ran to greet him, on the first day of the new term, with I suppose much of the exuberance of a freshly weaned puppy.

The shock I got carried me, white-faced and panting, clear into the ladies' loo; and some very odd looks and odder questions came my way before I was in command of myself again. All that day, nearly all that week, I lived in a whirling world, prey to a jealousy so intense its stabbings took my breath like the pang of the falling nightmare. On its heels came rage; such a rage as even I had never felt before. For my body, so secret and precious, to be laid in memory with others; to see my transcendental experience reduced to a mere drop in an endlessly roaring ocean, was nearly too much for me. I had probed Griff's mind only too effectively; it was all I could do not to hiss out the name, age, the hated statistics of his newest conquest. Why I had imagined I, so far from being his first love, would be his last, I have no idea; but I could neither face him nor speak, the sheer perfidy of the thing took my breath. For his part he was intrigued, trying by various means to probe the reason for my altered attitude. I prayed he would not touch me or come near; I knew I would be unable to control my hate.

The climax came one morning when he fondled me casually in passing, squeezing my breast tip suddenly beneath my shirt. I was within an ace of lacerating his arm with the scalpel that lay before me on the desk; my fingers had closed on it before, at its very peak, the rage was gone. In an instant of time I saw how very nearly I had once more fallen into the pit dug for me; I remembered he had been my tool and nothing more, a five-sensed, pallid creature I had used and discarded. I saw the suspicion bubbling in his brain, beneath it the dark-red pulse of an anger I would wake at my peril; so I caught his fingers and pressed them to me, rubbed my cheek against his sleeve before pushing him daintily away. I was sweet with him after that and gentle, acting the part of contrite fallen angel, projecting a shy and becoming friendship. He was charmed, and soothed; and I saw what in my haste I had overlooked, that he had by no means escaped from our encounter unmarked. I still filled a gratifying percentage of his thoughts; I nurtured his incipient love, latching by the hour on to his brain. From my superhuman vantage point I had already tried him and passed sentence; before I was through, I would see him writhe in hell.

Over that summer I insinuated myself into the so-called smart set of Northerton. No rally or treasure hunt, no dinner dance, no twenty-first was complete without Elizabeth Maynard, violet-eyed, hell-raising Innocent. I learned to drive, quite illegally, on a TR2, the property of one of the wealthier young men of the town; I learned sex too, competently and thoroughly. I took another boy, and another, and another after that; each of them I broke, carefully and scientifically, before moving to the next. One of them indeed, after a singularly vicious jilting, almost ended his life in a canal. I dissuaded him, at no little cost in personal inconvenience. What I needed was proof of my power; I was not yet ready to kill. I made my victims dance; but carefully, deviously, training myself for better things. I took care never again to lose sight of my objective. Compton Deverell was in my mind; a great quiet house, won by my own efforts, that overlooked the sea. Meanwhile my fame spread subtly and far; when Libby raised her frock, empires fell.

Griff of course had long since become aware of my intentions. My exploits, archly repeated, caused him quite remarkable pain. He retaliated in the only way he knew; but each conquest, each laying at a Saturday village hop, only spurred me to greater excesses. For over a year our strange, silent battle went on, through summer and the winter term, another Ball, another bitter January. It was as if we waggled masks at each other, ever more bloody and gruesome. Eventually, one of us must break; and I was determined it would not be me.

I had thought him incapable of rousing me to anger again; but I was wrong. One night towards the end of January we chanced to be the only students at the evening Costume Life session; the tutor dismissed the model, we sat round brewing coffee and smoking, hearing the wind rattle the great mansards of the studio roof while he refought for us his battles of World War Two. The chatter mellowed me; it was a faint shock to turn out into the rainy, blustery night. We leaned on the rail of the bus stop opposite college, waiting for the service that would take us down to town centre. Above us tall pollarded limes gave partial shelter; the shadows of their branches and twigs moved restlessly on the wet road. I was probing Griff's mind, seeing over and again the strangest image of myself; like a Renaissance Madonna, white and pure, lit it seemed by an internal flame like a lamp glowing through alabaster. Try as I might, I could see no farther; of late he had developed a trick of blocking, almost as if he knew or had guessed something of my gift. So the picture went and came, fascinatingly, like something glimpsed in the bright coals of a fire.

The bus was late; we boarded it finally, climbed to the upper saloon. He settled beside me, swinging his satchel between his feet, lighting a grateful cigarette; instantly the picture was back, coupled with a sweeter, hotter thought that despite myself set my heart thumping, the blood racing in my veins. I studied the shifting patterns of rainspots on the windows, expecting him to speak; but we were half-way to our terminus before he said gruffly, 'Coming for a drink, Lib?'

He knew as well as I did I'd missed my connection, I had an hour to kill. I half shrugged, sensing the sudden flaring hope.

'Where?'

'You name it, love. Royal?'

I hesitated again; then smiled suddenly, warming to him.

'Yes, all right. Like to. Thanks.'

The bursting of his thoughts was nearly like an anthem.

The bus ground to a halt almost opposite the hotel. He steered me into the lounge bar; we sat in half-strained friendship, glasses of Scotch on the table in front of us, talking over what to us had become old times. The whisky made me drowsy; I leaned closer to him, wishing with a strange passion that the cup might pass from me, that I could sleep and wake a normal, five-sensed being. He misconstrued the gesture; his arm slid round me, pulling me to his side. He talked then, openly, of his growing need for me, the wrongness of the pain we had caused each other. I relaxed, leaning my head on his shoulder, closing my eyes. It was good to be still for a moment, and not have to fight; good, too, to scent victory, albeit in an unexpected shape. Then in that instant of fulfilment came disaster. The image was back, purer and sweeter than before; and I realized, with a horrid shock, that it was a picture not of the present but the past, of what I once had been. It was as if, half-dozing, I had startled myself awake with a nightmarish dream. I understood, instantly, the blocked emotion that had been churning at the back of his brain. I sprang from him furiously, scurried for the door shoving people aside, leaving behind me indignant shouts. That he, that any half-sensed thing, should pity – pity me, for what he thought I had become – was more than I could bear. I ran down the street, hair flying; but he caught me before I had gone a hundred yards, swung me to a panting halt. I squalled at him then, startling the passers-by, trying to wrench free; and he shouted back, angry at last, that I was a fool. A fool and a child, spoiling my life for a bunk-up in a bloody van.

I was not conscious of hitting him. I felt no sensation in my palm, was unaware that I had moved my hand; but I saw his head snap back, the surprised red marks spring out across his face. I saw too the pain and rage scintillate in his brain; even while he laughed, turning his head and pointing, proffering impossibly the other cheek. I broke from him then, fled blindly through traffic and din till his hated, triumphant thoughtstream ceased to vaunt behind me. One thought only hammered in my mind; that he had beaten me, in some way that as yet I could barely understand. After that I dared no longer look into his brain; though I faced him at school and spoke to him, I tried to shut him from my thoughts. It was he now who used me gently, projecting not hate or love but a Christian and unspeakable charity. He ceased even to flaunt his prowess; for that mercy alone I could have clawed out his eyes.

The affair, if affair it could be termed, ended in March. We had had a late, heavy snowfall; it lay one morning in great wet brilliant drifts, crusting the Doric façade if the school, hanging in gobbets from bushes and the eaves of houses, turning roads to a churned morass of slush. I had taken up the option on the TR2 once more, had arranged to be picked up from school for a lunch-time drive. My escort duly arrived, hood down, red-faced and cheerful; I ran out grabbing for gloves and duffel and pom-pommed hat, climbed aboard as he revved impatiently in the car park. We skated down the drive beside the school, moving far too fast; and twenty yards from the road gates was Griff, standing alone. My boy friend sounded an imperious blast; and he turned, grinning with a new and dread familiarity. In his hands was a well-packed ball of snow; I would undoubtedly receive an earful as we thundered by, last blow to my already fractured dignity.

I had no intention, as my driver accelerated, of gripping the wheel-rim, yanking it savagely across; it seemed my body acted independent of my brain. The car slewed, throwing up a plume of whiteness while the boy beside me fought panic-stricken, yelling at me for a crazy bloody bitch. There were railings beside the drive, topping a low wall; Griff sprang convulsively, grasping one-handed, drawing up his feet as the bonnet lashed beneath his heels. Then we were past, surging into the road; and a cluster of students, who had so very nearly seen murder done, stood blank-faced and watched us go.

I heard later they took Griff and poured a stiff brandy into him; he was grey-faced with shock, all he could do was hold the glass and shake his head and mumble, 'Why, why ...' I was late back to school; when I finally slunk in, classes were under way and a brooding silence hung over the place. I was afraid to join my group; I sat in the women's cloakroom and hugged my knees and shivered. In time a girl came, and took me to my bus and saw me home. She spoke to me, asked what had happened between us, what I wanted done, but I was too bemused to answer. Now it seemed images of Griff crowded back to me; I heard his voice, the lewd, uproarious jokes he made, the silly, vivid things he had said and done. I asked myself, as he had asked, why; how what we had owned could have turned to such poisoned hate. There was no answer; save the will of that God who had broken at least my life in jest. I lay in my bed and wept into the night, secret and silent; because for a second time I had looked on death. The death of emotion, as real, as poignant as that other ending I had seen. We had cured ourselves of each other, finally; I knew already, as only I could know.

'Silly Libby Maynard, silly Libby Maynard ...'

The voice was a whisper, nearly too faint to be heard.

Just a year and a half after that nearly fatal episode, and twelve months after quitting Northerton, I drove through golden autumn woods into the sprawling market town of Allingbury. Sprawling because London's bursting population had already spilled out to drown the place in a sea of Developments, of factory and trading estates and mile on mile of snotty rowfoot terraces. What was left of the original town seemed in any case somewhat less than prepossessing, a shoddy and ponderous monument to Victorian materialism. The tower of a pretty Restoration church thrust up forlornly from the jumbled mass of building, there was an oasis of trees, beyond them some fine old shops; but then the road was crossed thunderously by a railway bridge of latticed iron, and the drab mechanical jungle began again. I stopped once to ask a direction, arrived eventually at a tall old mansion set back some thirty or forty yards from the London Road. The home of Hill Studios, a small but thriving film unit presided over by one Jack Franklin, I later came to know it sardonically as The House That Jack Built. It contained maybe little grain; but there were within it cats and rats enough.

I pulled the car in beside the front door, parking next to a somewhat battered Sprite. Beyond were a Ruby, ancient but trim, a Mark Two Jag, a brace of small Fords. I climbed out brushing my skirt, lifted handbag and folder from the rear seat and looked round. The appearance of the place was a little better than I had expected. The road was screened by a row of massive pollarded limes; the garden, mostly under grass, was leaf-strewn but otherwise tidy while the house was freshly painted in white and a not-unattractive ochre green. Curtains partly obscured the windows of the nearest bay; craning, I saw the corner of a drawing-board, the head of an Anglepoise lamp. Beside the door the lowest of three tarnished plates carried the style of the company; beneath it, strapped to the brickwork, an ungainly wooden box bore the legend LABS in white stencilled lettering.

There was an ancient bellpull; I tugged at it, producing no result. Traffic grumbled on the London Road; from a daylight basement a few yards away came the sporadic light clatter of some machine. I tried the bell again a couple of times before tiring of the sport. I eased the front door open and peered inside. I saw a staircase flanking a long hall, white-painted and floored with stout brown linoleum. Against one wall were ranged three uncomfortable-looking straightbacked chairs; two were occupied, one by a heap of hastily torn open envelopes and packages, the other by a stack of five hundred foot film cans. Above them on the wall was a fine stag's head. It looked a little strange; peering, I saw that somebody had skilfully sabotaged it, turning its lustrous glass eyes inwards till they had assumed an absurd and violent squint.

While I was considering this phenomenon there proceeded from the landing above a species of agonized yell. It was followed closely by an avalanche of tin cans of all sizes and shapes; they bounded past me, striking the front door with a desultory clatter, rolling about across the linoleum and beneath the chairs. I waited, patiently enough, for enlightenment. It was not long in coming; a bearded, stout and dishevelled personage descended the stairs in their wake, kicking irritably at the mess with sandalled feet. I had it seemed 'spoiled his take', in some way that was never fully made clear. I saw now the heavy mike suspended by a short length of flex above the stairs; I projected my most pretty confusion. I had already identified the disappointed technician by the fruity north country timbre of his voice; this was Jack Franklin himself, I'd phoned him from Northerton the day before to arrange an interview. The great man was suitably mollified; I was conducted to his office, through an aggressively contemporary ante-room presided over by a bad-tempered young woman in sweater and off-the-peg tweed skirt. I was left to myself while Jack slopped off bellowing for tea. I lit a cigarette, look ing round me thoughtfully at the display cases of ancilliary products, toys and books, the big frames of mounted stills and specimen cells. Behind the desk a smaller case showed half a dozen plaques and trophies; my prospective employer was apparently a man who preferred to surround himself with the tangible evidence of genius.

The tea duly arrived, followed a short time later by Mr. Franklin, re-equipped now with collar and tie and with his dark blond hair more or less brushed. I sat and listened to his schemes for, among other things, the reformation of the British film industry before he finally turned to my specimens of work. He flipped through them, making the odd appropriate noise, but his interest was desultory to say the least; he was concerned almost completely with me. For my part I had already decided Hill Studios would serve my immediate purposes admirably. Small enough to control with ease, it was still well enough known to serve as a useful springboard in a year or eighteen months' time; it would take me that long to assimilate all I could usefully learn and gain a practical background in the industry I had decided suited my curious talents best. I would move on then either to some fairly high-powered executive position or what was already more to my fancy, an establishment of my own.

I had determined soon after quitting Northerton that I would make some branch of the film business my next objective. I would be working in an atmosphere more or less highly charged with emotion, a factor I deemed imperative. I filled in for a time at a variety of jobs, anything from barmaid to children's nanny; that and a few commissions for paintings, wheedled for the most part from my extensive social contacts, enabled me to possess myself of an elderly but tolerably reliable Morris Minor.

Thus armed I trundled south, leaving behind me all but a few essentials. I told my mother to expect me in a few days; in fact I had no intention of returning, and as things turned out I never saw her again.

Some question from Jack recalled me to the present. We had reached the stage of haggling over salary; his wife and co-director was in London for the day but he felt sure we could reach an agreement. I too had little doubt. I had been examining his shrewd but curiously immature brain in some detail; an accomplished seducer of the very young, he had already begun his first ploy, projecting the image of a benign father-figure. The process was nearly automatic in him; later would come the phase of confidences, of confessing to his prospective victim how beneath his bluff exterior he truly needed her. Usually success came at this stage but there were other gambits in reserve, notably an absurd but ingenious spiel about running away to sea. Starting Again in some foreign clime. I saw that he justified his philanderings to himself as the natural disappointment of twelve years of childless marriage; had he had son or daughter on whom to focus ambition and hope, how different his life might have been! While there was some validity in this, it was as annoying as all such half-truths tend to be. I nodded sympathetically, hearing the outward words while I systematically explored and catalogued his brain. His was to my mind a sly and more than usually despicable mentality; shifting, untrustworthy, hypocritical even to itself. I stepped delicately into the web he spun so glibly, trying to restrain my amusement; he would find, before I was through with him, that in this instance the spider was less poisonous than the fly.

The discussion concluded satisfactorily for me at least, on a figure just under double what he had initially had in mind. I left him more than a little baffled, already concocting excuses that he hoped might justify his extravagance to his wife. The arch conman had in his turn been conned; I had pushed him hard, latching on to his brain, watching it flare and hope as I backed my arguments with those hundred and one little promises of eye and body and lip that I had always withheld from Griff. I was well pleased; my first encounter with the film world had turned out better than even I had expected. Soon, now, I would whistle the moon down from the sky.

I had no intention of engaging in a dreary round of flat-hunting; I made a couple of telephone calls to friends of friends, and as a result spent a pleasant week at a farmhouse ten or twelve miles outside Allingbury. By the end of that time my new acquaintances had managed, through the offices of an estate agent friend, to install me in a small but quite pleasant apartment not much more than half a mile from Hill House. I moved in, and settled down to work. Marjorie Franklin, a tired, mousy, chain-smoking creature, detested me of course from our first encounter, as did Jack's current mistress, a wild and hirsute village wench at present tenuously employed by Hill. Both, I decided, would have to go, the wench at least permanently. A word in the right quarter would rapidly settle that; for it was a curious aspect of Jack's nature that, profligate though he himself might be, he expected considerable fidelity from his tarts. In time I would arrange the matter; for the present I let the girl be, contenting myself with subtle gibes against which she was powerless and that roused her to flaming heights of rage.

The staff of Hill were mostly young, a fact that Jack explained ensured continued enthusiasm and freshness of approach; it also of course enabled him to pay minimal salaries and to remain undisputed king of his tiny domain, though these were aspects he was perennially less ready to admit. The one exception to his rule was Tom Thomas, his studio manager, a dapper little man whose knowledge of the film racket was apparently inexhaustible. Thomas had seen service with the RAF in the last war, in memory of which more spacious time he still sported a large and to my eye somewhat insanitary moustache; he was a sad creature, a lonely bachelor living on the ghosts of glories past as he bounced jauntily into middle age. His was the red Sprite I had seen at the door the day of my arrival; he was frequently to be seen bumbling round Allingbury and the surrounding district, hood down and scarf flying, symbol of a youth he no longer owned. The exhibition made me feel depressed and a little sick; I would have ignored him completely but for one curious fact. I couldn't read his brain; over his thoughts played a continuous bright pattern of interference, a shifting, altering rhythm I could neither understand nor penetrate. I had seen its like before at odd times, but never so clearly or persistently. I studied him, striving to pierce this unconscious guard; he reacted warmly, misconstruing my interest as affection. In truth he seemed to stand in need of friendship; for Jack habitually treated him like dirt. I put myself a good deal into his company; I had determined to learn the whole process of film making, from costing onwards, and of all those at Hill, Tom was best qualified to teach it to me.

I had as I said given myself a maximum of eighteen months at Allingbury; I rapidly realized I would milk the place dry long before that, in spite of the complexity of its operations. Franklin had sprung into prominence, like many others of his type, with the expansion of British commercial television; much of his work was still concerned with advertising, but unlike the majority of his contemporaries he had had the wit or good luck to diversify. He now produced in addition educational and entertainment material in an impressive variety of techniques, cartoon, stop-frame and the like. Altogether the place was as good a training ground as I could wish for; and my appointment as assistant art director (assistant to whom I never discovered, as there was no art man at Hill) allowed me ample freedom of action. I took full advantage of it, moving from department to department under Tom's guidance, committing to memory such techniques as I felt might be of future usefulness. In this way I learned the rudiments of animation and layout work, rostrum camera operation, cutting, dubbing and the host of other skills that make up that most technical of all art forms, the art of the moving picture.

Meanwhile I had of course become Jack's mistress. Ours was no clandestine, hole-and-corner affair, I saw to that from the first; I flaunted the relationship, making it clear to my workmates that in me they had acquired a new taskmaster. Marjorie, after a brief and vicious battle, retired to an Olympian height of contempt from which to watch this latest and wildest of her husband's passions progress to its inevitable end. In that she made a serious mistake, totally misunderstanding the nature of my hold over Jack Franklin. Within weeks of joining Hill I had subjugated him completely; after six months he would, had I desired it, have eaten from my hand.

My technique was simplicity itself. Buried deep in his brain I had discovered a schoolboy's dream, an image of the perfect girl; she had haunted him more years than he cared to remember, teasing and mocking, flirting her pretty tail just out of reach. She would, I decided, be an interesting part to play; I studied her carefully, adjusting my manner and appearance, delighting Jack till his baffled mind could think of nothing else but me, his long-sought vision moving and speaking. I was, I learned, a creature made all of opposites; intelligent but not self-willed, practical and mystical, level-headed, gentle, deliciously passionate. Feminine to a degree but nonetheless a lover of masculine things, food and wine, good books, boats, cars; I could cook a dinner, mix a cocktail, change a sparkplug, sail a dinghy, corner an Elan. Some of these skills I owned, others I set myself conscientiously to acquire; I stepped down from ten thousand advertising hoardings, sparkling and glinting, into Jack's arms. I added to my wardrobe, bought slickly tailored suits, soberly fashionable dresses, denim slacks and striped sailor sweaters, swimsuits of primeval scantiness, senseless pretty shoes. No detail was too small; I cut my hair, taking great pains to ensure an exactly proper curl beside each ear; I changed my way of walking, eating, talking, assessing carefully the effect of each modification. My price was an office of my own, a hitherto unheard-of expense account. I set about a complete reorganization of the firm, disposing of those of the staff of whom I disapproved or who had been most vocal in their opposition to me, bringing in fresh people as our plans and commitments expanded. Nowhere but in the film business could I have run such a hectic course. Our overdraft reached classic proportions; Tom Thomas protested, long and vigorously, but was howled down. I considered the advisability of removing him too from the scene of his labours, decided finally against it. The operation would be fraught with difficulty; he had been with Jack for many years, long enough for a strong and to me incomprehensible relationship to have developed between them. In any case he could do me no harm; I ignored him, turning my attention to more pressing matters. I had put aside enough for the deposit on a better car: I bought myself an eighteen-month old Alpine, a stylish scarlet beast of which I was inordinately proud. It was the first good thing my gift had brought me, a reward for years of pain.

Most weekends I spent now with Jack, either quietly at the flat or in drives down to the coast; I worked on him viciously and persistently, determined finally to break him. Inwardly I raged, feeling for the first time a wide and swelling sympathy for my sex. Were we, I asked myself, nothing but properties, pegs for weak men to hang their silly dreams? I had gone to Hill to learn; before I left I would teach a lesson Jack Franklin at least would never forget. Already he had begged me, this time in earnest, to leave with him, start a new life; he was in fact hoisted, neatly and ironically, by his own petard. His world had centred on me; I rehearsed the clipped, brutal phrases that would tear it apart. The decision involved no emotion; I played, conscientiously, the part it seemed had been created for me at my birth.

A year after joining Hill I learned, through the impersonal offices of the police, of the sudden death of my mother. The news reached me one Sunday evening, brought by an embarrassed and awkward probationer constable. Jack had spent the day with me, talking and drinking and making love; I was still half naked, lying luxuriously before the fire. I struggled into a skirt, swearing at the persistent ringing of the bell, padded barefoot down to the door. I stood dumbfounded while the boy jerked out his stilted message. Mrs. Maynard had been admitted to hospital, had passed away, as he put it, the previous afternoon. He knew no details.

My first feeling was of little more than aggravation; my schemes would be interrupted now by a dreary round of form-filling, of interviews with solicitors, undertakers, clergymen. I disposed of Jack, summarily; when he had gone I ran a bath, sat and smoked cigarettes and soaked while I decided what to do. The house and all its effects must be sold, that much was certain; I wanted nothing more to do with my home town, then or ever. I wondered, callously, just what the estate would be worth; the money at least I could put to good use. I dried myself and retired to bed, lay until the small hours planning details. my charcoal grey would serve for the funeral but I must buy black shoes; first stops must be police station, hospital . . . By the time I slept I had my operations planned in detail; I rose early, packed what I would need and scorched north, determined to dispose of the matter with all possible speed.

It was dusk before I parked the bright car outside what had been my home. I sat for some minutes before I could bring myself to open the door. The day had been hectic, too hectic for thought; now there grew on me, projected it seemed from the empty house, a fearsome desolation. I remembered the folk I had spoken to; the stolid police sergeant, the blandly indifferent coroner's clerk, the houseman at the hospital. I remembered his words, white and aseptic. Extensive haemorrhage, cerebral origin ... For all his talk, he could not keep me from horror. In that airy, pretty place, they had danced the Masque of the Red Death.

The neighbours had been watching for me; before I reached my door I was intercepted by a worried, fussy little woman who insisted on giving me tea. I sat in the living room of her featureless house, sipping and smoking, sensing her unease at this remote, brilliant-eyed stranger, sensing too an unvoiced condemnation that drove into me like a knife. I managed finally to escape, refusing an offer of accommodation for the night; it was of paramount importance that I be alone. I clipped a parking light to the window of the Alpine, carried my grip up the diminutive drive to the house. The privet bushes beside the porch needed cutting; I noted the fact mechanically as I unlocked the front door. In the hall I was greeted by a faint, cold smell of new paint. My feet scuffed newspapers and a letter; I picked the papers up, carried them to the sitting room and turned on the light. The place looked nearly alien; fresh paper on the walls, fresh cushion covers and drapes, a new runner on the tabletop. the television still stood on its corner table, beneath it an old chocolate box that I knew contained sewing silks and cottons. A fire was laid in the grate; beside the big easy chair a tidy held newspapers, and a wad of knitting. There was fruit on the table; one apple was spotted, I took it through to the kitchen meaning to dispose of it. The kitchen too was freshly decorated; it seemed in her efforts to keep hands and brain occupied my mother had worked through the entire house. I walked up to my bedroom knowing what I would find; new paper and curtains, fresh paint, new coverlet on the bed. The paper wasn't bad, a Regency stripe in palest tangerine.

A radiator was plugged in to the wallpoint; I switched it on, sat on the neatly-made bed and lit a cigarette. Rubbed my eyes, wearily unbuttoned the top of my dress. I sat an hour, smoking and brooding, trying to remember where to start and what I had to do. Finally I turned to my wardrobe. I emptied it, laying each article carefully on the bed. There were old dresses, far too small for me now; pleated grey school skirts, a blazer I had worn at Compton Deverell. On the top shelf I found a boat, a tennis racquet, a forgotten and dusty tie. The heap grew; I worked faster, digging through memories like an archaeologist through the stacked layers of Troy. I unearthed my gym kit, an ancient doll, stacks of exercise books, boxes of trinkets. There were oddments of silver, earrings and a necklace; a cairngorm brooch set round with cloudy amethysts, gift of a half-forgotten relative; black choker ribbons, relics of an art school craze. There were letters and papers, school reports, correspondence from college; a fragrant note from Moira, Griff's awful Christmas card, an old and still-mysterious Valentine. Things barely remembered, cross-sections of the seemingly endless years. I lost the sense of time; it was early morning again before I washed and undressed, lay between the faintly sour-smelling sheets. I left the fire burning, a spark of comfort in the night; as my eyes became accustomed to the dark it lit the room again with a steady orange glow, details standing forward distinct and clear. Save for the faint singing of the element, the house was totally quiet; I closed my eyes, and once more the ghosts began to parade. It seemed there broke in on me a dead susurration, world-wail of the life of pain; it was as if the fabric of time itself wore thin, bringing old events and older folk within the compass of my arms. Towards dawn I slept, to be plagued by one persistent spectre. I woke sweating. No well-shod young buck it was that had haunted me, splashing his blood and clanking his chains; but a grey thing, complaining and lost, mooning through its ghostly supermarkets, buying its ghostly jam.

A fortnight passed before I turned south again. What had at one time seemed an impossible task was completed; I left the house brooding and empty, stripped of furniture, carpets and drapes. I had intended to bring nothing away; instead the car was crowded nearly to the roof. With useless things for the most part, mementoes of college and school and childhood, clothes and books, old games and toys. I drove fast, impelled by thought streams it seemed I could no longer fully block; they had woken me night after night, beating and thundering like an endless dull-grey sea. I bypassed the town centre of Northerton, chafing at the slow crawl of the traffic; once clear of the place I built up speed again, heading for Allingbury and the south. The cryings moved with me, half-heard through all my senses, darkening the sun.

After the inquest and funeral I had driven away the jackdaw-pecking neighbours and relatives, shut myself in my mother's house for days. As I searched shelf after shelf, cupboard after cupboard, the strange mood into which I had fallen was intensified. I spent an entire day reading old letters. It seemed other Libbys spoke to me from the scrawled lines; there were other suns, bright childhood meadows, other hopes. I wept finally, praying to the God I had once despised, longing, not for the first time, for Faith, the blind power of a mighty church, the benison of confession.

Into the cold, clock-ticking silence a single idea seemed to steal. In my foolishness it seemed God had indeed answered me. I knew that once more and finally the circumstances of my existence must be changed. I must leave Allingbury and my little conquests, the whole tipped-up, cocked-up, aniline-tinted mess I had thought was life. Perhaps I would teach; I felt a sudden longing for the clear bright water of children's thoughts, an urge to recapture an innocence that had I been less exalted I might have realized I had never owned. I saw myself now lower and more shallow than the folk I had despised, my grand designs reduced at last to piddling *bourgeois* dreams. It was as if a weight was lifted from me; thought where I would go, how I would finally come to terms with a hostile world, I had no idea. Increasingly it seemed every hour was precious; I worked far into the nights, burning what I could neither sell nor carry away. When I had finished I was filthy and aching and had lost pounds, but at last I could leave. I turned off water, gas and electricity – it was like stopping the heart of the place – lodged the key with the estate agent handling the property and drove away, not even waiting to change from my grubby shirt and jeans.

I reached Allingbury at midday, ate a hurried cafeteria meal and drove to my flat to pack. On the way I stopped off at my bank. I had already advised them I intended to close my account. I let myself into my room. The phone was ringing; I answered it, with a stab of apprehension. It was Jack. I had left him no forwarding address, he must have been hopelessly calling me for days. Marjorie had finally left him; I would undoubtedly be named in an action for divorce.

He was not at the studio; work there was at a standstill, he hadn't been near the place for a week. He insisted on seeing me at once; I agreed mechanically, drove the couple of miles out to his home. He met me at the door, was instantly shocked by my appearance. I was I know white-faced and feverish-eyed. I fended him off when he tried to take me in his arms. What I needed was a drink; he fixed it for me, brain whirling. Two Scotches steadied me enough to talk; I lit a cigarette, wanting nothing but to get away.

I had intended to confess to him, as I had confessed once before, reveal the bizarre fraud I had practised. Now I knew I couldn't do it, I lacked the courage. I hedged desperately, agreeing to that and this; I promised to live with him, marry him, leave the country with him, anything to keep him from knowing the truth. Night fell as we talked. With the dark a sullen rain began, lashing at the window. I escaped finally, pleading I had to clean up and change, that I had to be alone to think, promising to telephone him first thing in the morning. He planned to raise money on the camera lenses, risk everything in a crazy dash abroad; my head was spinning, it seemed meshes were closing round me, I couldn't think straight any more. Whatever happened, one dismal fact stood clear. For a decade, he had been the driving force behind Hill; now he was close to breaking point. The studio was through.

I drove back to my flat. I rented a garage at the rear of the place: I left the car on the hard standing in front of the door, scuttled back upstairs. One suitcase was all I could take; I packed it hastily, flinging clothes about in confusion. Most of the stuff I would have to leave behind. I turned the lights off, locked the door. I could mail the key back later. Halfway to the Alpine, lugging the heavy case, I stopped. I saw quite plainly the bright, thudding thing ahead of me, like a beacon in the night. Once, many years before, I had run from such a trap. I knew now I couldn't run again. With the knowledge came a weariness that deadened feeling like an anaesthetic. I walked forward again to where Tom Thomas was waiting.

He had the MG slewed across the tail of the Alpine, blocking the way. He stood beside it, shoulders hunched, a darker shadow in the night. Behind him, high on the wall, a solitary lamp burned in its wellglass, throwing a streaky fan of light across the damp-stained brick; the rain still soared sullenly, the spots banging at my shoulders, dimpling the puddles on the asphalt. There was no other sound.

He seemed embarrassed by his mission, hanging his head as he talked, refusing to meet my eyes. He spoke of the studio, and Jack, and what he had watched me do; he talked of a love I had never been able to see, the strange love of man for man that passes all understanding. I saw at last the monstrous joke that had been played on me; I put my head back, feeling the rain on my face, and began to laugh.

I surfaced slowly from the black depths of a sea. Above me, very far away, was a blaring of noise and light; I floated towards it, trying unavailingly to check the upward movement, sink back to the deep silt bed of unconsciousness. For a time it seemed I might be successful; but the harshness and shrieking, the flarings that were neither light nor sound, were too insistent. I opened my eyes, and instantly it seemed the uproar was redoubled. It was as if a dozen motor horns had jammed, shrieking into my ear. The sound pulsed and throbbed, developing new and hellish dissonances; as my head cleared fractionally it became the noise of voices. The voices, it seemed, of all the people in the world.

I was instantly sick. The spasms started bursts and flashes of pain. I hugged myself, panting and uncomprehending, trying to force my brain to work. I saw I was lying on wet asphalt, which seemed an unconstructive thing to do; my clothes were soaked, my face pushed close to the gritty tyre of a car.

In time the pain eased a little. I reached above me carefully, fingers slipping on wet steel, touched the shank of a wing mirror. I edged myself up, still with that deadly uproar ringing in my ears. At all costs I must get away, find a place to be alone and quiet. I levered with my knee, and pulled. Somebody drew a tooth without anaesthetic; the shock sent me sprawling across the bonnet of the Alpine. I clung to it face down, feeling now with a phantom dullness the beating of the rain on my shoulders and back. Round me the noise surged again, rose to fresh bright peaks that dug like lancets at my brain.

This, I told myself absurdly, would not do. I was embarrassed by my predicament and obsessed, I suppose like any injured animal, with the notion of shelter. I knuckled my face feeling a soapy smoothness. I seemed to be covered with mud. Some of it had got into my mouth; it had an odd taste, metallic and hard. I spat, and tried to be sick again. The retching was brilliantly painful.

It was obviously important to get upright. I pushed with my hands, giddy again and panting. I made it, stood swaying. I thought that was very good.

The mess on my face was actually blood. It was stupid of me not to have understood this before. I pulled myself along the car till I could reach the driving door. There was a box of tissues; I wriggled a handful free, splashed them in a puddle and wiped. They were not much use. There was a headscarf in the cubby. That was better. It didn't come in pieces when it got wet.

My case still lay where I had dropped it. I couldn't lift it; I pushed it with my foot, against the Alpine's wheel. The scarf was wet and sopping; I held it across my nose and tried to think. I must reach my flat; once there I could shut the noise away, lock and bolt the doors, huddle in bed where I couldn't hear the shouting. It was absurd for there to be so much noise; the whole town seemed to have gone wild. The voices that screamed at me seemed to pull me a hundred ways at once, standing against them was like leaning into a gale. I counted my footsteps; anything to take my mind from that awful din. The key seemed wrong for the lock; I panicked, huddled whimpering before forcing myself to be calm. Each step of the stairs started bright, forked pains. I reached the upper door at last, slammed it with shuddering satisfaction, stood leaning on it gulping huge breaths. Listening to the roar that seemed now to split the darkness of the room.

I think for pure terror that final moment of understanding will never be equalled. The realization that the beating had broken more than lips and teeth, that it had snapped some deep thing in my brain, seemed to burst on me; I was wide open, jammed open, encompassed by the thought-din of the whole colossal world. I screamed, though whether with throat or mind I cannot say; some great noise certainly, a wail of ultimate fear and pain. Instantly it seemed the voices answered, the jabbering and howling, crying, lusting, screaming, redoubled themselves. Flooding in on me as a focus, flooding from farthest horizons, from the sunlit edges of the world; voices of children and women and animals and men, voices of the hopeless and unwanted, the lost, the desolate, the mad; voices of the unborn and the frightened, fading dead.

If I fainted, as seems possible, unconsciousness brought no relief. The din raged in my brain, waking me within seconds. I staggered to the lightswitch, clicked it on, glared round at unreal things; at walls and floors that doubled, shimmered, quadrupled, flowed apart to run together again in a mad confusion of impressions. Already it seemed I knew what I had to do; I was amazed that I had not understood the problem and its answer before. I fumbled my way to the bathroom, pulled at my clothes with a sort of clumsy urgency till I was naked. There was a long mirror; I saw the bruises on me, my muzzle still bright-striped. To this I had come, to grovelling and fighting, crawling in puddles and dirt. I clawed at the bathtaps, dunking my head, not waiting for the thing to fill. The sea in my brain still thundered and roared. I must have quiet, at any price; but the body I had been so proud of, and that had served me so well, could not be left scruffy with dirt and mud. I dried myself, brushed and worried at my hair, washed my face again. My nose finally stopped bleeding; I scrambled into clean clothes, fresh pants and bra, a newly-pressed skirt and blouse. I tried, hopelessly, to repair the damage of the night with lipstick and powder. Then I could delay no more; every second added to my nonsensical pain. I left the flat in disorder, half the lights burning. The bath had been nearly boiling, the heat had drawn some of the pain from my limbs. I walked carefully back down to the garage, started the Alpine and drove it in.

The carport was awkward to close from the inside. I swung it down finally as far as it would go, switched on the car's headlights so I could see to work. At the far end of the place was a heap of junk, left by some former occupier; I had never bothered to clear it away. Among it I remembered seeing some lengths of that flexible piping sometimes used for exhaust systems. I found the longest, bent it into a shape that might just reach the passenger window. It was short by a foot. I sleeved another piece inside it, jammed the end over the tailpipe. The joints would leak of course, but the thing would answer my purpose. I wound up the Alpine's window, trapping the end of the tubing beneath the hood. The noise in my brain seemed duller; I realized with faint surprise that I was drowsy already. I climbed into the car, lay back listening to the thudding of the exhaust. In the confined space the beating was disturbingly loud. I tried to breathe more deeply, was alarmed by a sudden pang of sickness. I had no desire, after all I had done, to soil myself with vomit. I forced my eyes open. The lids seemed nearly too heavy to raise. I saw then what I had forgotten, the telltale blaze of headlights from the wall in front of me. I tried to reach out to the dash, found I could not. My hand moved in my lap, fell back; my brain, already stunned, could no longer translate will to action. So this was death; I experienced a sudden sense of sorrow, a pity for my blameless body that would now dry and rot. But the emotion was over in seconds; I fell smoothly into a well of night, and the voices and poundings were still at last.

I woke to that same hellish din. Once more I cannot adequately convey the horror that flooded me at the realization that beyond death and the grave there was indeed another fearsome Life. The panic was succeeded by a futile rage at that God who could so condemn His creature for the faculties He Himself had given her. Tears squeezed from me; I tried to scream, struck out with my fists. My arms were instantly gripped. I opened my eyes, saw above me the pale billowing shapes of His angels. There were bars too, dimly visible to either side; so it seemed I had been imprisoned for my crimes. I arched my body, yelling and laughing. The angels moved round me; I felt a stabbing, a quick shock of pain, slid back swiftly to unconsciousness.

Even there the voices reached me in a mumbling roar. I moved and muttered, whirled through countless vivid dreams. I saw Compton Deverell, stark now in an appalling light; and Moira, Saint Cath's, Dave, the beach, the bright MG. I ran to the car, desperately; but Tom Thomas rose up from it laughing, hands ready to hurt and tear. I turned back, moving with the underwater slowness of nightmare, and the cliff crumbled beneath me, plunging me once more through tunnels of dark and stars. then I was at the Palais, dancing and dancing with Griff in the hot pain of spotlights; round me a vast half-seen company swirled, mumbling and masked and rotting, holding up hands turned to old bleached bone. I screamed to Griff but he was gone already, tumbling into a coloured void while the roof and walls of the place split and cascaded into ruin. Moonlight squirted through them; the moon itself was spinning, throwing off blood and pale smoke. But the moon was a lamp in a ceiling, brilliantly white. The ceiling zoomed down at me; then the sea came again and the crashings, the lightning-shot dark. Sometimes voices from the real world reached me, and hissing fragments of thought. The faces above me receded and advanced in their turn, darker faces of men among the starched ships that were alternately nurses and clouds. As my understanding grew the laughter became unstoppable. That they should have taken me, put me once more in a hospital, a place of pain and shrieking; the joke was worthy of my cosmic trickster. There were wet patches to either side of my head, made by the laughing: I tried to tell the faces I was slipping toward death, that not all their bright machines and medicines and stinging needles could keep me back; but they didn't understand.

There was a void.

In it, voices called. They came it seemed from great distances, night and stars in the timbre of them and empty moonlit roads. There was a chattering, a probing, an excitement. Then quiet again; and one insistent calling, low and clear and sweet as a bell.

Elizabeth . . .

And it seemed I was gently shaken.

I woke abruptly, lay waiting for the voice, the dream, to come again. It didn't. I moved my head restlessly and opened my eyes. For the first time I saw my surroundings clearly. I was lying in a tiny ward equipped with just one other vacant bed. There were tall curtained windows; in the ceiling a single lamp glowed like a distant sun. The bars that had puzzled me were cot sides strapped to my bed. Beyond them I saw a side table, cream-painted; above it on the wall a thermometer in a holder, the panel of a radio relay system. A tall stand carried a bottle of some solution; tubing led from it, taped neatly to my splinted right arm. I frowned, examining each object in turn. Lifted my free hand, flexed it. It looked white and pale, like the hand of a ghost. I tried to raise myself from the pillow. The effort met with no success. I lay still frowning, trying to remember. The little room was hot, heavy with the sickly-sweet smell of anaesthetic. The hospital was very quiet, no echoings of footsteps or voices, no clatterings from kitchen or sluice. I listened carefully, and understanding came with a rush. The din that had plagued me was gone.

But not gone completely. Concentrating, I detected a faint mumbling, far away and harmless as the summer-noises of insects. Or the sound of a sea beyond some great strong wall. Inside the wall I was safe. I tested cautiously, opening my mind, tasting the air. There was nothing. Just the quiet.

The air spoke to me.

I lay rigid, not breathing, unable to believe. But I had to believe, the air did speak, I knew it spoke because I heard it with my inner ear, it said *Get up, Elizabeth . . .*

But it was difficult to think. I wondered if I was finally mad; I tried to ask the air, the Otherness, what are you, what are you, where, where . . . Instantly the chattering was back, and the excitement. *We thought you were dead, we heard you crying then you were quiet, we thought you were dead, get up, Elizabeth . . .*

I shook my head, still dazed, trying voicelessly to talk, tell Them, the Others, the Others like me. About the tube in my arm and the faintness and how I couldn't move. They laughed and shouted, exultant now; and the air became a sword, the bright tip touched my brain. GET UP, ELIZABETH . . .

Quiet again. And the first voice, the gentle voice that had called, soothing and explaining. A gabble then, quick and bright as the chatter of children. There were children, suddenly I knew that.

Where is she?
In a hospital . . .
I can't see, let me see . . .
She's very ill . . .
Is she pretty?
She's very pretty. Hush . . .
Let me see . . .

There was a . . . linking. I heard Others join in, dimly, and others, and still more. There were questions, quick instructions. I saw now how They were holding back the din that had terrified me. I called to Them, told Them be quick, please be quick. They answered; and there was power.

I lived a silver dream. My body moved; They moved it, I could not. It seemed I hung above it again, floating and safe. I saw my fingers flex on the rail of the bed, uncertain at first then more and more sure as They gained control. The left hand closed the taps of the drip, very gently, very careful and slow. the fingers moved down, stripped the dressings from my arm, withdrew the bright needle. A spot of blood followed it; the fingers wiped, and it was gone.

In the air, a hushed tension. A watching, frowning, biting of lips. Somewhere a voice squeaking. *Hurry, please hurry. Before someone comes . . .*

My body moved again, a sleepwalking impossibility. It unlatched the iron grid from the bed. The thing dropped with a muffled clang. Tension again, a waiting; but the corridor outside stayed quiet. There was a cupboard, built into the corner of the room. The wraith-Libby found clothes, dressed herself. Edged to the door, eased it ajar, waited trembling.

The hospital was haunted; there were Other ears listening. Other eyes that watched and stared. Libby slipped through the door, huddled in shadow. There was a pause, a tensing, a moment of strain; and the corridor lights blinked out.

I was back in my body, feeling it pant for breath. The darkness spun; I swayed and stumbled and instantly the power was back, holding my arms and guiding. I was scurried forward, down steps, through an unseen door. They knew the place so well; They had watched and prowled, listening, searching, trying to find me. I knew I could never do what They wanted, walk out of that huge building on my own. I tried to tell Them; there was laughing, and more power. *See,* they said. *You are walking, Elizabeth, you are walking. . .* The Otherness flowed ahead of me, seeing, feeling, tasting. There was no sensation of movement; I was buoyed up, it seemed my feet barely touched the floor. There were other lights burning now, but sparser and dimmer; and people scurrying. Another flight of steps, a long, cool corridor; and I felt the movement of night air on my face. There was a car park, white under a clear high moon. I crossed it, flitting through brightness and shadow. A car was coming for me, I saw it distinctly; long and black and low, snarling at the road, hurrying from the West. *Walk, Elizabeth* They said. *Just a little more. Walk, Elizabeth* ... And I walked. Their power moved my limbs, but it was my strength that raised my head. For I had found my own folk, after a weariness of time. Already I understand that I was a new being; Libby Maynard was dead.

The Everything Man

1

The pub was an old posting inn, high-ceilinged. Ceilings and walls, once white, were stained with the golden-brown glaze of nicotine; the walls, timbered and coarsely pargetted, were enlivened with plaques and ornaments, trays and medallions of brass. Among them were curious rural relics; a set of quoits, chained and chrome-plated, stirrups and harness and crossed hunting crops; heads of foxes and a badger, grinning in dusty agony. Curlicued wall lamps, their shades replete with pebbles of coloured glass, supplied a species of light.

Across the main bar ran a head-high partition, its upper half set with panes of muffled glass. In one of the rooms so formed half a dozen locals muttered round a late spring fire; the other had been taken over by some twenty strangers, girls and young men. They wore jeans and faded shirts, leather jackets and duffle coats, high boots, sombreros. The disposition of the group had secured for them possession of darts board and billiard table. On both, vigorous games were in progress. The landlord, a burly, bulbous-eyed man in shirtsleeves and cravat, watched darkly, occasionally confiding to an unseen in the snug that the influx did not in his opinion represent the best possible class of trade.

At a corner table, immediately beneath the petrified trophies of the chase, sat a slim, bearded man in a light blue anorak. Its hood, slung at a negligent angle across his shoulders, imparted a vaguely monastic air; round his neck, suspended by a variety of crossing straps, hung a flash gun, an Agiflex camera, the leather case of a telephoto lens. His long, corduroy-clad legs were thrust out negligently in front of him; at his elbow was a battered pewter mug, from which he swigged occasionally with a nonchalance that hinted at considerable practice. His hair, dark and slightly waved, clung close to his long skull; his cheeks were marked by deep creases that seemed to pull back the bright red lips in a permanent sardonic half-smile. His eyes, deep-set under heavy brows, were a strikingly clear light blue. He seemed considerably older than his companions; in fact someone, more literary than reverent, had once called Roley Stafford the Horned God of the Campers.

He frowned now slightly, sipping from the tankard again and holding a letter up to the light. The envelope, grubby and dog-eared, bore an overlapping tangle of addresses and directions. "Try 13A, Southampton Buildings, SE8.' 'Not known here, try *Bull and Butcher*, Southwark . . .' The last alteration, in a woman's backward-sloping hand, had rung a faintly miraculous bell. 'Try Camping Site, Oldford St John, Herts.' The thing had arrived that morning, thanks largely to the tenacity of the postal authorities, ending its voyaging at The Travellers' Friend.

Its recipient tried to place the handwriting, gave up with a faint shrug. Could have been any of a dozen people half known and less than half remembered. He slit the flap, drew out two pages of close-set writing. He found the signature, screwed up his eyes and nodded, turned back to the start.

> Roley, you old bastard,
>
> So you sometimes read your mail! I sent a dozen of these things all over Town, glad one finally caught up with you. Where are you hiding out these days? And how are you, you old devil? Still whooping it up, or are you married with a dozen kids and a wife helping you read this, wondering what a funny lot of mates you used to have?

The billiards game finished noisily, the landlord shouting at the players to mind the flaming cues. Roley looked up vaguely, fingers closing reflexively on the pot at his side. A blonde girl in scruffy tight-fitting jeans tried to grab the pages from him. He fended her off absentmindedly, not looking at her. He scanned rapidly, taking in paragraphs of the past.

> I got married, after I lost my father . . . Remember that old pub behind Praed Street, what the hell was it called, the place we used to shift eight pints a night and set the world to rights . . .
>
> We made a deal once there, a long time back. Don't suppose you even remember. First one to get a pub stands the other a month's free booze. Well I got my place of ill repute old son, got it years ago. Now I'm calling your bluff, there's four weeks' supply of cool fresh-from-the-wood West

Country bitter down here pining for your company, all you have to do is collect . . .

Roley frowned slightly, scratching his cheek with a lean forefinger.

All you have to do is travel. But there's something else, and believe me this is for real, there's something damned important I got myself tied up with. Remember those nights in Town when we yapped about making a better world, about letting the artists have a go at it, something crazy like that? Well there's a chance of doing just that and I mean it, we've got a Problem down here with a big red cap P and I can't think of anything I'd sooner have along on it, anybody that'ld be any good at all. It's big enough to take hold of everything you ever knew and turn it inside out and rattle it, and that's no goof. So try and make it will you, if only for old time's sake. And in case you haven't changed –

The reader turned a page.

– In case you haven't changed, I'll dangle a final carrot. There's a job waiting for you that'll earn you more than you'll ever scrape anywhere else in this nasty world; unless you've got better at being civil to your inferiors, which I doubt . . .

Roley grinned, folding the sheet to read the last paragraph.

. . . Don't bother to let us know, just Blow In. And I hope you don't mind me raising delicate subjects but if you happen to need an advance for Christ's sake yell. Money isn't a problem any more, not compared with this.

I'll keep my fingers crossed.

Yours ever,
Jimmy Stringer.

Roley put the letter away carefully. Lit a cigarette, leaned back to blow a smoke-ring at the ceiling. The grin got worse. The blonde girl pushed a Nordic profile at him and crooned. 'It's from his lover to tell him she's run away with a Race Problem . . .'

He slapped her backside softly, still thoughtful, and jetted another halo into the thick air of the bar.

2

The little train moved steadily, clattering in sunlight, winding its way between green hills; the hills of the West Country, gentle with age. Roley lowered the newspaper to his lap, sat brooding, dribbling smoke between half-parted lips. On the front page twenty-line caps shouted war. He folded the thing, tossed it on the seat beside him. Fresh confrontations in Pakistan, Chinese and Russian fighters over Kashmir; and India, that old land of gold, a new and appalling trouble spot. Talk of a peace mission; Mohindru to fly to Moscow, Pekin. Some Boston Terrier of a President in the States, barking warnings; England lining up with America, the whole world taking sides. Escalation was the term they used these days. He shook his head. Years ago he'd marched those fruitless miles along the Great West Road, behind the banners, with the jazzbands and kids and prams and sweating coppers; then it seemed he could grasp, in moments of fury, just what fresh war meant, what they planned to do to this land, to each other. Now there was nothing but weariness. Maybe he was getting old.

Across the compartment from him a pleasant-faced, middle-aged woman knitted steadily, carrier bags beside her on the seat; apart from her the little train seemed empty. He wondered what there would be, here, if it came. A grumbling behind the hills, the rising flare of an earthbound sun? Or nothing, just flash and flame?

'I don't believe there can be another war.'

He had spoken aloud, not really intending to. The woman smiled and nodded, answering pleasantly. He smiled back, rose to push the carriage windows open to the sunlight. Leaned his elbows on the dark wood of the frame, rocking slightly to the movement of the carriage. The ancient 0-4-4 that drew it came momentarily in sight on a bend, chuffing in reverse like a sooty, overlarge kid's toy. The whistle sounded; a plume of whiteness whirled back over the carriage roofs, lost itself in the deep blue of the sky. He indulged a pleasing fantasy; it seemed the rails wound not physically through space, but backward into Time.

The little engine shouted at the hills.

He was close to his destination. He lifted jacket and rucksack from the rack. Beneath the rucksack the pewter mug swung and clanked, attached by a snap fastener of its own. He smiled again at the oldster as he caught her eye. Stubbed his cigarette, sat and watched as the station buildings came into sight. They were stoutly built of creamy-grey stone, overshadowed by massive decorated chimney stacks. Scots pines leaned toward the track; there was a lattice footbridge painted a faded green. Beyond the station the roofs of the village humped and clustered, spotted with a rich orange lichen. He narrowed his eyes. Over the place, looming sudden as a blow, reared the wall of a nearly perfect shell keep; it squatted on its *motte*, watching with windows that were eyes of sky. Beneath it, on the fresh steep green of the slope, he saw goats grazing, jewel-tiny in the still air; then the thing was gone, lost behind a clustering of trees.

The train hissed to a halt. He climbed down, feeling the sunlight on shoulders and neck. He handed his ticket to a faintly inquisitive porter, carried his kit through the barrier. Beyond was a little forecourt, cobbles shrouded with macadam. A rusty siding branched into it; on it stood a line of antique coaches, wooden-built, their wheels trapped by balks of timber bolted to the tracks. They fitted their surroundings with a kind of ponderous grace; beside them a noticeboard proclaimed the delights and economy of Camping Holidays with British Railways. Beyond, cars were parked; an Austin, a rusty Packard, a dashing XKE. There were cottages, creeper-covered, little gardens exploding with colour that burst between fence rails and posts to sprawl across the path.

He walked forward, still conscious of the warmth on his back. He took a pair of sunglasses from his pocket, propped them on his nose. Ran his fingers through his back hair. He'd been meaning to get a trim before leaving Town. Forgotten. Behind him the engine hooted briefly, began to move away. A white car growled past into the forecourt, swung in a half circle and stopped. Spitfire Three, drophead, driven by a girl. He half turned toward it, meaning to ask a direction. But the pub couldn't be far.

She called him, leaning across the cockpit.

'Mr. Stafford?'

He stopped, easing the strap of the rucksack.

'The same.'

His voice was quiet, with a hint of sibilance.

She opened the door, swung her feet to the ground. 'Jimmy asked me to meet you,' she said. 'Sorry I was late. We aren't used to Fred being on time.'

He walked toward her, carrying the pack by the strap. 'That's all right,' he said. 'I only just got in.'

She opened the boot of the car. 'I think that'd better go in there . . .' She held out her hand. 'Pleased to meet you.'

He believed in first impressions. He absorbed this one, carefully. Short intensely black hair; little straight nose; eyes of an odd deep colour that just failed to be blue. White shirt, crisply laundered, skirt neat and brief. Slim arms and hands, sunbrowned. Jimmy had done well for himself.

She shook her head, grinning. 'I'm not his wife,' she said. 'But she's pretty too.'

He lowered the rucksack gently, as if its contents consisted entirely of eggs. The bootlid creaked a little as she closed it.

He stood back to look at the car. 'Nice motor,' he said. 'Very pretty.'

She said, 'We like it.'

He opened the driving door for her, waited as she smoothed the skirt under her thighs. He walked to the passenger door, slid in beside her. Flipped the top of a twenty of Embassy. She shook her head. She'd put on sunglasses; all she was showing was short nose and smile.

'Good trip from Town?'

'Not bad,' he said. He leaned back, lighting up, still studying.

'Jimmy's away on business,' she said. 'He'll be back this evening. He said to say he was sorry. Do you think you'll like it here?'

'Can't tell,' he said instantly. 'If you ran me round a bit I might find out.' He glanced back at the boot, where resided his rucksack and a faint, nagging mystery.

She laughed, twisting the ignition key. The engine barked sharply. She swung the car in reverse, gunned it across the square. The exhaust note splashed back from close stone walls as she turned into the village street. 'This is High Street,' she said. 'Also the only street. Practically.' Acceleration squeezed at him as she prodded the throttle.

'I saw the castle,' he said. 'From the train.'

'Do you believe in castles?'

'Yes,' he said. 'I'm very romantic at heart.'

She grinned again, teeth white against her skin.

The pub stood halfway along the street. She pointed it out to him as they passed. It was old and heavy-timbered, erratic-fronted. There were low windows; boxes of flowers beneath them, bright against the white walls. She waved briefly to some-one, accelerated again. The derestriction signs surged past; she flicked the car to sixty with a faint burr from the catseye studs as she chose her line into the first bend.

The second bend she took stone blind, wheels clipping the offside verge. And the third. The speedo needle played with eighty. He watched her carefully, brushing at the hair that blew across his forehead. She flung a question at him.

'Worried?'

'No,' he said. 'Should I be?'

'I'm glad,' she said.'I hate nervous passengers.'

Another bend, embellished with double centreline. She lay well over to the right, tapped her brakes, swung back to her own side. A Mark Ten passed instantly, travelling well. She took the full road again. 'We're lucky today,' she said. 'Not much traf-fic.'

The castle shell loomed ahead. She circled it, turning from the road on to a rutted earth track. Stone frowned down, close and huge; the thing was a monumental Presence in the after-noon. One of the goats raised its head, staring with its yellow-guinea eyes. 'I'll drive you back tomorrow,' she said. 'You'll have more time to look round.'

She turned back the way she had come. A mile on she swung left into a narrow lane. The road dipped instantly, dropped into a steep and unsuspected coombe. Became a paved track, grass sprouting along its centre. She held her speed; the little car lurched and bucked, racing between dank walls of stone. There were tree roots, gnarled and twisting, thick banks of moss. Branches interlaced forty feet above, cutting back the light of the sun. She snicked into second, through a hairpin little wider than the Spitfire. He called across to her.

'Is this one-way?'

She shook her head. She seemed to be enjoying herself.

He lowered his eyes from the vertical rushing of the banks, to the hem of her skirt. 'I'm a little nervous now,' he said. 'Can we slow down?'

A bursting of sunlight. The car climbed from the green gloom, abruptly. Fifty yards in front a heavy tractor, approaching with flatbed in tow, lurched on to the verge to let the Spitfire pass. The girl laughed delightedly. 'Beat him,' she said. Then with a quick sideways flick of the head, 'You're a liar.'

He sat back, imagining the nose of the Fordson looming round the hairpin. He didn't speak again as she drove through the village. She cruised sedately, swung in beside the pub. There was an arched gateway; she eased the car through, coasted to a stop by the far wall. He climbed out, looking round. There were fresh-painted white walls, dark blue woodwork. Above a tumble of roofs, orange and pink and green. A blue Victor estate car drawn up beside a stack of crates. Two upended barrels, marked as ullage. Round their rims, neatly chalked, STRINGER. LANGDON ARMS. Across the yard the sunlight lay in broad stripes and lozenges. It was very quiet; just tourist voices from the street, a child calling. In the distance, the bumble of traffic. The modern midsummer hum.

She was waiting for him, smiling. 'Nice ride,' he said. 'Thank you, Not-Jimmy's-Wife.'

She looked upset. 'God,' she said, 'I'm sorry. It's difficult sometimes, you forget . . .' She held out her hand again, formally. 'Maynard,' she said. Then, twinkling, 'My friends call me Elizabeth.'

He chalked up another mental query.

He took his gear from the car, thinking about the Mark Ten. She'd been showing him something. Not that she wanted to die. He shut the incident from his mind. In due course, he would find out.

The pub was as neat inside as out. Smelling of flowers and brass and wood. Elizabeth led him through an outhouse, floored with red brick. More crates stood by the wall. 'The cellar's through there,' she said. 'It's too small. We can't rack as much as we'd like.' She ducked under a door lintel. She was tall; five-nine he decided, maybe a little more. 'This is Anne,' she said. 'Anne, Roley Stafford.'

She was shorter than Elizabeth, fractionally. With a pretty, young-old face. Little deep-etched creases at the corners of her mouth. She was wearing an apron and old, scruffy shoes; one strand of sandy-grey hair had fallen across her forehead. 'Sorry things are a bit hectic,' she said. 'It's delivery day, we always get behind.' She took his hand, smiling, eyes flicking forward and back across his face. 'I'm glad you could come,' she said. 'Jimmy's told me a lot about you.'

There were children. Three of them; two short, dark-eyed boys who could nearly have been twins, a blonde girl of twelve or thirteen in skimpy jeans and suntop. They had materialized quietly, stood studying him. 'Dawn,' said Anne. 'Bevis and Mark. Bevis is shorter and noisier. Otherwise it's a job to tell them apart.'

He was adding to his store of problems fast.

'I was late,' said Elizabeth. 'The train got in on time.' Then to Roley. ''Scuse me if I tear off. I've got some shopping to pick up in the village.'

'Dawn will look after you,' said Anne. 'If you need anything, just yell. There'll be some tea on in a minute. OK?'

'Fine,' said Roley. 'Fine by me.' The children preceded him silently up the sairs.

The house rambled, was bigger inside than it had appeared from the street. Three storeys of wavy-floored rooms crowded and shoved each other, stairways wound between odd levels, ceilings sprouted pillars and unexpected angles. He followed the girl's neat behind as she opened doors, trotted along passages. 'That's the bathroom,' she said. 'If you fill it too full it comes through the skylight in the bar. The John is straight on through, through the other door. That's Anne and Jimmy's room. That one's spare, we think it's haunted. That's where there used to be a coffin chute.'

He tapped the wall experimentally.

'If somebody died upstairs they couldn't get the box down,'

she said. 'It's quite logical. You're an artist, aren't you? Jimmy told us.'

'I do a lot of things.'

'You were at Royal,' said the child. 'You were a *Prix de Rome.* I paint a lot myself. So does Mark. He's better than me at the moment. Less inhibition.' She opened a door at the top of the final flight of stairs. 'This is yours,' she said. 'I hope you like it.'

He swung the rucksack on to the bed, crossed to lift the net curtains from the diminutive window. He looked down across a frozen sea of roofs. 'It's great,' he said. 'Thank you, Dawn.'

She perched on the bed, straightbacked, crossing her legs like a Buddha. 'I expect you'll want to freshen up,' she said. 'Can we help you unpack? If we're being a nuisance we'll go. We're just naturally inquisitive.'

He took soap and towels from the rucksack, watching her speculatively. 'Stick around,' he said. 'Be my guests.'

The children were still in residence when he got back. They had opened drawers and wardrobe doors, sat waiting patiently. He stowed his gear quickly. Last out of the pack were the camera and accessories. The girl took the Agi, handling it delicately. 'What a beauty. Is it yours?'

He had paused, cigarette between his lips, half-minded to take the thing from her. Touching his camera was like stroking a dissected nerve. But her fingers were very gentle. 'Yes,' he said. 'It's mine. I always have it with me.'

'Do you make money with photographs?'

'Sometimes.'

'What sort of things?'

He hesitated. 'Road smashes,' he said. 'They're worth a fortune if you get there first. And the shunt's bad enough.'

'Yes,' she said. 'People are like that I'm afraid. Thank you.' she handed the camera back, carefully. 'What's this?'

'This' was the flashgun. The strange children seemed intrigued. One of the boys piped up. Probably Bevis.

'How does it work?'

Roley took it from him, twisted a control. There was a faint whistle of h/f as the charge began to build. 'A light comes on when it's ready,' he said. 'Then you shoot.'

Abruptly, the children's hands were over their ears. They glanced at each other, eyes wide, then back to the thing in his hands. A brief fizzing, a crack; and he dropped the gun hastily. It had become extremely hot.

The children were watching blankly. He picked the ruined thing up, laid it on the windowsill. 'We're sorry,' said Dawn. 'It made a funny noise. Is it broken?'

'It's all right,' said Roley gently. 'It happens sometimes.'

She stood up, still watching him, and twitched at her jeans. 'I think your meal's ready now Mr. Stafford,' she said. 'Would you like to come down?'

Anne had laid a farmhouse tea in the back parlour of the place; there were scones and butter, dishes of thick yellow cream, jam. He ate quietly, mind busy. Mainly with the burned flash gear upstairs. 'I don't know what's happened to the dray,' said Anne. 'They must have changed their round. It's the season of course, they get terribly behind. Dawn, run and see if they're coming will you? And you'd better change, if you're going to the Waters'.' Then to Roley, 'Elizabeth's down at the house. She said to tell you she'd be back in later on.'

He started, conscious suddenly of incivility. The child Bevis spoke before he could. 'Mr. Stafford's a little tired,' he said. 'It's a long way on the train.' Roley glanced at him. He was looking bland. Beside him Mark applied himself studiously to a large slice of cake. He was saved from answering by a rattle and clash in the yard, the arrival of the long-expected dray.

He insisted on helping. Anne told him there was no need; but the work was by no means strange. The barrels they trundled through the back of the pub, to the awkwardly-placed cellar; the bottled beer was off-loaded beside the door. He carried the crates in as they came from the lorry, restocked the bars under Anne's direction. A half hour, and the job was done. He had worked up a thirst; he drank beer, with the drayman and his mate, leaning in the empty coolness of the bar. The drayman was an unusual personage. He was tall, taller by half a head than Roley, and immensely broad. A grubby shirt, open from the shoulders, disclosed a chest and belly that were a mass of hair; on his head, half-lost among a tangle of dark-blond curls, was perched an ancient, high-peaked cap. He wore a full beard; the eyes above it were a brilliant, direct blue, the nose straight with well-shaped, sensitive nostrils. His voice, Roley imagined, might come rumbling from that mass of bone and fat like the distant noise of an earthquake; but it was oddly soft, lilting and gentle. The children hopped round him excitedly, tapping for sweets and lemonade, till Anne shooed them away. She told Roley, after he had gone, his name was Brian; he had never, as far as she knew, answered to any other. He usually drank in the pub of an evening. Elizabeth liked him; she called him Weland, swore he was the Smith of the Gods.

He stocked the bar fridge with lager. Trundled a fresh three X into the saloon, tapped the barrel that stood waiting. Half a pint, and the beer ran clear; he straightened up, pleased, and heard a car pass the door.

Jimmy was heavier than he remembered him. But there was the same faintly worried air, the same wave of dark hair hanging across the eyes. They were stilted with each other at first, old friends long parted. They loosened up over pints in the back bar. The street doors were open by then, a few shirt-sleeved tourists shifting halves of mild in the Public. 'We get a hell of a trade four months of the year,' said Jimmy. 'Live off our fat for the rest.' Then, catching the direction of his glance, 'You, you skinny bastard . . . You wouldn't believe' – turning to Anne – 'that he's a profligate at heart.'

'I've got a fortunate metabolism,' said Roley. 'Where are the kids?'

'Upstairs watching the Box,' she said. Wiping a glass carefully. She glanced momentarily at Jimmy, frownlines creasing her forehead. 'They're not ours,' she said. 'We adopted them.'

The car in the yard was Elizabeth getting back. She'd changed, sometime or other. Shortsleeved turquoise blouse, off-white skirt.

Matching accessories.

'It's all happening,' she said. 'Tourists, tourists; and still they come. *Pyyouch . . .*'

'Drink?'

A half of cider followed a well-worn track. Rough, at that. Another fortunate metabolism. She leaned on the bar, elbow touching Roley's. Frankness, not flirting.

She had asked him if he'd settled in, were they looking after him. He dragged his mind back from a distance. He'd been meaning to ask about the house. 'The beast,' he said, 'is fed and watered. Very adequately.'

'Good,' she said. 'Jimmy, can I borrow him a minute? I want to show him round.'

They wandered along the village street. There were the usual shops. A tobacconist and newsagent, still doing a good trade; a grocers, closed now, a radio and television store. Its windows boasted bright painted shutters. And an antique showroom; there were coloured prints of the castle, a spinning wheel on display only, a case of foreign butterflies. Gruesome china cats and pigs, souvenir chamber pots for the less discerning. A bad chandelier.

He found one thing that pleased him. A hairslide, African made; a pierced leaf-shape of beaten copper spanned by a sliver of wood. He bought it, handed it to Elizabeth. She looked faintly disturbed. 'For Dawn,' he said. 'I thought she'd like it.'

'Yes,' she said. 'Yes, she will.'

Outside, very distant and high, was a noise of aeroplanes.

There was a children's playground, an open space behind the houses. Seats surrounded it, there were swings and a Wicksteed roundabout. A covey of local kids played a ragged game of cricket; they kept up a shrill squeal of argument, like grasshoppers. The sky colour was deepening, imperceptibly; an early bat swung low, zigged out of sight. Far away, miles high, contrails sketched a symbol against the evening. She said abruptly, 'Mr. Mohindru's dead.'

'Who?'

'Mohindru. The UN Secretary General.'

The great peacemaker. He felt, momentarily, something like fear. Something chilling, touching the heart. The grass waved, rustling.

'It was on the news,' she said. 'This evening. It was on a plane. They think it was . . . sabotaged, someway. They can't tell.'

'I didn't hear it,' he said. 'I forgot to listen.'

The shadows had lengthened. His senses seemed abnormally acute; he saw, with the clearness of hallucination, those same shadows lengthen across rubble. The growth of lichen, the little harvests of the stone; aimless trundling of a wood-louse, after the men had gone. A trilobite, lost under an ocean of air; old fossil, jarred from rock, piping again.

She was watching him. Her face had paled; she looked older, lines showing under her eyes. But it was the light.

She was still holding the hairslide. It was soft copper, she'd squeezed it out of shape. 'Look,' she said. 'Look, what a silly thing . . .'

He took it from her, straightened it gently. Pressing with his thin, hard fingers. 'What's the house?' he asked.

'House?'

A pause.

'It's a . . . place we had built,' she said. 'You must come and see it. It's rather fine.'

'Where?'

'On the coast. A mile or so away.'

He polished the hairslide with his thumb. 'Who's we?'

'Us. Jimmy, Anne.' She looked helpless. 'Us.'

'Elizabeth,' he said, 'what's going on down here?'

'Jimmy will tell you,' she said. 'When he's ready. I mustn't. I don't think I could. I wouldn't know where to start.'

She stood up, smoothing her skirt. 'I must get back,' she said. 'I work evenings in the bar. They rely on me.'

Across the hills the traffic roared. Or maybe, he realized, it was the sea.

He sat in a corner of the snug watching Elizabeth work. She was a village celebrity, that much was obvious; by his reckoning the young bloods of at least three counties came to spend their money with her. She had a word for all of them, a special smile for Brian. He sat still tousled, belly it seemed ever ready to burst from the restriction of a fresh white shirt, face scrubbed and glowering. At ten he left. Roley followed shortly afterwards, walked to the end of the village. Beyond the last of the houses was a stile. He climbed it, followed a field track to where he could see the castle a long way off, a mounding of darker sky against the stars. Day had not yet finished with his little world; to the west, low down, a turquoise streak still gleamed. He smoked a cigarette, brooding. Reached no conclusions.

The children were still around when he got back. Dawn better covered, and wearing the slide. He helped with the glasses on the bar. As yet he'd had no chance to talk to Jimmy. That would come later. He'd sort this thing out if he sat up half the night.

They had supper in the back bar. A light meal, biscuits and cheese and coffee. Elizabeth sat close to him; the beer he had drunk fumed slightly in his brain, making it careless of images. Twice she turned to him, faintly startled. He told himself, rapport doesn't exist. It's an artist's dream, the great pathetic fallacy.

His patience snapped.

He walked upstairs feeling he was going to meet Fate. He half expected the flashgun to have vanished. It still lay on the windowsill where he had left it. He carried it back down with him, set it on the table. Conversation stopped. Six faces stared at him; and there was Strangeness.

Then Elizabeth was on her feet, eyes glowing. 'Dawn,' she hissed. 'You little *beast* . . .'

Dawn hung her head.

'Leave her,' said Roley. 'It wasn't her fault.' Then quietly, 'One question Jimmy. *What the hell goes on here?*'

Jimmy picked the charred thing up, turning it in his fingers, brackling fragments from the case. 'Nothing,' he said. 'Nothing you can't understand, Roley.' He looked up smiling. 'We'll square with you for this.'

Cups jumped as Roley banged the table. 'What the hell does it matter?' he said. 'The price of a bloody thing like that? I asked you a question, Jimmy. *What goes on?*'

'It's a long story,' said Jimmy wearily. He brushed at his hair. 'Anne, love, would you make us some more coffee? I think we shall need it.'

They talked, while Roley sat eyes narrowed, smoking cigarette after cigarette till the tray at his elbow overflowed with stubs. They told him of *Gestalt* after *Gestalt*, centred here, centred there; and more springing up, all over the land. 'We don't know,' said Jimmy. 'We don't know whether it's a breakthrough, a mutation, what it is. We none of us know. There's nearly a hundred Groups now, more maybe we haven't picked up. We're the smallest, nearly the youngest. Because it's getting to the kids. I'm the sort of . . . co-ordinator, Roley I know this is crazy but take it in, let it get through – Anne's the eyes, the children are the hands, Elizabeth's the brain; she's the smart one, there's a script of hers upstairs she wants you to read. Put you in the picture better than I could. She plays the stock market, if we need a few thousand. Another house, new car . . . There's nothing to it, nothing at all –'

Roley held his hand up for quiet. Across the table the children watched, sleepy now, eyes brooding and dark. He felt the rise of a new weariness.

'It hangs together,' he said finally. Looking down at his cup. 'It makes a logic. The logic is crazy. You have a group delusion.'

He didn't want to be convinced. He knew, as they knew, what must happen.

The knife rose from the cheeseboard, hung spinning to streak down, slam into the wood beneath his hands. Then the cups and plates, dancing a mad ballet. The pub was haunted, poltergeists rampaging through the room. His mind screamed for out, levelled. There was quiet.

He sat still, face down, a vein pulsing in his forehead. When he looked up his eyes were bleak as ice. 'All right,' he said. 'Get on with it. Let's have the rest.'

The rest. After what they called the first phase, the phase of self-awareness, had come a time of consolidation; the Groups linking, deciding, choosing their territories. The first fear gone, they had settled down to the business of living.

'The life of Reilly,' said Roley, watching down at his fingers. 'What's part three?'

They told him.

He heard them through; then he shook his head. Very steadily, slow and cool. 'No,' he said. 'You're playing it wrong. You won't make it. It's all wrong.'

Were the faces angry, or appalled?

He rose from the table, after a long, long wait. 'Well,' he said. 'It's been a hard day.'

And that was all.

He was lying on the bed, not asleep, watching the moon stream through the windows of the little room. The scraping of the door disturbed the stillness. He waited. An oblong of blackness; from it a voice spoke softly.

'You asleep?'

He shook his head, knowing the other could see.

'Can I come in?'

He shrugged, still lying with his hands clasped behind his head. 'It's your pub . . .'

Jimmy lit a cigarette, squatted on the end of the bed. Tossed the packet down. Roley found it with his hands. His ordinary, human hands that had to grope and touch. 'I'm sorry,' said Stringer. 'Sorry you're mad at us.'

There was silence between them. Roley lit up, inhaled, saw the pink reflection flare and fade on the ceiling. The weariness was still on him, a great dulling weight. Weariness at the task ahead, the changes there must be in human thinking, acting, feeling. Now that *Homo Superior, Homo Gestalt,* had come to stay. It was too much. Too much for him, too much for any of these shut away behind their Mountains Green. Finally he spoke.

'Where's Elizabeth?'

'Gone to the house. You frightened her.'

A little noise, half between a laugh and a snort.

'I know it's a shock,' said Jimmy.

'Don't make platitudes,' said the long man on the bed. 'Anything else, Christ. But platitudes yet.'

Jimmy was still hunched, studying the burning tip of his cigarette. 'What the hell else can I make?' he asked.

Softly.

Bitterly.

Roley stirred suddenly. 'Why'd you mix me in, old mate? Why me?'

Simply. 'You were the only one I could trust.'

Another long wait. Then, 'Why're you so mad?'

Roley clicked on a shaded light beside the bed, looked up squinting. 'I'm not mad,' he said. 'You silly bastard, I'm not mad.' He got up and walked to the window, stood leaning on the frame looking out and down. 'It's just that you're a rat,' he said. 'And you find an elephant stampede's on the way. That's all.'

'You'll get over it. I did.'

'Yeah,' said Roley. 'In forty-eight hours.' He moved across the room, pulling a jacket round his shoulders.

'Where're you going?'

'Out,' said the bearded man shortly. 'I'm going out, I'm going to walk, I'm going to watch the dawn come up like a lovelorn child. Haven't done it for years. I'm going to Adjust, to being the inferior species.'

Jimmy gripped his arm. 'I haven't got much of a Talent,' he said apologetically. 'I just got caught up in this. That's all.'

The other punched his chest, softly. 'You're a bastard,' he said. 'One month's beer.' He slapped his pockets, located cigarettes and matches. 'The brainpickers are off duty,' he said. 'Union rules.'

'They're off duty.'

'They'd better be,' said Roley. 'Better be, boy.' He turned back halfway down the stairs. 'I'm going to find the sea,' he said. 'Always liked the sea. One day it'll be all there is left.'

Jimmy heard the click of the side door as it opened and closed.

The sea was farther off than he'd reckoned. He walked an hour, dim shoulders of hills showing to either side, before he realized he'd missed the road. He turned back. There was a side track, badly surfaced; a sign, bright in the moonlight, that said *Johnson's Pool.* He followed the lane, setting his feet cautiously as the slope steepened. The hills ahead loomed blacker, more solid; there was a fresh breathing on his face, a harder, cooler wind. Then the smell of water, old and huge, the sense of openness. And a great dim horizon, glimpsed through a vee-cleft in high banks. He stood and listened to a stream trickling through some runoff in the rocks; then eased himself down, carefully, wetting his feet in puddles. The sea was flat calm, darker than grey. Miles out was the dim flaring of the horizon. He sat and tossed pebbles, heard the splashing of them in the making tide.

He was very tired. Sometime he curled sideways in a patch of wiry grass. Shut his eyes.

The gulls woke him, white scraps of life, their screams exploding above his head. He sat up rubbing his face. His mouth felt dry and harsh. He looked across the water, saw the early sun working through veils of mist. To right and left high rock jutted at the sea, enclosing a shallow bay. There was a jetty, a moored yacht. He laughed; at the sea, himself, everything. Human life, chittering and piping. The world too big, uncaring. This one little bay, in the dawn light, flattening his soul.

He got up. There was a shadow-figure above him on the rocks. Behind it, a shadow-house.

So he couldn't get away.

She came down carefully, sandals slapping on the path. She was wearing an old cotton dress, floral print, too short for her. He sat watching her, hands between his knees, still chuckling. 'Come on,' he said. 'Where's your boar spear?'

She was shivering. She looked at him in the dimness, and there was pain. 'This is difficult to say,' she said. 'You won't understand. I was afraid of looking. Looking properly.'

'Try now,' he said. 'Open up, Elizabeth.'

A moment of tension. Then she sat down abruptly, put her face in her hands. The skin of her forehead was damp. 'I'm such a fool,' she said. 'Such a bloody fool.'

He put his hand under her arm, lifted gently. His fingers were wiry and strong. 'I'm all right,' she said. Brushing at her lashes with a palm. 'Jimmy told me about you. He . . . said what you were like. I'm just a fool.' She smiled at him, unsteadily. 'There's coffee,' she said. 'Might manage cornflakes. You hungry?'

He nodded. He'd seen enough of the sea.

The house squatted, staring across the rocks. And it was a flyaway house, of concrete and steel. He looked at it, still half-bemused with sleep. 'It was a . . . present,' she said. 'You won't understand. Not properly. Not just yet. It wasn't what I wanted. What I thought I wanted. But they knew better.'

She'd lit a fire. It crackled faintly in the centre of the one great room, beneath a copper cowl stained brilliantly by heat. He stood and looked round him slowly. A glass wall, low and wide, showed him the sea, bright now with the dawn. He saw smoothly worked cream stone, steel girders painted cobalt blue. Lush fitted carpet, smoky-blue; fossils and shells in alcoves, a model ship. To one side, a bright surprise; the Spitfire, nosed into a recess in the floor. Round one wall ran an exploding mural, blue colours that burned and hissed and just started to be a bay and rocks and a boat before dissolving into Light. Opposite was a sleeping gallery, reached by slim wooden companion ladder.

He walked forward, looking at the mural.

'We let the kids loose on it,' she said. 'In swimming trunks. Then Jimmy pulled it together.'

'He's got better,' he said. 'Maybe there's hope.'

'I know you,' she said. 'You were a *Prix de Rome*.'

He pulled her close. Carefully, frowning. Rumpling her skirt, squeezing the big muscles of her behind. She rested against him, motionless and warm. 'You have to take my word,' she said, 'for my part of it. Just my word . . .'

Her mouth was generous, and soft.

He unbuttoned, slowly. The vee of skin went down, and down, and down. She pushed him aside, gently. He thought, for an instant of pain, that she was sending him away. She climbed the ladder to the bunk, holding the frock half round her.

The sun reflections spread across the water, twinkling in miles-long silver skeins. He lay seeing the mural, how it burst away at its end to blue flecks that vanished against stone. Drifting into sleep and back from the edges of it, Elizabeth giggling at the thoughts he sent and nipping like a cat. She got up sometime in the morning, staggered into a sweater and climbed downstairs. He followed, and the bacon was spoiled. Half-naked women shouldn't try to cook breakfast.

3

He drove the Victor out of the pub yard, waved briefly and swung right, accelerating along the village street. The day was overcast, ragged clouds chasing in from the West; as he passed the derestriction sign a spatter of water lashed across the road. He used the wipers. The spots of water smeared, blended into an oily diesel scum. In time the screen was clear.

He passed the shell of the castle. A map lay on the seat beside him; he glanced at it briefly, swung right and began to climb. Joined his route five miles farther on. There were crawling lines of traffic. A Jag flashed him; he edged out, closed up behind a rusty-fendered A40. Its roofrack was piled with luggage, partly protected by a flapping polythene sheet; in the back window were pennant stickers and a jigging doll. He allowed his mind to wander. In time the A40 vanished.

The boat had been a four-berth Rayner, Volvo-engined. Two thousand and eighty-five quid ex-yard. They had dropped out from Johnson's Pool at midday, used the engine to get them clear of land. He had the tiller; Elizabeth sat by him in jeans and heavy windcheater, hair blowing in the keen sea breeze. There were long slabs of rock beyond the eastern headland, needles of stone they called the Dancers. He could hear the surf round them over the throbbing of the boat. Clear of them, he killed the engine. The yacht lay rolling and slapping as they hoisted the sails. She heeled to the wind then, became a live thing.

They stayed out too long. Elizabeth was talking love. And she would cook hamburgers.

Dusk brought heavy cloud. And a crawling, rolling fog. They heard a horn call and call, miles away. She said, 'Like an empty bed the night long.' She'd read her Bradbury. He laughed at her. No more empty beds.

Not now.

She was worried by the fog. She sat close to him, tensed, turning her head. Calling he knew, listening to God knew what, coming from the land. They closed the coast; but the Other eyes couldn't see. Because of the fog. Elizabeth edged forward, out of his sight. The engine thumped steadily, water creamed and slapped beneath the keel. Nothing to see; just the fog, moving and coiling, the red and green ghost-glare of the sidelights. Endless slap-slap of halliards as the boat rolled, crabbing across the tide.

And there was the surf-noise again, the sighing and booming. Away to his right. He swung the tiller hard across, clawing off the land. Seeing in his mind the Dancers, the looming shapes of them like Brocken-spectres in the mist, the waves seething at their bases. Lifting up, slow and long, crushingly down. The fear he felt was for Elizabeth.

She called him instantly, reassuring. The voice from the dark was confident now and quiet. He turned back unwillingly toward the land; and there was the still blackness of the Pool, movement of figures on the jetty, a bobbing light. Elizabeth poised at the bow, coiled line in her hand. The *Gestalt* was whole again.

He had held her close that night, afraid of losing her.

The A40 was back, braking. He avoided it, edged out. There was a clear road. He took a line of six, opened up. The car moved well.

He stopped for a beer, after two hours driving. The pub

looked dingy and old. He sat in a corner of the snug, eating high-priced sandwiches, brooding into his glass.

There were many images of Elizabeth. He saw her sitting over the fire with the great copper cowl, face flamelit and solemn; curled in a deep corner of the settle, watching the Box that flickered across the lounge; dancing, arms dropped loose across his shoulders, the big voices from the hi-fi filling the night. Ella and Louis, the smoothway and the rough. Stars fell in Alabama.

Another time she climbed a clay scree out of the bay. Knees muddy, skirt blowing up showing small white pants. She was eminently undressable, existed just for him.

He got back on the road. The traffic had eased a little, he made better time. He was balked for a while by an artic; eventually the flashers called him through. He was driving in shirtsleeves, windows down and quarterlights open, deflecting a cool breeze into the cab.

He'd always promised himself he would marry the first woman who could swear without being coarse. But that was before he got too old for love.

She wouldn't wear a pyjama top, not for all the world. He chivvied her about it till she retaliated, flinging taunts.

'Breasts are nothing. I wonder you get all worked up.'

'I don't.'

'You flaming well do . . .'

He grabbed at her, and missed. She padded along the gallery, reached to draw curtains against the night. The great seaward window they left uncovered, for the moon.

'You're a tit man,' she said. 'I'm disappointed.'

He lay laughing silently, pulling back the corners of his mouth. 'I'm nothing of the sort.'

'I'm sorry you don't like me. I don't think you're very nice.'

'You aren't very nice.'

'Then I shan't come to bed. And you'll be sorry.'

'I could see through your shirt this afternoon,' he said. 'We shall both get jailed.'

'Then you're what I said.'

'I like everything,' he said. 'It's the way I'm made.'

She wriggled alongside him, fresh and smelling of night air.

Pulled to make him roll on top. '*You're an everything man,*' she whispered. '*That's what . . .*'

He woke early, soon after dawn. Lay wondering what had disturbed him. Then he heard it; the throb of huge engines, miles high. It reached down to the house, buzzing faintly in wood and steel. He got up, walked to the window. The bombers were too high to see; the contrails shone, catching light from over the shoulder of the world.

A breath at his elbow and a sound. He held her close, fingers against her hip. It seemed a shadow crossed the land; he saw folk running, tiny and scuttling, boiling like ants. Over them, drifting and slow, fell a mantle of twinkling blue. And the people heaved and were still; and all the rocks and trees and boats and homes of men were still. Quite still.

He swore, knowing she had seen. He asked her, 'Do you know what they're carrying? The aeroplanes?'

No answer.

His face was twisted as if in pain. 'It's dirt,' he said. 'Shit.'

She nibbled at him, to make him go back to bed.

Jimmy had been crisp, forced into an unwanted role. 'Here's the main concentration,' he said. Tapping the impossible map with its bright clusterings of rings. 'All round us, right here. Here's a secondary grouping. Centred on the New Forest. And another here, here . . . We can link, for a while. Puts our range up thirty, fifty times. We can't hold full power for long but it'll be enough. You, Roley, you're the go-between. The only Normal we can rely on. We don't like indirection, any of us. And we're none of us fools enough to think we can stop a war. Maybe we won't even make a ripple. We see ourselves as a diversion. Something to make folk stop, re-think their priorities. Anything that does that is good.

'But to do it we have to stay free. That way we're an unknown quantity. Potential spanner in the works. Once we show ourselves we've had it. *Kksss.*' He drew a finger across his throat. 'Locked away somewhere working for the State. This or another. That's not the way we want to play it.'

Round him the faces watched; the ordinary faces, dozens of them, faces of fishermen, farmhands. Each infused with that same odd light. Through them, the Groups listened.

'What we want from you's a report,' said Jimmy. 'Daily,

when things hot up. You've got your schedule. *Poste restante,* different office every time. We don't expect that'll last for long. When they rumble us we'll have to think again. Or maybe by that time there won't be any need. There'll be a security clamp-down right from the start of course. That won't matter to us. What we want from you's reactions. What folk are thinking, how they talk. How far we are from winning. We shan't have any time to run opinion polls. Sure you can supply?'

Roley nodded, silently. He hadn't spent years round the Fleet Street pubs for nothing.

'OK,' said Jimmy. 'If you've got any other problems, trot 'em out. We'll fix a drawing account. How about ready cash?'

Roley shrugged, mind busy. 'Could make do. Advance might be handy.'

'Elizabeth,' said the other, 'give him five hundred. That enough? Plenty more if you need it.'

Roley nodded again, drily. 'It'll do for a week or so,' he said.

She wouldn't watch him leave. She'd run upstairs, to the bed-room; he followed her, awkwardly. She was warmth and satin skin and salt of crying. He could lose himself in her now, feel as he kissed the brief sensation of falling. She was trembling, she pushed away and swung to the window, stood, eyes shut and hand rubbing her throat, smudging the tears there. He left her, silently; went down, stowed his kit in the estate car. The Victor smelled of pvc: a new, sweet stink. He shook hands with his friends, not wanting to meet their eyes or minds. Knowing already what he had to do. He started up, edged past the Spit-fire. Jimmy stood at the pub door, and the kids; Dawn had her hand to her hair, touching the slide. He drove out of the yard, waved briefly and swung right, accelerating along the village street.

At Marlborough he joined the Great West Road. Ahead the sky was dark; behind him a haze of sunlight still lingered. The mirrors caught the brightness, trapping orange chips of it against the night. He drove fast, trying not to think any more. Knowing his hands might yet turn the car, race it back toward the light. At Newbury he met a Mobile Column, truck after dark green truck speeding down toward the West. Another holdup outside Theale; he saw army vehicles, the swathed shapes of field guns. He wondered what the hell they thought they were going to do with those. He worked his way through Reading, opened up again, branched on to the M4 a mile or so from Maidenhead. He passed London Airport, drove into Chiswick. At a quarter after nine he parked the car in the mews outside his flat, locked up and wearily climbed the stairs. The place smelled stale; somewhere a cat mewed, scuttled from the noise of his feet. He unlocked his door, kicked aside a jumble of newspapers and bills. He brewed coffee, smoked a cigarette; wondered briefly about a meal, decided against it. He undressed, lay down and closed his eyes. Beneath the pillow were letters. To the *Times, Guardian, Telegraph.* For good measure the *Express, Sun, News of the World.* He'd post them in the morning. Then the wheels would start to turn.

And never stop.

4

Phase Three, in operation.

On a grey hillside, secluded behind formal grounds and trees, sat a grey country house. On the lawn before it a group of beehives roared softly. The roaring was not the noise of bees.

Below the house, deep inside the hill, the Regional Seat of Government bustled with activity. There was a constant ringing of telephones, a coming and going of army and police personnel. Corridor after corridor echoed with footsteps; children wailed as families, dependants of the local *élite,* tried to establish themselves in the new world of the bunkers. Soon the shafts would be sealed against the death that would come from the air.

In one little room, grey-painted and bare, a WRAC corporal stood quite still, books and papers in her arms. On the wall in front of her was a long blackboard, polished and as yet unused. Below it a tray held assorted sticks of coloured chalk. She watched quietly as the sticks shuffled and moved. One dropped to the floor; another rose, hung uncertainly, moved to the surface of the board. Rapped once, began to draw. The scraping sounded loud in the room.

Her mouth opened slowly, wide and wider. The scream was soundless. The thing on the blackboard grew, shaky and uncertain at first then more firm; till there gleamed in stark impossibility the red circle, the joining legs, of the Sign of Man.

The books hit the floor with a thud. Seconds later the lights failed through the bunker system; a slow whine sounded as the air conditioning died.

The radar tower stood among trees, two hundred feet of dully-shining duralumin shell. The great dish at its top stared blankly, pointing at thc zcnith of thc sky.

Round it, forces sparked. The struts wobbled, twanged. The structure was too strong for the thing that wrestled with it. It quivered, there was a sense of strain . . . and nothing.

The forces groped downward. Ran across the tower sides, nearly-visible ripplings in the metal. Reached underground, far and deep; found conduits, burrowed along them into busbars and fuseboxes. CR tubes imploded, burst with cracklings and rushes of sparks. Their operators scurried, helplessly. Main lighting blew, then in quick succession the twin emergency systems. A hooter blared, was cut off; the place was confusion and darkness.

Except where a lead, torn triumphantly free, splashed blue fire, burning the Sign on the fresh concrete of a wall.

In a room below Whitehall a stout, grey-haired man sat staring, hands pressed to the green leather tabletop in front of him. Round him filing cabinets emptied themselves, phone-leads tore from their sockets, mounds of paper reduced themselves to Most Secret confetti. Ashtrays danced, carpets rucked where Nothing ran along. An electric fan leaped from its bracket, hung screaming a foot from his face before crashing to the carpet. The blades jammed, quivered for a while; the motor hummed and was silent. A wisp of smoke rose from the casing before the circuit blew.

Somewhere, there was fire. It ran along carpeting, licked at the torn paper, busied itself with drapes and the backs of chairs. Tentative at first then brighter, spreading.

The man was unaware of it.

And across the country presses stopped as the machines refused the news they had to run, spat paper from their tall innards in whirling coils. Flash doors ground shut along the deep tube lines of London, sirens howled, in a thousand police stations Early Warning monitors burst into warbling alarm. *Red Alert, Red, Red, Red Alert* ... Men hammered at phones as the lines burned in their hands; distributor caps split, engines flashed into flame as petrol from torn lines dowsed their blocks, computers rebelled, barraged their operators with lunatic results. An army of poltergeists was loose, ripping and snapping, jamming beyond all repair the machinery of war.

'*Why . . .?*'

The newsman leaned on the corner of the bar, nicely drunk, drawing faces on the counter with piecrust chips and beer smears. Roley was sober. He'd had a poorish time; Reuter's man had thrown him down the stairs, his contacts had one and all turned to sedentary syphon-feeders.

'Tha's the *why*,' said the reporter. 'But the *how* ... peeeww, *Jesus*. S'curity? Tha's a dirty word.' He held his hands up, forefingers opposed. 'Guns 'is way. Guns 'at way. Cordons. Poop, poop . . .' He giggled, helplessly.

London was under siege. Armed troops on the street corners, tanks grinding through the Mall. 'Poop, poop', said the newsman. 'Highly entertaining . . .'

He wagged an admonishing finger at Roley. 'M'boy,' he said, 'tomorrow, I shall be hung. You will be al-alongside. Mauve, and kicking.'

'*You'll forget me*,' she'd said, '*The first time you pass a cathouse . . .*'

He'd made her promise to grow her hair. He wanted as much hair as possible, over her face, in her mouth, everywhere. Then he would paint her. It was important, he'd said, to show she was a female animal. The painting would be bad. He knew that before he started.

'Doing about it?' said the newsman. 'Now you t-tell me, what you'd do about it. Got a new weapon. Who? Us, them? The Russkies. T-tell you what, it's the bloody Russkies ... Know what I'd do?'

'No.'

'Poop off a few nukes,' said the other, leering. 'Afore I – hic – lost the flints . . .'

Roley got out.

The pavements were hot, and the tarmac of the roads. London stinking and shimmering, a noisy mirage. There were letters to be posted. More letters, to *The Times* and the rest. By now the Groups would be moving West, concentrating. Homing on Elizabeth's h/f beacon.

He tried to wish that he had never known her.

He read the newsbills, bought papers. There was the war-talk still, final Notes exchanged, threats and undertakings. The Church clamouring; the Pope would speak, on the Eurovision link. Tonight. Nowhere a word of what had happened. The clampdown. The truth was too frightening.

Or childish.

He fought his way home, through the tube. Then out to Hammersmith to unload his mail. The last salvo had been fired from Stepney. The game was played through, it had been at the start. They'd search London, with fine-tooth combs. Then the country. Then the planet, if they had to. They would be professionals. Nothing he or the rest could do would cover for long. The machine was slow because it was big. That was all.

A world in panic. One little country buckling at the edges. Every new weapon is an Ultimate Deterrent, for a little while. How long would *Gestalt* last, caught in an asymptotic progress curve?

He went back to his flat and painted. Just a sea, blue and spreading, stretching out for ever. He tried to lose himself, hypnotize his mind with the rhythmic movement of the brush. Like the child-Dali drawing the cherries on the old door. When he'd finished the canvas showed him a bland bright eye. He had nothing to say.

He'd planned a Drunk once, meticulously. One of the times he'd needed to die.

His London was a subterranean world of cellars and clubs and bars. Frenetic now, with death so close. There was great jazz being played. He didn't hear it. He saw the huddling bodies, flash of eyes and nails and hair; painted brickwork, purring fans, red-daubed bulbs, posters from Spain. The vibration in the walls was like the noise of planes.

Somebody had a transistor, in one of the dives. It squawked about evacuation, Government assurances. Somebody else ground it under their heel. There was a fight, savage and pointless. He saw glass used, edged out on hands and knees. There were loudspeaker vans touring. Saying go to your homes. He was ignored. One drunk in a drunken town.

It was easy, after all, to set one foot in front of the next. At the centre of him was a knot of cunning; it controlled his body, making it perform, walk in straight lines. There were more people. Sprawling people, drunk people, junked-up people lying in tangles of legs and arms. Somewhere there was a woman. She didn't care for what he had to say. He was flung out. Or hauled out, feet tap-tap-tapping on stairs. They left him in the street. He lay face down, nursing his great and witty truth. That she had not been Elizabeth.

Where was Elizabeth?

He wondered, looking for her. He found her quite soon, and cried into her lap. She wiped his face and mouth; he whispered to her, to her alone, secret things that only she might hear. Bought her jewels and strapped them to her feet, opened her dress to find the gay, surprising nipples. But the nightmare took her, altering and changing. This wasn't Elizabeth either; Elizabeth wasn't old, and her face wasn't lined, and she didn't stink of powder and sweat. He screamed at her, and men came running. Eager to hunt. Father forgive them.

The shells, the hemispheres of the bomb, approached critical mass. He pushed them apart with his hands, knowing he would die. But they closed and closed in spite of him. Blue bright stuff inside them cascading and joining, and soundless flashes. He died many times.

He lay listening to the lap-lap of waves inside his mind. Wanting Elizabeth, who had run away from him. He groped slowly, exploring the cold cobbles that were her body.

But that was wrong too.

He shook himself from the iron dream. Sat up. There was a harsh light, unfocused. Great shapes, planes of bright grey. Above him were warehouses; over them, soaring, agoraphobic, the iron tips of cranes. In front of him was Tower Bridge, mightiest of Follies. Reaching up to mist.

He fell back again, shaking, feeling the pounding inside his brain. He was lying on a wharf, downstream from the Bridge. Couldn't quite remember how he'd got there. He opened his eyes again, cautiously. His vision was blurred, tear-streaked it seemed. There was the river, sullen and broad. At the wharf edge, a tiny backwater. In it an oily scum moved, slapping and gurgling, rocking the white hull of a fag packet. There were leaves, shells of old spring buds from trees.

He got up, walking and reeling. There seemed to be some altercation. Above him, on the Bridge. Solid lines of traffic edged and hooted; there was a shouting man in white shirt and gold-braided cap. Another running, bloody-faced. He was wiping at the brightness, showing his hand to people who wanted to see.

He walked beneath the Bridge, unsteadily. Through an archway guarded by great iron-studded doors. In the confined space the rumbling from above was very loud. There was a ship in the Pool; water boiling under her stern, a tug at her side crying. He looked up at soaring girders, miles high.

He walked on towards the Tower of London. The Little Tower now, cringing and lost. The cannon were still there, black lines of them. He leaned on the great butt of one, pressing his mouth to the iron. It seemed the Bridge was moving. But that couldn't be; the bascules couldn't rise, not with crashing and thunder, vehicles tumbling from their backs like children's toys. He laughed at the absurdity, groped round his neck for the straps of the Agi. It was gone. He must have left it somewhere.

He turned away, tired of the din. There was an archway in a wall. Spiked, and round-topped. Above it a notice-board, screwed to the stone. He tried to read what it said. The letters swam and danced, shifting annoyingly before his eyes. He solved the riddle eventually and started to laugh again. This was the Traitors' Gate.

At midday he walked into New Scotland Yard.

5

He lay in a plain room, concrete-built, its walls painted a flat, pale green. His hands gripped the iron rail of the cot behind his head. He was motionless. He'd been motionless for hours.

Above him a lamp burned steadily, out of reach behind an armoured wellglass. A conduit led away from it, saddled to the ceiling. He knew the lamp; the porcelain holder, the reflector, the wing nuts each side that held the fitting closed. He knew the ceiling, the marks of shuttering across it, pocks and pits in the concrete that the lamp threw into relief, distant and tiny as the mountains of the moon. He knew the room; the one functional steel chair, canvas-backed, the table screwed to the wall. On the table stood a polythene water-jug and tumbler; beneath it was an untouched stack of magazines. There was an iron-sheathed door, studded with bolts. In its centre, at head height, a rectangular spyhole guarded by bars. Through the hole he could see the bright-lit passageway outside. Sometimes the shadow of a guard. At the end of the corridor was a toilet. If he knocked he would be taken there. The door had to be left ajar.

He lay listening to the hiss of the air conditioning. The inlet was a painted grille set just under the ceiling. The hissing was the only sound in the cell. He moved his eyes back to the lamp. Once in twenty-four hours it dimmed to a glow, twelve hours later brightened again. He had tried to use it at the beginning, to count the progression of nights and days. But they'd taken his watch, and it was difficult. He lost track, and raved, and gave it up. Now he had no hobbies.

He'd been met at first with incredulity. It hadn't lasted long. Faces changed as he reeled off dates and times and places. Information classified, information unknown. The reaction had been fast.

They brought his things from the flat. But not to give him. Everything was searched and labelled, carried away. He asked for receipts. They gave them to him.

It was night before they moved him. He was taken to a car; a big saloon, rear windows darkened. He saw motor-cycle outriders. He sat back dully, not caring. His senses reported, arbitrarily, the progress of the vehicle through blocked, panicking suburbs. Once he thought he heard firing; once saw, briefly, the light of flames. It showed him Mr. Johnson's bland, pale face.

He'd asked the others who he was. They didn't know. Or wouldn't say. Mr. Johnson with his dark City suit, anonymous tie, quick, friendly eyes. Pale hands, neatly manicured, thin, clipped moustache. He looked like an overworked GP. He'd said how pleased they were he'd come to see them. Been sensible. He'd said, just tell me a little more about yourself Mr. Stafford. All the little things. It all helps, you know.

They were holding him, were they not?

Yes, unfortunately. For a little while.

He asked the charge. That was a little difficult. Mr. Johnson hoped he wouldn't be difficult. He asked about a lawyer, *habeas corpus*. But this was the twentieth century. Mr. Johnson looked vague.

Maybe he didn't have Latin.

When they told him he was leaving he held his hands out for the cuffs. Mr. Johnson looked faintly disturbed. He said, 'Don't be bloody silly.' There was a slight holdup. 'Afraid I've got to sign for you,' said Mr. Johnson. 'Damned unnecessary.' Getting into the car he caught his bowler on the top of the door-frame, and swore again. 'Got it in a sale a few weeks back,' he said. Brushing anxiously at the nap. 'Two quid. Cheap, for a bowler.'

They travelled country roads, in the dark. Two hours later the motor finally stopped. Roley got out. There was a big house, dimly seen. A flight of steps led up to the front door. Things purred on the lawn, groups of housings. His eyes were used to the dark. They looked like beehives.

He walked through the door, along a hall. Two Redcaps treading close behind. There was a lift; Mr. Johnson steered him into it, one hand on his arm. The thing whined, dropped it seemed a limitless distance through rock.

There was a surgery, bright-lit. Through a half-open door he saw the end of an operating table. Two doctors checked him; pulse, temperature, respiration, blood pressure. They dressed his cuts, drew his blood, peered at his eyes. Mr. Johnson waited patiently. He'd sent for cigarettes. Gauloise. His favourite brand. He gave him two packets, and a box of safety matches.

They guarded him as he shaved. Afraid he might cut his wrists.

There was no news of the outside world. He saw no papers, heard no radio. Instead, there were the questionings. Hour after hour, endless. Sometimes he was woken in the middle of the night. When he accused them they laughed. Showed him a twenty-four hour clock that said it was midday. For a time he was certain he was right. Then he became less sure. Through it all Mr. Johnson offered little services. Would he like to paint? He would need special pigments, Mr. Johnson believed, and canvases. Anything he wanted would be supplied. Brushes; hogshair, were they not? Mr. Johnson had dabbled in painting himself, over the years.

He wanted nothing. He wanted Elizabeth Maynard.

Mr. Johnson was sorry, that was difficult.

What would happen? What was happening? *What had he done . . .*

Mr. Johnson was sorry. He wasn't allowed to say.

The light in the cell dimmed, and brightened.

The patrol car cut out abruptly from the line of traffic, siren blaring, took the bend ahead with a protesting squeal of tyres. The Spitfire accelerated instantly, seeming to hunch between its wheels.

Verges and hedgerows blurred. The little car howled, overdriven in third. The Wolseley wouldn't leave it. It worried it, a mastiff behind a terrier.

Bee-bah-bee-bah-bee-bah . . .

The sound dopplering down as the thing stormed by.

'What'd they want her for, Charlie?'

The observer, shouting over the radio noise.

'Don't ask me. Try the bloody CID . . .'

Sliding the saloon through another bend.

The observer reported. Position, direction, speed. Ahead were roadblocks. The pursued one loses, nearly every time.

There were more bends. The castle showed on the left; a stone face, aloof and high. The Spitfire eased; instantly the big bonnet was alongside, roaring. There was a choice. Let the Wolseley go or use gas, hit the first corner just twenty miles too fast.

The road snaked then seemed to flick away, fast as the cracking of a whip. The little car rose slowly, mounting the bank. Hung wheels churning, showed its chassis as it rolled.

The Wolseley skidded to a halt. The observer ran across the road, shirtsleeved, boots crunching on gravel. Scrambled through the hedge. A coil of wire snagged at him. He stopped to pick it free. There was white metal, torn and oil-splashed; then a thud, the quick bright bursting of fire.

'What happened after College?'

'I think I told you,' said Roley distantly.

Lying on the bed.

'Just a check, Mr Stafford. Get all the facts.'

'Agency work. Here and there. In Town.'

'Names of the agencies?'

'You wrote them down.'

'Yes,' said Mr Johnson. 'I know. How'd you spend your evenings, Mr. Stafford?'

'Drinking. In bed with women.'

'No hobbies? Recreations?'

'Don't be bloody silly.'

'Who were they? These women?'

'How the hell should I know?'

'They had names.'

'It's been a long time ago.'

A pause.

'Why'd you join the CND?'

'It seemed a good idea at the time.'

'That's a quote,' said Mr. Johnson. 'Not very original. Did you think you were making any difference?'

'What to?'

'The country. Marching up and down the Great West Road.'

'We only marched up it,' said Roley. 'Never down.'

'It seems a waste of time to me.'

'It would.'

'You've seen all the right films, haven't you?' said Mr. Johnson. 'You know all the answers. You're smart.'

Silence.

'You know something, Mr. Stafford? You make me sick. You make me want to puke.'

'There's a bowl over there,' said Roley. 'See it gets washed.'

Mr. Johnson lifted him by the lapels, and shouted. He often shouted.

'*Who set you up?*'

The noise rang in his ears. He wanted no more trouble. Not now.

'You're bloody fools,' said Mr. Johnson. 'All of you. You

had it made. You had a good life. You threw it away. For nothing.

'Who set you up?'

Blazing.

'I told you, I bloody told you . . .'

'Where'd you get the money?'

'I told you where we got the money . . .'

'Who were the women?'

'I don't know, I don't know, I don't bloody know . . .'

'You're a Commie. You're a Commie, boy . . .'

'Go to hell . . .'

'Who set you up?'

'Go to hell. . .'

'You're a Commie. . .'

'All right,' yelled Roley, 'All right, all right, for Christ's sake, I'm a Commie. . .'

'Who set you up?'

Silence. A panting of rage. Roley fell back, hopelessly.

'Look at it my way,' said Mr. Johnson. 'I see a group of nice, talented people. They've got money, they've got pull, they've got everything they want. And they throw it all away. One bright morning. That's not the way the world works, Mr. Stafford. Not the way at all.'

Roley was silent.

'You're thinking. "He wouldn't understand",' said Mr. Johnson. 'That's why you make me sick, Mr. Stafford. You've got the corner in thinking, haven't you? You people with your blasted little banners? You bleed if you're cut, don't you? Nobody else.'

'Where's your war?' asked Roley. 'That war you were going to have?'

'I'll let you into a secret, boy,' said Mr. Johnson. 'I'll put you right in the picture. There never was going to be a war. There won't be a war. There'll never be a war because nobody can afford a war. Only you're too damned stupid to see it, you've got to wave your flags and chant your bloody songs. You're a pacifist, aren't you?'

Silence.

'Would you say you were a pacifist, Mr. Stafford?'

No answer.

'I'd say you were,' said Mr. Johnson. 'That's why you don't

want war. You don't want to see the little children fry. How many children have you got, Mr. Stafford?'

'I'm not married.'

'Don't beg the issue, Mr. Stafford. How many kids? Any we don't know about?'

No answer.

'Maybe there's some you don't know about yourself.'

'*Get out. You bastard . . .*'

Mr. Johnson said, 'How I detest that word . . .

'So you haven't got any children. I've got two. You're worried about mine. That's nice of you. But I don't want you to worry about them. I'll worry about them myself.'

Roley turned away to face the wall.

'You took everybody else's responsibilities,' said Mr. Johnson. 'On your own broad back. You didn't have the guts to get any of your own. Your sort never do.' He hauled Roley back to face him. 'This is going to come as a shock,' he said. 'Better brace yourself. *You're not Jesus Christ after all . . .*'

He crossed to the table, poured water into the cup, brought it back. 'I'm roughing you up,' he said. 'It'll get rougher. There's no way out. Not for you. Because you're nothing, boy.' He cracked his fingers, under Roley's nose. 'Not that. You sold your friends out, right down the river. Now you've got nothing. You've talked some, you're going to talk the rest.

'*Who set you up . . .*'

The lamp dimmed.

The door was a bright rectangle against the half light of the room. Mr. Johnson walked in quietly, pulled up a chair. Roley was lying huddled, face to the wall. Once he tossed and muttered. The other watched him a time then reached across and shook him. Roley woke with a start, turned dazed eyes at the light. The eyes focused.

'She was with you,' said Mr. Johnson softly. 'She was with you, wasn't she boy? Right with you. But she got away.'

Roley licked his mouth.

'It's getting to you,' said Mr. Johnson. 'I can tell.' He was carrying a bottle of Scotch and a stack of paper cups. He poured two measures carefully, held one out.

'Water?'

'Christ almighty,' said Roley. 'Don't you so-and-so's ever kip?'

Mr. Johnson shook his head. He lit a cigarette, tossed the packet on the bed. 'Mr. Stafford,' he said, 'you are causing me confusion and grief.' He capped the bottle, sat turning it in his hand. 'This,' he said, 'is what they call Pull. Do you know, I'm Breaking the Rules? You aren't supposed to get near glass. You might overpower me, and cut your throat. You won't though, will you?'

'No,' said Roley. 'I won't do that.'

Mr. Johnson chuckled. 'It wouldn't be smart,' he said. 'You're saving yourself for better things.' He set the Scotch on the floor. 'The bottle I can sign for,' he said. 'But the cups must be paper. We live in a crazy world.'

Silence.

Mr. Johnson proffered the cup again. 'We don't drug Scotch,' he said. 'Not in my department. It isn't considered the done thing.'

Roley sat up.

'Plenty more where it came from,' said Mr. Johnson. 'All at Her Majesty's expense. Might as well make the most of it.'

'Yes,' said Roley. 'I will.'

Mr. Johnson shook a cigarette from the packet. Gave him a light. 'I had my boss on my back this afternoon,' he said. 'I push you, he pushes me. It's the way it goes.'

'You're thinking I'm a bastard again,' said Mr. Johnson. 'I am. I'm paid to be. But I'm also your Only Friend.' He sipped Scotch, and made a face. 'Doesn't it taste foul,' he said, 'from paper cups?'

Roley flicked ash, carefully.

'The way it works, you see,' said Mr. Johnson, 'is we isolate you, break you down. We yell at you, shine lights in your eyes, drive you round the twist. Then I come along with a drink. Tell you all my troubles. Ask you to be a good boy. It's childish. Completely. Unfortunately, it works. You can feel it working, can't you? I'm your Only Friend. You'd miss me if I wasn't here, wouldn't you?'

'Yes,' said Roley. 'I would.'

They'd sent books in, in the afternoon. Mr. Johnson reached across idly, picked one up. 'You know,' he said, 'that's a beautiful play. I saw it on the stage. Went straight out and bought it.'

'He wrote it for ten years,' said Roley. 'When it was finished he died.'

'Drinking Scotch in a New York bar. I read the preface.'

'How many artists have you got in the bunkers?' asked Roley.

'Very few I'm afraid,' said Mr. Johnson. 'Better for them to stay outside. They'll do much better work as they cook.'

Roley laughed, suddenly. Not knowing why.

'What's she like?' asked Mr. Johnson.

'Who?'

'Your girl.'

Silence.

'I know I wrote it down,' said Mr. Johnson. 'But words don't say a lot, do they?'

'No.'

'Tell me about her.'

'I can't remember her,' said Roley. 'She's fading away.'

The other laughed. 'No,' he said. 'No she isn't. What colour's her hair?'

'It's in the record.'

He waited.

'It's black,' said Roley. 'That's all the words will do. It's black.'

'She's going to grow it for you.'

'Not now.'

'She will,' said Mr. Johnson. 'She will.'

'Where is she?' asked Roley.

'She could be next door.'

'She isn't.'

'No. She isn't. But she could be. I saw her this afternoon.'

'You're a liar.'

'How can you tell?'

'There'd be a light on your face,' said Roley. 'Like Moses on the mountain.'

Mr. Johnson poured more Scotch.

'Why did you give her away?'

'I didn't.'

'No,' said Mr. Johnson. 'I don't think you did.'

A pause.

'Keep talking about her,' said Mr. Johnson. 'Life's still good when you're talking about her.'

'Her name's Elizabeth,' said Roley. 'It's all in the word. Elizabeth.'

A waiting.

'I want to buy her a present.'

'What sort of present?'

'Little pearl earrings. And a big cuddly bear.'

'She'll like that.'

'No,' said Roley. 'No, she won't.'

'She's growing her hair for you,' said Mr. Johnson. 'She's coming, Roley.'

'What?'

'Look at the door.'

'I've seen the door,' said Roley.

'Look again. Listen.'

'What to?'

'The footsteps.'

'There's nothing there,' said Roley. 'Except the noises in one's head. And that bloody fan.'

They did drug Scotch, in Mr. Johnson's department. It was very clever. He could hear her walking now, if he concentrated. The click of her heels a long, long way away. Very cool and sharp and clear.

'It's getting to you,' said Mr. Johnson. 'It's getting you hard. You need her, boy. She's coming. I'm fetching her for you.'

Then very softly,

'*Who set you up . . .?*'

Mr. Johnson was his friend.

The door opened, silently.

'We're moving you on old chap,' said Mr. Johnson. 'Company orders I'm afraid.'

He swung his feet off the bed, picked up his jacket. An escort waited in the corridor. The inevitable Redcaps. They trailed him into the lift. The journey up seemed shorter than the long trip down.

Outside the house the gravel drive was white with sunlight. Roley screwed up his eyes. There was the car again, waiting. He got in, laid his head against the back of the seat. Mr. Johnson sat in front with the driver. The saloon moved off, swung between tall gateposts on to the road. Half an hour later it entered a town. Roley kept his eyes shut. It no longer mattered where he was.

There was a garage, a shabby little place in a backstreet. Its doors stood open. The car turned in, stopped. Another was waiting. Roley got out, stood looking round. 'You change the plates,' he said. 'And respray them.'

'Something like that,' said Mr. Johnson.

Opening the rear door for him.

Abruptly he was seized by cramp. He'd been getting a lot of stomach pain. He doubled up silently, leaning on the car. Johnson dropped a hand on his shoulder, pulled him upright. He said, 'I need a loo.'

Johnson nodded to his driver, silently. The other took Roley's arm. There was a lavatory, a little caboose stuck in a corner of the shop. He went in, pushed the door shut. Leaned his forehead on the downpipe of the cistern. The bowl was stained, an unravelled cigarette end floating.

'Don't lock it,' said the driver.

There was a wad of torn newspaper, stuck on a nail in the wall. His eyes noticed it dully. He reached across, pulled the top sheet away. There was a fraction of headline. THROUGH MYSTERY CORDON. And a picture of a car, well crumpled. Numberplate visible.

Not much information, really.

He flushed the lavatory, unhooked the chain from the cistern and dropped it in his pocket. He opened the door, walked back to the car rubbing his stomach. They drove out, swung right. Back into the town. He said, 'Where are we going?' Mr. Johnson answered briefly.

'London.'

Beyond the town was a dual carriageway. He saw a signboard. LONDON 60. The day was cloudless and bright; there seemed to be very little traffic. The driver opened up, climbed to the statutory seventy. The pain came again; Roley swore, doubled over on the seat.

Mr. Johnson was concerned. He leaned across, pulled at his shoulder. He asked, 'Do you want a doctor?'

The chain, flailing, caught him across the eyes.

Roley flung his arms round the driver's neck, wrenched. A screeching, a whirl of sunlight, a huge jolt. He lost his grip, was flung violently into the back of the seat. He thought they had stopped; but the second jolt was worse.

He sat up, dazed. The driver was slumped against the dash. Mr. Johnson was fumbling at the side of the car. His fingers were red. Roley opened his door awkwardly, climbed out, leaned drawing shuddering breaths. They'd spun a hundred yards from the carriageway, tearing swaths across the grass verge. Crunched a wing on a concrete fencepost, come to rest in a field. On the carriageway a car passed unconcerned. Maybe it hadn't seen.

Mr. Johnson was hurt. He held one hand to his forehead; in the other was an automatic pistol. So people really did carry such things. Roley wondered what calibre it was. The muzzle seemed very large.

'Slowly,' said Mr. Johnson. 'Slowly now. Go round the car, Mr. Stafford. Don't go fast.'

He did as he was told, lifted the driver. In his forehead was a dark-red dent; blood ran from it indignantly.

'He's hurt,' said Mr. Johnson. 'Lift him down.'

It was difficult to get his feet away from the pedals.

'Good boy,' said Mr. Johnson. 'Sit in the car now. You drive.'

He obeyed, leaned across to open the passenger door. He was remembering about undressing Elizabeth. He thought, 'Poor Mr. Johnson can't see.'

The other moved round awkwardly, steadying himself on the bonnet. His fingers groped for the windscreen pillar. Roley slammed the door on them.

The gun exploded, let daylight through metal panelling. He kicked the door back open, heard a thud. Ran round, risking the gun, and kicked again twice.

Hard.

There was no traffic in sight now. He started up, slammed into first. A groaning, chafing of rubber on steel. He bounced across the grass, accelerating, fighting the wheel. Half a mile on there was a side road. He stood on the brakes and turned, nearly rolled the saloon. A mile down the lane he realized he'd never make a proper criminal. He'd forgotten to steal Mr. Johnson's gun.

The car was hot. He supposed that was the term he ought to use. And she wouldn't take him far, not with the wing flaying the wheel. He reached a tee junction. The placenames on the signpost meant nothing to him. He turned right. A half mile on was an ancient-looking barn, roof nearly fallen in. A gateway beside it, nobody moving that he could see. He opened the gate, ran back, nosed the car inside, stopped out of sight of the road and set the brake. He threw the ignition keys over the hedge, laid a spanner round the distributor. No reason, except he was getting used to destruction.

Mr. Johnson had been his friend.

He started to walk, trying not to let his mind swirl into panic. How long had he got, before they came after him? Not long, he decided. Not very long at all.

He was in luck. An Anglia carried him a dozen miles. There was another main road. Heading West. A Consul stopped for him. Driver was a rep, a cheerful, balding man in his fifties. Roley said he'd been hiking, got out of touch. Left his kit to cover his last night's digs. He asked what had been happening. There seemed to be little news. More Notes exchanged; the UN trying to set up last-minute talks. Things had cooled off sharply. Maybe there wouldn't be a war after all.

He made another forty miles, wondering when his luck would run out. It was dusk as his benefactor drew up. 'Well,' he said, 'that's about it. Turn off here, old boy.'

'Great,' said Roley. 'Thanks a lot.' He swung out, jacket over his arm. Crossed in front of the bonnet, turned back to the window. He said, 'Did you know you'd got a flat?'

The door trick was good. He yanked the handle again and his victim hit the road. He'd been carrying a weighted hose in the cubby. It came in useful.

There were lights approaching, half a mile down the road. He towed the limp weight off on to the rough. There was a ditch; he bundled the driver into it, crouched till the car was past. Under the Consul's dash he'd seen a coil of plastic-covered flex. He ran back for it, bound the stranger's wrists, tied them to his ankles.

This car might stay clean.

He saw the checkpoint a mile before he reached it. The road descended on a long curve, high woods to one side, open fields on the other. Ahead was the line of tail lights, bright blue flashing of patrol cars.

Trust the cops to ball things up.

He killed his lights, U-turned and drove back looking for a side road. If the manoeuvre hadn't been seen he might still get clear. There was a road, a mile farther on. It carried him through silent villages. He twisted and backtracked, sweating. Eventually he found an AA board. It told him what he wanted to know. He had fifty miles to go.

The second roadblock also signalled its presence with flashing lights. White and amber this time. He turned back once more. He remembered passing what looked like an old quarry. It was on a bend, his lights had swept the sandy face of it. He found it again, slowed cautiously. It looked deserted. He drove the car in, away from the road. There were high bushes of bramble; he forced the Consul between them, knowing he was wasting his time. It would be seen fast enough in daylight. He searched the dash. There were two bars of chocolate. He put them in his pocket, climbed out. The night was moonlit and bright. He climbed a gateway, took to the fields. Following as nearly as he could the course of the road.

Towards dawn he knew he was beaten. He'd passed the line of roadblocks, he was sure of that, but he couldn't go on much longer. He'd worked back to the road; he was stumbling along it, not caring now if he was caught or not. He felt delirious; he remembered being thirsty, trying to suck a pebble. He'd read somewhere that was the thing to do. It seemed a daft trick. It had certainly brought him no relief.

He was crossing high moorland, bushes and clumps of gorse to either side. The morning was clear and bright, high streaks of cloud lit orange by the rising sun. He was very tired. He fought the notion of sleep for a time before giving in. He left the road, crawled into cover. Closed his eyes.

He killed Elizabeth.

The dream was confused. At first it seemed he was fighting Mr. Johnson, trying to take his gun. He seized his arm, wrestled; but the other's muscles were strong as the sinews of a machine. The pistol came down, and down, and down; then, without transition it seemed, Roley was holding it, pumping at the trigger. But it was Elizabeth standing in front of him. He willed his hand to stop. It wouldn't. A roaring; and the terrible look in her eyes, of disbelief and pain. He screamed then, praying to undo what he had done, turn the clock back just one second. It seemed such a little thing to ask. But she was falling, brushing at him as she fell . . .

He sat up, eyes wild. In front of his face other eyes stared. Liquid, and terrified. Then the rabbit turned, crashed back through brambles and was gone.

There was sweat on his face. He wiped at it dazedly. He knew now she was dreadfully hurt. He ran back to the road.

There was an artic, rumbling steadily. Trailer piled square and high, the load lashed down and covered with bright green tarpaulin. He flagged the lorry, heard the fierce splash of air brakes as it slowed. He ran down the road to it, swung up beside the cab. He said, 'I'm going West.'

A long moment. The diesel clattered heavily, idling.

'Alright mate,' said the driver. 'Make it snappy.'

He ran round, half-believing. Climbed up, slumped in the deep leather seat. Across the cab from him the man ground his gears. A jerk and they were under way.

He hadn't slept for long. The sun was still low, flinging the big shadow of the truck ahead along the road. He lay back, squeezed the bridge of his nose, rubbed his eyes. He looked round him. There were stubbed ends of cigarettes on the ribbed rubber floor, a jacket on a hook. A rucksack, thermos protruding from its flap. There was a bouncing mascot, a cancan doll; above the windscreen a pinup of a bare, black-haired girl. She looked a little like Elizabeth.

The driver was watching him, sidelong. He stiffened, and the other shook his head. 'I shouldn't, mate,' he said. 'Not if I was you.' He nodded at the cubby, arms spread on the big wheel. Roley followed his eyes, saw the shaft of a heavy wrench. 'You're a rough bugger, you are,' said the driver. 'I'm another. Don't start nothing.'

He sat slackly, feeling drained. 'Why did you pick me up?' he asked finally. 'If you knew who I was? Going to turn me in?'

The other shook his head. He was thick-necked and stubborn-jawed, wispy light hair blowing across his round skull. His hands were heavy, calloused. They lit a cigarette now with practised speed, flipped the pack to Roley. He lit up gratefully, inhaled.

'Had your picture on the Box you have,' said the driver. 'You're right up the ruddy spout. Six times you was on, last night.' He removed the cigarette from his lip, spat a shred of tobacco overboard. 'What do they want you for, mate?' he said. 'Apart from knocking some bloke over the head?'

Roley swallowed. 'You'd better put me off,' he said. 'You don't want trouble with the law.'

The other laughed, shortly. 'Stuff the law, I says. And stuff the flamin' government an' all.' He glanced sideways again. His eyes were a bright, piercing blue. 'Panics,' he said. 'Strife an.' flamin' confusion. There's goin' to be a war. There ain't goin' to be a war. The situation's under control. What bloody situation, I'd like to know. But that ain't for the likes of us to find out.'

He nodded down at the road. 'I'd got you sorted out,' he said. 'Soon as I saw you. "That's the bloke they had on the Box," I says. "He's mixed up in it, for a flamin' pension." You could tell, the way they was goin' on. "If there's anybody as knows," I says, "It's 'im ...' So I'm asking you, ain't I? What bloody well goes on?'

'Some friends of mine,' said Roley slowly, 'didn't want to see another war. They tried to do something about it. That was all.'

'You're joking,' said the driver. 'Stop a war? Nobody ever stopped a bloody war mate, I can tell you that. I went through the last lot. My old man the one afore that. I ought to know.'

'No,' said Roley tiredly. 'I don't expect they did stop anything. But they tried.'

'How?'

He tried to tell him.

The other heard him through, narrowing his eyes at the road. When he had finished he shook his head. 'Christ,' he said. 'If that ain't the biggest load o' cods I ever heard. Like something in my kids' ruddy comics.'

'I don't expect to be believed,' said Roley. 'I only half believe it myself.'

'I didn't say I didn't believe it.' The driver blew his nose one-handed on a grubby scrap of cloth. 'Take something like that to start this bloody shakeup, wouldn't it?'

'What shakeup?'

'Christ,' said the other again. 'To start with they evacuates half Oxfordshire . . . Where you bin, in the nick?'

'Yes,' said Roley. 'In the nick.'

'Well,' said the driver. 'Stroll on . . .'

No word of the demonstrations had as yet been released to the public. Instead massive troop movements had begun, culminating in the hurried evacuation of area after area of the country. Military cordons had been set up; the biggest, ten miles across, evidently ringed Jimmy's headquarters. Roley yawned and shook his head, unable to explain.

'You don't know a sight more than me,' said the driver. There was a layby; he pulled into it and switched off. 'There's some shaving stuff down by your arm,' he said. 'In the bag. Better use it. You'll have to make do with it cold. About the only chance you've got. Otherwise they'll pick you up as soon as look at you. I don't reckon you'll get through anyhow. They're only letting essential stuff in. Rest has to detour.'

Roley said, 'I'm very grateful.'

'Don't be,' said the other shortly. 'Maybe what you said was a load o' balls. I just get fed up bein' left in the dark. If we're in for the chop let's know about it, says I. I ain't the only one this time either. Not by a bloody long chalk.'

He poured coffee while Roley shaved, set the cup on top of the dish. He produced a packet of sandwiches, shared them meticulously. Roley ate hungrily. He'd had nothing except chocolate for twenty-four hours. 'We're nearly down,' said the trucker. 'Have to chuck you off in a mile or two. You'll be just short o' the cordon. Don't try it in daylight, they'll probably blow you apart. Haven't seen nothing like it since the war.'

'Thank you,' said Roley. 'Thank you very much indeed.'

The lorry dropped him five miles on, at a bend in the road. He got down stiffly, waved. The driver raised an arm briefly from the cab, revved; within minutes the artic had grumbled out of sight. He was alone again.

He was still in downland. He struck off at an angle from the road, moving cautiously, keeping to what cover he could find. A mile on he came in sight of the cordon. It stretched as far as he could see; there were vehicles dotted across the grass, men moving about. In one place troops were busy stringing wire. Away to his left the roadblock itself was overshadowed by a heavy tank. It stood foursquare on the verge, facing the direction from which he had come. There was a striped pole, a guard hut, a clustering of tents. Lorries were waiting, and a private car. He saw the car turned back, peremptorily.

He lay up through the day, trying not to think about thirst. Towards evening he moved off again, following the line of the cordon. An hour's walking brought him to a secondary road, climbing the downs between high banks. There was a signpost; he read it, sat by it awhile to get his breath.

He knew where he was.

The brewery was a dark grotto, many-storeyed, thick with the sweet stench of working beer. Round it ran galleries, connected by spidery iron stairways. Lights burned here and there, throwing gaunt shadows, striking gleams from the sides of the great vessels that clustered under the roof. There was a constant splashing and tinkling, the thud and bang of falling spots of water.

The big man climbed steadily from floor to floor, setting his feet carefully on the slimy metal treads, whistling tunelessly between his teeth. He paused by each vessel in turn, lifting the thermometers from the thick yeast, working the wheels that dropped the cone-shaped chutes down through the scum. The overflows fell with thunderous slappings, into the waiting troughs. The man in the shadows spoke softly. 'Nice brew, Brian,' he said. 'Working well.'

The other stiffened, fingers curled on the edge of a vat.

'Don't overplay it,' said Roley. 'You knew I was here.'

There had been a village cricket match, on a little pitch set round with elms like the famous pitch in the story. There was even a slope behind the wicket up which Brian had pounded, redfaced and ferocious. It was one of Roley's best-ever days. The first ball sang past his ear; the second he lifted into the outfield hay. The third he dispatched to leg, square over the boundary hedge. And the fourth and fifth. The sixth clean bowled him, cartwheeled his off stump.

'Don't hurt him,' Elizabeth had said.

'What, me? *Him?*'

'You could,' she said. 'Please, Roley. For me.'

He had never decided, whether or not he let that last one through.

The big man was still standing, staring into the froth. Below, the last of the overflow flopped and slobbered.

'I'm sorry, boy,' said Roley. 'There wasn't anywhere else to go.'

The other said thickly, 'Get out.'

'I can't.' Roley detached himself from shadow. 'I've got to get to her,' he said. 'I've got to get through.'

'You've done enough,' said Brian. The thick fingers clenched on the side of the vat.

Roley said, 'Get me through.'

The other took his arms, carefully. The grip was like the grip of a machine. He turned slowly, slammed him into the guard rail. The iron tubing clattered in its stanchions.

'Over the top,' said Brian. He swallowed, face dark. 'Nice and easy. Five floors.' He shook him. The rail clattered again. Then he let go. 'Get out,' he said. 'You've got the chance.'

Roley leaned on the rail, pale-faced. 'Sorry, boy,' he said. He half laughed, painfully. 'Get me through.'

The other turned away, back to the vat. Stood leaning, head down. 'Do you know what it's like?' he said. His voice sounded smothered. 'What it was like listening to you?'

Roley licked his mouth. 'Yes,' he said. 'I do.'

They hadn't told him everything. They'd been smart.

'I've got nothing,' said Brian. 'Nothing. She talks to me in the night. When I can't sleep.'

'It's the way the world goes,' said Roley. 'You drew a course of hell.' He moistened his lips again. 'Get me through.'

The big man turned to face him. There was sweat on his chest and neck; his eyes were suffused, as if with tears. He stared a long while; then walked to the first of the ladders, not looking back, and swung down.

Essential services passed through the cordon.

There were two drays in the yard. One empty, one loaded and tarpaulined. Brian worked silently, lifting crates aside, building a space between them. He said finally, 'Get in.'

Roley swung aboard, wriggled into the niche.

'You're hers,' said Brian. 'Ours. Not mine.' He yanked the tarp forward. Roley crouched in darkness, heard the load ropes drawn tight. 'Tell them I'm coming,' he said. 'They'll know what to do.' The other paused with his work but didn't answer. Ten minutes later he heard the crunch of his boots across the yard, the clang of the outer gate.

It was a hard thing, being a God.

He slept finally, in spite of his cramped position. Sometime in the early morning he was woken by the clatter of an engine. He raised his head, cautiously. There were footsteps, a voice calling. The other dray moved out and revved, he heard it back up to the loading bay. Ten minutes later creaking and faint movement told him his own driver was aboard. The engine fired, settled to a heavy pounding. The lorry moved, lurching over cobbles. Swung heavily to the right, through the yard gate. Within minutes it was clear of the town, slugging up the long slope he knew lay beyond.

In front of him the tarpaulin edge, working loose, gave him jazzing glimpses of blue and green. He lay on his stomach, mouth on his wrists, feeling the pounding from the flatbed transmitted through knuckles and jaw to the front bones of his skull. The load shifted, crates digging at his elbows and sides. In time, the lorry stopped.

He felt giddy and sick. He edged forward fractionally, hearing voices raised in argument. He saw khaki-trousered legs, the lowered muzzle of a rifle. The legs moved out of sight. More arguing, a pause; and he heard the rasping as the load ropes were slackened.

He lay still, not believing. The tarpaulin was gripped, pulled. There was a bursting of light.

He scrambled for the side of the truck, rolled off. His legs, numbed, refused to take his weight. He landed jarringly, got up and began to run across grass. Hands grabbed for him. He evaded them; then the earth seemed to rise, bump at his knees. He fell again, wonderingly why they didn't fire.

He was lifted by two soldiers. The lorry stood in bright sunlight, engine idling; beside it two more men held the driver. The pole of the roadblock was still lowered; there were bivvys, a green tent with an awning rigged beside it, a heavy Command vehicle. He was taken to the tent. Beneath the awning was a stack of crates. He sat on one, put his face in his hands. Somebody brought him a drink. Coffee, laced with rum. It revived him a little. He watched, dully, the coming and going of men across the grass. There seemed to be a great deal of activity. Somewhere a telephone was ringing shrilly.

An MP collected him, hustled him to the Command truck. A tired-faced major met him, scanned him briefly and shrugged. 'Stafford,' he said.

An answer didn't seem necessary.

'You've been sent for,' said the major. 'It's out of my hands. We've laid a car on. Take him to it, sergeant. Look lively.'

He stepped down from the truck in a daze.

The car was an open Champ, plentifully spattered with company and battalion insignia. He got in. A shirtsleeved private climbed in beside him, started up. A couple of minutes driving and the gaunt shape of the shell keep showed above the trees. He hadn't realized he was so near the village. The Champ joined the road he had travelled with Elizabeth. As he passed the castle *motte* he saw more canvas rigged inside the ruin. There were ambulances drawn up, and what looked like a mobile kitchen. Over the keep flew square red flags, like the warning flags on a firing range. There was another checkpoint. The pole lifted as the vehicle approached. It drove on into the village, turned right, pulled up in the station square.

He stared round him. The old carriages were still there. Beside them a line of caravans. Mobile canteens, a radio truck. The whole place was a camp.

There had been no room, in the village, for all the People who had come.

He was taken to the first of the caravans, pushed inside. The thing was stripped, set up as an office. There were telephones, of various hues; filing cabinets, maps on the walls. A desk and chair. On the desk was a pack of cigarettes. He opened it, took one, struck a light. Behind him, a shadow fell across the doorway.

'Hello boy,' said Jimmy.

He looked up, slowly. Their eyes met and locked. While the Power that was loose in the place boiled and fizzed, raising his back hair. A long wait; then Jimmy reached out, grasped his wrists. 'You poor old bastard,' he said. 'I'm sorry, Roley.'

He had been searched, as he stood. His brain scanned, analysed.

And found . . . acceptable.

'It's alright boy,' said Jimmy. 'We knew we were wrong. But you couldn't have told us. We had to be shown.'

Roley licked his mouth. He said quietly. 'They didn't pay me any silver.'

'It's alright,' said Jimmy again. 'Roley, we're like fresh kids. Just born. We knew we could walk. We didn't know how fast we could run.'

Roley said, 'Who won?'

The other laughed tiredly, brushed at his hair. 'Nobody wins,' he said. 'Not in this life. You heard about Oxfordshire?'

A nod.

'We had a dozen, working shifts,' said Jimmy. 'We call 'em the demolition gang. You see the flags? Up on the castle?'

'Yes.'

'They're bivvied there,' said Jimmy. 'It's quiet. They put a nuke together. Sat two days with their fingers on the tit. They've got enough stuff at Brize Norton to make Britain an atoll. It took two days. It's OK now. Charlie's back on the shelf.'

Roley nodded, slowly.

'They shouldn't have hurt Elizabeth,' said Jimmy. 'She yells.' He examined his fingers. 'We got six contacts in France. The same night.' He looked up, smiled wanly. 'Surprised?'

'Yes.'

'So were we. There's been more since. Dawn learned Swedish. Overnight. We think the Other Side's got their problem children too.'

He turned to the door. 'I didn't send for you,' he said. 'It isn't me you've got to answer to.'

Roley followed him outside, back across the square. An o/b unit was operating; there was an interviewer, familiar-faced, a long-haired lad in sweater and jeans. Monitor screens repeated his words. 'We're Royalists, and Liberal,' he was saying. 'We're not a political group in any sense but we're having to thrash out a sort of Party Line. We're Pro-Russell on birth control, we asked for a Ministry. The Medical Council's going along with us but so far we've had no luck with the Church. We're meeting the PM again this afternoon and we're hoping we can speak to the Queen. We're drafting out a sort of formal resolution of loyalty. We shall be setting up regional centres for most of the

Groups. Some of us will definitely be staying in the southwest. We haven't got any final details on that . . .'

'We may still get blown to hell,' said Jimmy. 'If we do, God help everybody.'

The Champ was waiting. He said briefly, 'Take him up.' He gripped Roley's arm again. 'See you later boy,' he said. 'Take it slow.'

A cool wind blew across the castle mound, ruffling his hair. He walked across the grass to the first aid post. Behind the ambulances an awning had been set up, protected from the wind. He stopped when he came in sight of it.

She called him. She was lying propped up on a camp bed where she could see across the little valley, back to the village roofs. There was a tray beside her with glasses, bottles of fruit juice. A transistor, a stack of magazines. He walked up to her, stood looking down.

'I was smelling of being ill,' she said. 'I got them to bring me up.'

He said, 'You've got it made.'

She put her arms out to him, mouth quirked. He held her, kneeling, kissing mouth and eyes, ruffling her hair. 'It's alright,' she said. 'It's alright, I shan't break . . .'

There were a million things to say. No words.

'It's alright,' she said. 'I know, I know . . .'

He laid her back, gently, not letting go her hand. 'They made a good job of me,' she said. 'There won't be any scars. It was the first time they'd done anything like it. They were very pleased.'

He realized now how the doctors and surgeons would clamour. There were new vistas opening, everywhere.

'We were . . . stupid,' she said. 'So very stupid. That's how I felt when the . . . car went. Silly, and small. So much I didn't know.'

'*Elizabeth . . .*'

He peered up, under the edge of the awning. Dawn sat atop the nearest of the ambulances. In suntop and jeans. She waved to him excitedly. 'Big car coming . . ..'

'Yes,' said Elizabeth. 'I know.'

She was squatting, Buddha-fashion, shielding her eyes. Peering down at the roadblock. She said, 'It's got a flag on it.' Then, disappointed, 'It's a man. It isn't the Queen.'

'It's alright,' said Elizabeth. 'Tell them to let it through.'